ANYWHERE, ANYWHERE

Tim Barrus

Stamford, Connecticut

Designed by Graphic Arts Associates
Cover photo courtesy of:
    Save the Children Federation, Inc. 50 Wilton Rd. Westport, CT 06880

Published by Knights Press, P.O. Box 454, Pound Ridge, NY 10576

Library of Congress Cataloging-in-Publication Data

Barrus, Tim.
    Anywhere, anywhere.

    1. Vietnamese Conflict, 1961-1975—Fiction.
I. Title.
PS3552.A7414A84   1987   813'.54   86-27374
ISBN 0-915175-21-5

Printed in the United States of America

Portions of this work have appeared in *Advocate Men* and *Christopher Street*.

January 1, 1987: San Francisco — This book is dedicated to my daughter, Kree Bjorn, who has gone through more wars and lovers (staunchly, stubbornly) at her less than sane father's side than any child should have to face. Thank you for being there for me, through thick and thin, darling, when tis I who should have been there for you. You will always be the love of my life. Love me tender. Love me sweet. Never let me go. — daddy.

—jungle moonlight ran
   hot through our indigo boyveins
   like toy princes we
   ran through jungles
   slaying beasts and
   other toy princes running
   cool through moonlight
   our lungs full of
   pyrotechnics
   life and napalm blush running
   naked often enough
   into one another breathless
   through the jungle rain leaking
   from our eyes sweating
   bloodrivers running into agony
   into defeat into the glitterball
   of madness running
   metastasized moonlight
   arterial cool running anywhere
   anywhere—

Part One

ANYWHERE, ANYWHERE

—boy princes on horses
toy soldiers like soft
nighttime kisses
boys on daddy's knee
engaged in battle
summoned by dreams
by demands
that blood run
through the fields
through the streets
hot through the veins
of boy princes
on horseback with swords
engaged in battle
with daddy a flood of duty
toy soldier blood
running faithless
and moral
a tidal wave of prince blood
running with manic laughter
anywhere anywhere—

I'S ONE FOR THE MONEY, TWO FOR THE SHOW, THREE TO GET READY, NOW, GO-CAT-GO. GET OFF. AND DON'T STEP ON MY BLUE SUEDE SHOES. YOU CAN DO ANYTHING THAT YOU WANT TO DO BUT GET OFFA MY BLUE SUEDE SHOES. YOU CAN KNOCK ME DOWN, STEP ON MY FACE, SLANDER MY NAME ALL OVER THE PLACE. DO ANYTHING YOU WANT TO DO. LAY OFF, HONEY, GET OFFA MY SHOES, DON'T STEP, GET OFFA MY BLUE SUEDE SHOES. BURN MY HOUSE, STEAL MY CAR, DRINK MY LIQUOR FROM AN OLD FRUIT JAR, DO ANYTHING THAT YOU WANT TO DO. BUT, OH, BABY, LAY OFFA MY BLUE SUEDE SHOES . . . The blues the blues. Mama's rockin' and a rolling. COME ON, MAMA, LET'S ROCK . . .

I have tried many times to eradicate Vietnam from my dreams. But like a tenacious vicious bitch she refuses to stop haunting me.

Candy, soda, dirty pictures, boom boom dope. Elvis always Elvis . . .

Like the whore that she always was Vietnam clings to my rock'n roll nightmares with her junkie visions, her sweat, and the burning smell of death. Her music. The blues the blues. I used to go to great lengths to avoid having to confront sleep altogether. Drugs and liquor helped. Until they didn't help anymore. Drugs and liquor finally began to simply make the visions more intensely focused. I can sometimes taste my dreams. You came back to the States and you did whatever you had to do to forget. COME ON, MAMA, LET'S ROCK. GET OFF, GET OFF A MY BLUE SUEDE SHOES. ONE FOR THE MONEY, TWO FOR THE SHOW, THREE TO GET READY . . . There is no forgetting. SO GO-CAT-GO! Even the men who claim to not think about it anymore—ever—are lying. They know it and you know it. And they know that you know that they are lying. Sometimes we need our lies. Lies help. Until even the lies don't help anymore. Until they make the dreams more intensely focused. It was neverneverland.

Candy, soda, dirty pictures, boom boom dope. And Elvis. In my dreams most of the people I know die because most of the people I knew died. Bang, you're dead. And a lot of the ones who came back are for all intents and purposes just as dead. I am told that in my sleep I claw at my ears. My ears are frequently scratched when I wake up. The sounds from the dreams are intolerable. I spent some time in a VA psycho-ward when I got back, dancing at the glitterball, because I could not handle being back. Although I could handle the dancing. The walls of the psycho-ward were green and the floors were absolutely spotless. A whole lot more spotless than those of us confined there.

We danced the shuffle shuffle.

There are people who say that those of us who became crazy became crazy because we did not win the war. We lost. Yet the ones who seem so concerned with the masculine issues of winning and losing seem to be the ones who returned and stayed sane. The ones who while they were there held themselves together no matter what. The ones who returned and continued to hold themselves together. No matter what. The ones who didn't go crazy still think that if we had only done something—differently—we could have won the war. If only we had put more into it. If only no longhairs back home had protested. If only the politicians hadn't sold us out. If only—if only. The sane ones see it in black and white terms. You either win or you lose. Period. You are either sane or you are insane. Period. You are either a man or you are something less than a man. It takes a certain degree of sanity to think that any of it was at all noble. GET OFFA MY SHOES. If only we had won. It takes a certain degree of insanity to come to the conclusion that winning was never possible, that life is composed of more than winning.

It takes a certain degree of insanity to learn from having lost.

I was one of the luckier ones. The man in the bed beside me, a kid who was not much older than I was, really, cried constantly. It was all boyhero could do. The blues the blues. They told him to shut the fuck up, that it was making them sick to hear it, that he wasn't a *man* anymore, but all he could do was cry. It was an amazing thing to observe, this flawless clean capacity for grief. He was an officer. Officers aren't supposed to cry. Officers are supposed to be well past it. But from the minute he was awake in the morning to the minute they put him under at night all he could do was grieve. Dancing the shuffle shuffle at the glitterball. He let it all hang out like so many of the rotting human innards we all saw in Vietnam. And he didn't give a damn about who saw his pain. It was his and he wasn't about to let go of it. GET OFFA MY SHOES. It was like listening to somebody's guts scream.

While you were there—Vietnam—you survived. You tried your best not to have any thoughts around what it might be about. YOU AIN'T NOTHING BUT A HOUND DOG ROCK-IN' ALL THE TIME. YOU AIN'T NEVER CAUGHT A RABBIT AND YOU AIN'T NO FRIEND OF MINE. COME ON, MAMA, LET'S ROCK. You were afraid that if you listened to your dreams you might find out that the horror of it all wasn't about anything whatsofuckingever. But in the closed off part of your inebriated soul you knew. And you hated it. Your hate turned to rage and your rage turned to numbness. Or insanity because insanity was perfectly acceptable where numbness only felt empty. At least raving insanity was anything but empty. The people who held you together, the men who felt as sick with it as you did, the men who shared your emptiness, were your buddies, your friends; it went far beyond friendship. It went beyond rock'n roll. These were the bonds of anguish, of dreams, of death, of disfigurement. These were the men who held you in their arms when you needed them to hold you—just hold me. So they hated it but they held you.

And anyone who didn't think he would ever need to be held in another man's strong uncompromising arms because he was after all—a man—found out very quickly that he was indelibly wrong. It was a brotherhood bonded in blood.

Some of us came back with our minds scrambled like eggs-&-cheese for breakfast. The blues the blues. Some of us came back to lovers and wives and parents and children who tried their best to understand who and what we had become. YOU CAN KNOCK ME DOWN, STEP ON MY FACE, SLANDER MY NAME ALL OVER THE PLACE . . . Some of us came back to lovers and wives and parents and children who were not able to reconcile themselves with who and what we had evolved into. We needed them badly but it was impossible for many of the lovers, the wives, the parents, and the children to be there in the ways that we needed them to be there. FOR US! We needed them to hold us, oh, God, Mama, just hold me, please. We needed to be embraced even if we did not know that we needed to be embraced. And they were afraid. So many of us came back to discover that all we had here was essentially all that we had had there.

Each other.

You had your buddies. COME ON, MAMA, LET'S

ROCK. You lived for them, with them, around them, because of them, and often enough in spite of them. Take my friend and partner in crime, Christopher. Now, Chris is very much a *man*, there being very little about Christopher that isn't totally masculine. For one thing he's a big lunk. Six-six and most of it muscle. That's big. Sometimes he reminds me of a crazed Nordic viking what with his blond scraggle of a beard and his unstylishly long blond hair. I am very much in love with the man, Christopher, but it's the "little boy" in him that amazes me, intrigues me, continually surprises me, and makes me reach down into my own psyche to pull up hard hidden hurting parts of myself I never knew existed. The child-like part of me. It's Chris' sense of the insane that keeps him going. It's Chris' sense of the insane that keeps me in a constant state of simply keeping up with Chris. I always seem to be three steps behind him. Inevitably it seems to be Chris' insanity that has kept both of us from going mad, from dancing the glitterball shuffle shuffle until the music stops. Until mama can't rock no more. LET'S ROCK . . .

When you first look at Chris, you, of course, notice his size. But it's his eyes that ultimately present you with the first of his many inconsistencies. While you are, indeed, looking at a *man* it's his boy-blue rock-a-bye eyes that flash like a child's. Light blue eyes as intense as polar ice in the sea on a clear cold day at noon. It's his smile that lights up like a naughty flame. It's his laugh that tells you that as a man he is many things. Every time I think I know all there is to know about Chris he creates new facets to himself for me to somehow keep up with. How many times have I had to stop the merry-go-round, take a good, long, slow look at both of us, and wonder about where we've been together, and how the fuck have we managed to survive?

LOVE ME TENDER, LOVE ME SWEET, NEVER LET ME GO. How many times have I tried holding—both of

us—together? How many times has Chris asked me where our
lives are going? Going. How many times have I told him that I
do not know? How many times has Chris begged me not to
leave him? I have stopped counting. I couldn't any more leave
Chris than I could put a handgun to my head and pull the trigger. Sometimes I wonder who the crippled one is? Him or me?
In the beginning I think I hated his wheelchair more than he
did. When some people see Chris they inevitably see a
beautiful blond man in a wheelchair. Those of us who love the
bastard see Chris.

There is a difference.

YOU AIN'T NOTHING BUT A HOUND DOG CRYING
ALL THE TIME. YOU AIN'T NEVER CAUGHT A RABBIT
AND YOU AIN'T NO FRIEND OF MINE . . .

The blues the blues. Chris and I rarely talk about Vietnam
because talking about Vietnam has never made that experience make any kind of sane sense. It'd be like trying to define
the blues. Or rock. Or Charlie Parker. Or Elvis. Or mama. We
are politically incorrect. That doesn't mean we don't think
about that nightmare or dream about it. We do . . . WELL,
THEY SAID YOU WAS HIGH-CLASS. WELL, THAT WAS
JUST FINE. THEY SAID YOU WAS HIGH-CLASS. AND
THAT WAS JUST FINE. YOU AIN'T NEVER CAUGHT A
RABBIT AND YOU AIN'T NO FRIEND OF MINE . . . How
many times have I jumped up in the middle of the night,
drenched in sweat, Christopher holding onto me? "It's okay,
guy," he says. "It's okay. I'm here." It is not okay. A lot of
men can say, well, just fuck the dreams. But what do you do
when it's your dreams that are fucking you? For us it all
remains a rather specific horror.

Candy, soda, dirty pictures, boom boom dope.
Elvis . . .

It's just that we've reached the point where what is, *is*, and everyone else endlessly discussing their own reasons for what was isn't going to put a dent into what, for us, still is. If I take a deep breath and close my eyes I can still smell Vietnam. Definitely. Lush green, humid, tropical, indigo sunsets, rivers, napalm, blood, and death. Screams. Putting it behind us has always been easier said than done. Vietnam will always be a large part of who we are and what we became. For Chris and I Vietnam wasn't dinner table conversation after a half hour of viewing Walter Cronkite on the CBS Evening News. And then back to the commercials. Hey, Mama, take a look at the new '68 Cadillacs. Great-looking car. The war wasn't an in-depth pseudo-intellectual article written by a comfortable little staffer somewhere, someone who had never fired a gun, much less lived by one, someone writing for a publication as sublime as let's say *The Advocate*. For us Vietnam was not a semi-chic march on a university campus. It wasn't a cause. Hell no we won't go. There were many boys during that time who found themselves one day marching against the war, mouthing the words: Hell no we won't go. And the next day those same boys found themselves on their way to fight. LOVE ME TENDER, LOVE ME SWEET . . .

Candy, soda, dirty pictures, boom boom dope. Elvis. For us Vietnam was where Chris was shot in the back. His spinal cord was shattered. His beautiful back and his beautiful butt are covered with ugly raised red scars. We both know men who feel deeply that the scars they have, the knotted twisted sunken parts of healed wounds, are marks that are to be worn proudly—they were earned. We both know men, men we loved, who carry around their knotted twisted sunken scars inside their knotted twisted sunken personalities. Chris oozed out gunk and garbage from his wound for five years.

We both oozed out gunk and garbage from our minds for a lot longer than that. DO ANYTHING YOU WANNA DO—

BUT MAMA—GET OFFA MY BLUE SUEDE SHOES. We
sometimes wonder if scars are politically correct. He's lucky
to be alive. I thought for sure they were going to have to dump
him into one of those green plastic body bags. How I hated those
bags. Every medevac chopper had those bags. I remember trying very hard not to be hysterical when Chris was shot, and I
remember not succeeding well at all. I remember holding him.
It all happened so fast. Bang, you're dead. I remember shov-
ing him into a chopper. Go just go! Get the fuck outta here!
ONE FOR THE MONEY, TWO FOR THE SHOW, THREE
TO GET READY, NOW, GO-CAT-GO! And I remember the
feel and the smell of his thick warm blood. But Chris survived.
He just can't walk which is shit but it's better than being dead.
At least—sometimes—it's better than being dead.

   We were in Vietnam as buddies. It was somehow inevitable that we would wind up as "friends" back in the states. We
are more than friends we are lovers. It has been our friendship
and our love that has redefined us. Something had to. When we
came back to the States we should have been with girl friends
or wives or pussies. But no girlfriend no wife and no pussy was
going to understand. We drifted but we drifted together. We
needed to drift. The VA filled my pockets with valium, told me
to adjust, and released me. I remember standing outside of the
Bronx VA Hospital with my bag in the rain. Okay, asshole,
now what . . . ?

   Pull it together.

   Chris would get day passes from the hospital and we hung
out in several bars that surround Times Square. In the evening
I would dutifully wheel Chris back into the Bronx V.A. hospital where he was supposed to be receiving some kind of reha-
bilitative treatment. They were always pissed with me because
I always seemed to be bringing Christopher back sloshed to his
veteran tits. Drunk. But I was, of course, drunk myself. When
Chris was finally discharged he moved into my apartment in

Greenwich Village although I practically had to beg him to do it. He insisted that the last thing I needed was a faggot cripple in my life. His self-pity was tiresome. As was his use of his new term for what we now were—faggots. I once took a bottle of beer, poured it over his head, and told him to shut the fuck up.

He has no feeling in his legs. Screw the doctors. Chris isn't supposed to be able to control his bladder and there are, indeed, times when he can't. But those times are actually rare and he's declined the various surgeries they've all wanted him to have. Drilling holes and putting tubes and plastic bags into my beautiful babe in order to make him politely socially acceptable isn't part of our definition of wholeness. And if the bastard occasionally wets his pants—so what. Since I am a totally sick pervert I do not mind cleaning him up. We have reached the point where trying to explain our relationship is just about impossible and we rarely try. How am I going to explain something that is totally unexplainable? I don't know why I love Christopher. But we've been through too much thick-and-thin to not at least love one another.

Love is the fucking least of it.

Neither one of us believes in love, anyway. Chris says that we're too butch to love anyone. But I love him no matter what Chris says.

We do the most bizarre and silly things together. Things that make no sense. But these are things that make sense to us. When you live in a wheelchair long enough or you love someone who lives in a wheelchair you start giving up on things that make sense to everyone else. The trick to it is in not giving up on those things that make sense to you. And like Vietnam that is easier said than done. As it was in the war, survival continues to be a day-to-day proposition.

We grew up with the music of Elvis and we will go to our graves with his lullabyes in our rock'n roll heads. We take a lot of baths together. We listen to Elvis in the tub or we read, sometimes we read out loud to each other. We could sit in our old oversized antique tub for hours on end drinking beer, smoking bad things, eating chips, soaking our dicks, talking about whatever pervert things have surfaced in our cocksucker minds. Chris bought a big black notebook and he spends hours writing poetry. The black notebook is stuffed. And when he's finished with a poem he reads it to me. I am not an authority on poems, poetry, or crippled cocksuckers who feel compelled to write the stuff. But I listen because listening is half the trick. Sometimes his poems make me laugh. Other times his poems make me cry. He doesn't have a name for the black notebook filled with poems and the poems rarely rhyme. We simply refer to his work as "the book."

If Chris reads to me I also read to him although I do not write poetry because I do not believe in love and I am much too butch to write poetry. Reading to each other while soaking in our tub grew into a ritual. "I like the way you read to me," he'd say. And I'd ask him what it was he'd want me to read. "Surprise me," he'd say, and once I read to him the entirety of *The Wind in the Willows* as we soaked. Five solid hours. He would have to keep turning the hot water on to keep us warm and our cocks became as water-shriveled as two wrinkled brownish prunes. Christopher just closed his eyes and looked like a big kid as he floated in the water next to me with his big balls languidly drifting as I read to him all about the adventures of the Mole, the Water Rat, the Badger, and Mr. Toad. Chris said he wanted to be like Toad, live in a country manor, and have adventures up and down the countryside.

We laughed and considered ourselves lucky enough to have a top-floor walk-up closet-sized place with an elevator that at least works half the time, and where Chris can grow his pots of flowers on the roof and write poetry. I think that Chris secretly believes in love. I do not know why. We are politically incorrect. A really politically "masculine" faggot would never grow flowers nor would he use the word faggot. Or the word fuck for that matter. Nor would he own a black notebook crammed with obscure poetry. While we've marched in our share of gay pride parades in our minds we will always be poet faggots and poet cocksuckers because we are never allowed to forget that we live on the edge. The fringes. Not of just "society" but also of "gay society," and we do not believe in the word "community."

We are our own community.

We once marched and wheeled it down a gay pride parade where there was a dance after the parade at The Saint, a gay New York club. Very chic. They did not allow wheelchairs into The Saint. We are not correct and Chris grows flowers. We are crazy-cripple rooftop flowergrower poet-cocksuckers. We still listen to Elvis. Still. PUT A CHAIN AROUND MY NECK AND LEAD ME ANYWHERE. OH, LET ME BE (OH, LET HIM BE) YOUR TEDDY BEAR. I DON'T WANNA BE YOUR TIGER CAUSE TIGERS PLAY TOO ROUGH. I DON'T WANNA BE YOUR LION CAUSE LIONS AIN'T THE KIND YOU LOVE ENOUGH . . . I have never asked Chris what kinds of flowers he grows. I don't know jack shit about flowers or Elvis or Vietnam or the blues the blues. Although I now know a great deal about cocksucking. And craziness. We *like* our craziness our cocksucking our flowers. Sometimes living on the poetic edge is living in the only sane place left in town. Living on the edge is where even cripples can dance. It is a sight to see Chris slick back his hair (for dramatic effect) and play his guitar along with an Elvis record. He can't swivel his hips like Elvis the pelvis but it's the thought that counts. OH JUST LET ME BE YOUR TEDDY BEAR!

There is a small set of stairs that leads to the roof and it would be like Mount Everest to anyone else in a wheelchair.

But Christopher always just manhauls his body up those stairs using his strong lunk arms as he kind of drags the rest of him along. I made him an oversized skateboard to get around on up there and he'll spend hours just sliding around tending to his plants, watering them, talking to them, soaking up sun, and being politically incorrect in general.

Chris' solid pecs would put most bar-fly-boys to shame. Big delicious suck nipples for days. I have considered life without this man. It is not conceivable to me. If I couldn't be with Chris I would laugh, put a gun in my fucking faggot's mouth, and pull the sweet trigger. I love him. Even if I do not really believe in love. I was sitting at the kitchen table with a paper and a cup of steaming coffee in front of me. Chris was sitting on one of the kitchen chairs with a dumbbell in each hand and was working his arrogant muscles into a sweat. His warm juice was dripping down the middle of his slick chest. I was having difficulty keeping my attention glued to the sleazy news of the *New York Post* while Chris worked out.

"You're only with me because you feel sorry for me, aren't you?" he said. It was half-joke half-paranoia. Very typical Christopher. His chest was heaving and he was almost out of breath. He kept moving the dumbbells up and down as his sweat dripped. His blue eyes flashed. We were both dressed in our underwear.

"Yes," I said as I turned the page of the paper trying to basically ignore him, "the only reason that I'm with you is because you're a cripple and I feel sorry for faggot cripples who fancy themselves as poet-clones. If I didn't have you around I'd have to find a puppy dog who doesn't drool, and I can't afford the shots. Other than the fact that you have a big dick I can't think of any other reason why I keep you."

He smiled and lunged for me falling off of his chair. I ignored him and continued reading my paper. He crawled over to me and propped himself up on my chair. "You're getting in the way of my paper, Chris," I said. He pulled the paper out of my hands and put his muscular arms around me. I should have known better than to get within his reach. He is twenty times as strong as I am. And he pulled me to the floor with him where he held me squirming in one of his wrestling holds. Chris' sweat was soaking me. I struggled to get away from him but there is no getting away from the lunk when he has you where he wants you. Chris held me down to the kitchen floor and kissed me playfully on the mouth like the beast-animal he is. I tried pulling away but the strength of his arms just pulled me back to his face. Miss Greenwich Village Poet Weightlifter of 1987. He kissed me. I laughed. I DON'T WANNA BE YOUR TIGER CAUSE TIGERS PLAY TOO ROUGH. I DON'T WANNA BE YOUR LION CAUSE LIONS AIN'T THE KIND YOU LOVE ENOUGH. I JUST WANT TO BE YOUR TEDDY BEAR . . .

"What's so funny?" he asked.

"You're some cripple, Chris. I thought that molesting a defenseless homosexual who was once your commanding officer was against the law." I was trying to be funny. I didn't want him to ask the question again. His question. But my being either sarcastic or funny is never enough to stop him from asking.

"You aren't going to leave me someday are you, Boss?" He still called me Boss. I have asked him about a million times to stop calling me that but somehow the name sticks to me. I do not know why. I am not his boss.

"No," I said. And I looked into his eyes because it was a serious question. Chris could ask it a thousand times and while it was never politically correct or based in security it was serious. He meant it. Over eight years together and Chris still asked. Damn him.

"Say you won't leave me. Say the words."

"No one's leaving you, Chris." I wasn't going anywhere.
COME ON, MAMA, LET'S ROCK . . .
He was all I had in the world.

Nobody wanted to be there. Even the gung-ho ones didn't really want to be there. We were *men* and we talked to each other as if the most important things in the universe were cars, rock'n roll, girls, girls, titty, killing the gooks who had killed boys you knew, girls, pussies, nookie-always-nookie, and that close call you had last night when your bunker took a direct hit. YOU CAN KNOCK ME DOWN, STEP ON MY FACE, SLANDER MY NAME ALL OVER THE PLACE . . . And girls. And sex. And nookie. Which was interesting because in reality the most important thing in the universe wasn't pussy, it wasn't sex, it wasn't girls, and it wasn't that close call you had. The most important thing in the universe was mail.

Even the ones who said that they loved the war had to have their mail.

Mail was a link to something real where so much of Vietnam seemed so utterly abstract that it wasn't really happening. It was a bad dream. It wasn't real. It couldn't possibly be real. We had all grown up in the fifties and the sixties where reality was Elvis and a pair of blue suede shoes that you'd die for if it became necessary. Your biggest dream was to own a 1963 Corvette and drive around Route 66 with another guy, your best friend, a guy you secretly had a crush on, you wished he was your brother, you wanted to share girls with him, but you kept all of this to yourself. Our daddies all took 8mm home movies of us in the front yard. We were basketball players. We all went fishing with our older brothers. We were sand-lot baseball players. Not cold-blooded killers. Vietnam was a game.

It couldn't possibly be real.

We were told that we had to win because we were men. They were gooks. We could not and did not fathom the not winning part. You wanted to just get it over with. You wanted to live. You wanted to go back home. You didn't know why you were there. You didn't want to think. Or see what was happening around you. Bang, you're dead. We were not *dumb!* None of us were stupid. We were numb and empty and filled with despair. We came back and so many of us were smoldering with hate. Men seethed with it. Hate was what had kept you alive. You hated and you lived. I used to burn the leeches off Chris' legs with cigarettes. And then he'd burn the damn things off of me. Black fleshsuckers the size of a baby's fist. 707s would fly overhead, turn and bank, and we knew they were full of men going home. We'd stand up and cheer jump around. Most of Rhem were just kids. Motherfuckers, you're going home. COME ON, MAMA, LET'S ROCK . . .

Alive.

We were in our Greenwich Village tub together sharing a joint the size of Cucamonga because bathing together was our custom. So was smoking joints the size of Cucamonga. "I wrote a poem today," Chris said.

"You write a poem every day, Chris." I really wasn't in the mood for something as literary as poetry. I was in the mood for playing with Chris' big balls and smoking joints so immense that they boggled the imagination. Even imaginations from California.

"Listen, Boss." Chris opened his notebook which was now thicker than *War and Peace.* I could sense a serious poem forming itself somewhere on the emotional horizon. OKAY, MAMA, LET'S ROCK. "Running moonlight cool," he read from the book. "My legs in my hands. Running anywhere. Running junglehot through silent rivers filled with the brown blood of princes. The blood of boys. Running through remorse.

My legs are hideous and have turned into a coward's legs. My legs are running through moonlight running in my dripping hands. I carry my legs as if they are a burden. Like lead. Dead weight legs. Running for places where nightmares no longer push and dance doing the shuffle shuffle. Just running to no man's tune. Just running. Running anywhere. Anywhere." Chris looked up. "Well, what do you think?"

"I think that most poetry is way over my uneducated head."

"You shouldn't have to think when you hear a poem. You're supposed to simply feel it."

"Okay, Chris, I fucking feel it. It is anything but simple. But then you knew that. What do you want? Your legs can't run anymore. I'm sorry. But I can't do anything about that. And neither can you. Sometimes I just wish that you'd stop trying so goddamn hard. That's what I think. Now, hand me that joint."

"I can run without legs," he said.

"Stop pouting. I loved the poem. I love all of your poems. I don't agree with any of them. But I love them all madly." Chris gave me his best let's have an argument look. "I don't want to fight. I want to play with your balls and get high."

"You want to fight. You love it when we fight because you always win. And then you get high."

"Do not."

"Do too." There was a long silence between us.

"It's just that I think it's about time you started accepting the reality of your situation, Chris. It's p-a-s-t time. It's p-a-s-t time to stop running through remorse. And your legs are not hideous. They're great legs. They're better-looking than Elvis' legs although I don't think anyone ever saw Elvis without his pants on." I lifted his leg and sucked on his big toe.

"What would you say if I told you that I wanted to join a basketball team for the handicapped?"

"I would say that your brain is in worse shape than your legs, that's what I would say."

"And why would you say that?"

"Because there are no faggot wheelchair teams, that's why, Christopher. And you *hate* the word handicapped. If you're talking about joining the team I think you're talking about they are s-t-r-a-i-g-h-t. Watch my lips s-t-r-a-i-g-h-t Vietnam vets. And it's not like you are just getting out of the VA hospital anymore. You've driven that damn chair in too many gay pride parades and you wear your sexuality like a badge. You are insane. You have Post-Traumatic Faggot Syndrome."

Chris submerged his head and came out dripping. He pushed his hair back the way he does when he does his Elvis routine. "Do you think," he asked, "that Elvis ever sang House of the Rising Sun?"

"No."

"Never?"

"Never happened."

COME ON, MAMA, LET'S ROCK. I knew that he was going to do it. He knew that I knew he was going to do it. And he did it. Whenever Chris sets out to do something heaven, hell, Elvis, and mother earth combined cannot stop him.

Two days later I found myself waiting outside the rear of the St. Jean Baptiste Catholic Church at Seventy-sixth and Lexington. The rear of the church was the church school's gymnasium. I could not bring myself to go in. I knew that he probably would have wanted me to go in. That he would have loved to have shown me how well he could compete with the best of them. Run, Christopher, run. But I couldn't. It was almost as if I somehow knew what would happen. Men in wheelchairs passed me. Chris was the last one out.

The side of his face was bruised. It was swollen. Obviously he'd fallen out of the chair. I knew how much he hated to be strapped in. He didn't want to talk about it. "I want to be alone," he said.

"Let me take you home," I said.

"Fuck You!" he screamed. "I don't need you to take me fucking home! I can make it there myself. Leave me alone."

And I left him there. Obviously he hadn't made the team. And Christopher needed to vent his rage against something. Tilt at windmills. Perhaps it gave them some kind of masculine pleasure to reject him because he was a faggot—a cocksucker. He, of course, would have hid nothing from them because if Chris is about being anything in his new honest-Elvis life he's about not hiding. I hated his innocence. I hated his fucking new honesty. I hated him for making me leave. And I hated myself for not being able to do shit about any of it. If there was some way that I could have traded legs with him I would have done it long ago. The blues the blues. BURN MY HOUSE, STEAL MY CAR, DRINK MY LIQUOR FROM AN OLD FRUIT JAR. BUT GET OFFA MY BLUE SUEDE SHOES . . .

I walked downtown on Lexington, made a couple of turns, and found myself going south on Fifth Avenue. St. Patrick's Cathedral loomed up inevitably like a righteous abscessed giant as though it were built from the precious bones of virginal saints. Idolatrous visiting tourists lingered on the steps with cameras in obvious awe of being in the presence of such wonderous supplicated architectural sanctity.

I stopped at a liquor store because I fully intended to be totally inebriated by the time Chris came home . . . if he ever made it home. I had no idea how he would make it all the way to Greenwich Village. I usually helped with cabs and the subway if the subway was at all an option. It was well past midnight when I heard the elevator make its way to the top floor.

"How'd you make it, Chris?"

"By myself, of course. I wheeled it, babe. I wheeled it." And he laughed. But there was an edge to the laughter I didn't like. I had to remind myself that no matter what I really couldn't protect Christopher. It would be a terrible mistake. It would dehumanize him and his humanity was too close to me to try to protect him by putting him into a cage. Even if I had had a cage Chris would never allow himself to be pushed into any kind of protective custody.

That night he thought I was asleep when he crawled from his chair into our bed. I reached over to him and held him. "They said they didn't need any faggots on their team, you know," he said.

"I know," I told him.

"No," he said. "You don't know. You really don't." And he was, of course, absolutely right. I didn't know. I could never know. He ran his fingers through my hair. I looked up at him. "My legs are in my hands," he said. It was a line from his goddamn fucking poem. I wanted to burn the book. It was silly, really. Just stupid. The poem actually didn't mean anything. "Running anywhere running junglehot through silent rivers filled with the brown blood of princes. Running through remorse. My legs are hideous and have turned into a coward's legs. My legs are running through moonlight running in my hands I carry my legs." Chris paused. "Running anywhere. Anywhere." He looked at me with those eyes. Eyes the color of polar ice at noon on a cloudless day. "Let me run."

It was neverneverland. Candy, soda, dirty pictures, boom boom dope. Elvis. We used to go to Vietnamese whores because it's what everyone did. You screwed with whores or you were less than a man. Hey, GI, plenty goodtime. You numbah one GI. Number one GIs were the best. Number ten GIs were shit. Hey, GI, you want fuckee fuckee? How young you want? Me Vietnamese numbah one—VC numbah ten. I knew that Chris was seeing this particular whore. Most whores you saw maybe once. Twice if you were an idiot. But Chris was seeing this particular girl once, maybe twice a week. It wasn't until years later that he told me they never really fucked. They just talked. About everything except the war. She had a family somewhere north of Saigon and she'd send them money. Chris always paid her although he never fucked her. He simply liked her because that's who he was—is. She was her family's only form of support.

And then some soldier killed her. No one knew why.

Killing whores was common. It happened all the time. Maybe you'd just seen your best friend blow up. Maybe you'd just seen him step on a Claymore mine or a Bouncing Betty, and you learned to spit on the Vietnamese after a while because after a while they all looked like the enemy. You learned to hate all of them. So you found a whore because you were a man. And if she didn't please you, if she didn't put out the way you wanted her to put out, then you shot her. Or you beat her. You released your rage. Whores and rage went hand-in-hand. It happened all the time. The whores were just casualties. Victims. But then everyone was a victim. It didn't matter. "She's dead," he said to me.

"What happened?" I asked.

"I went over there," he explained with this kind of glazed look to his eyes—his eyes got that way. "And they wouldn't let me in, you know. 'No GI. No GI. GI numbah ten. GI numbah ten. She dead. GI shoot her. Didi, didi mao. Get away! Get away!' If I find out who did it I'll kill the bastard." But he never found out. She was a whore and it could have been anyone. In neverneverland we were all anonymous.

HONEY DO ANYTHING YOU WANNA DO BUT GET OFF GET OFFA MY BLUE SUEDE SHOES! Christopher wanted us to dress in leather and go to The Spike. So we hauled out the drag and went to The Spike. It's one of the better Manhattan gay bars, really, where we can maneuver the chair inside. And they don't mind him there. We cannot say the same for many of the other places which silently seem to object to a man in a wheelchair in their chic gay establishments. I guess it's not considered sexy or pretty. "I make a lousy stereotype," he said to me once as we were wheeling it o-u-t of a bar we had been asked to leave.

"Oh, I don't know," I said, "You'd look pretty normal standing at the bar until you fell on your face." And we were able to laugh about it. Maybe it should have pissed us off but we were past caring about being pissed off. We were past having to stand around in bars. Usually they'll just stop us right at the door if they don't want us dirtying up their fashionable environments. We have managed to find a couple of dance spots where a few times we've danced our booties off and I *love* shaking my dancing ass in Chris' face as we cavort around the dance floor. To say nothing of Chris who goes hog wild, taking his shirt off, showing off his massive pecs, and moving his beautiful hogbody and arms to the music. Chris dances with less self-absorbed phoniness from his chair than most men do on their feet.

The Spike was crowded with good-looking men in black leather. You could smell the leather in the smoke-blueish air. We maneuverd our way to the back and absorbed the scene. Several men hit on Chris immediately. And he always returned their cruising with his own version of subtle pouting. "You're going to make me jealous," I told him.

"Why do you think we're here?" he said.

That was the night that once again he made the announcement that he would be going home by himself . . . he wanted to do it alone. I didn't fight him. I gave the lunk a big kiss on his lunk lips and left him. It took Chris several hours to make it home. I knew that he was probably riding himself through the wet raining streets, that it probably had its own kind of thrill for him, and eventually he always made it back—although competing with cars from a wheelchair is slighly unsafe.

Crazed even. COME ON, MAMA, LET'S ROCK. WELL, THEY SAID YOU WAS HIGH-CLASS. WELL, THAT WAS

JUST FINE. THEY SAID YOU WAS HIGH-CLASS. AND THAT WAS JUST FINE. BUT YOU NEVER CAUGHT A RABBIT AND YOU AIN'T NO FRIEND OF MINE . . .

It was early in the morning and I was in bed. The sun had not yet brought Manhattan to its frantic sense of life. I had not slept. No Chris. I heard the elevator doors open but still no Chris. Then I heard the sounds of Chris dragging himself up the stairs to the roof. "Shit," I thought. "What's he doing at four in the morning on the fucking roof?" And I went up to see.

YOU CAN BURN MY HOUSE, STEAL MY CAR, DRINK MY LIQUOR FROM AN OLD FRUIT JAR. BUT, BABY, GET OFFA MY BLUE SUEDE SHOES . . . Christopher looked to be either drunk or crazy as sin. He was on the skateboard he used up there. He was throwing his flower pots violently against the brick wall of the raised side of the building. A small pile of dirt and flowers was on the roof. He picked up one of the pots and threw it over the edge. I heard it hit the concrete several floors below us. I asked him what he was doing and I was told to mind my own fucking business. He said that he was mad because he was mad. Period. I left him to his flowers, his depression, and his rage.

That morning he crawled into bed with me and I was very concerned about him. I pressed myself against him in the bed softly. I was amazed to bump into a raging erection. He laughed. "I'm mad as shit," he said, "and I don't even know *why* I'm mad. But look at what it's doing to me." And he looked down at his magnificent boner with fascinated curiosity.

"Maybe," I said, "you ought to get mad more often." YOU CAN KNOCK ME DOWN, STEP ON MY FACE, SLANDER MY NAME ALL OVER THE PLACE . . .

For the first time in a long time we made some heavy loving. LOVE ME TENDER, LOVE ME SWEET, NEVER LET ME GO. Chris was mad as hell and his cock had somehow come alive. I went into the bathroom after that. Chris' pants were on the bathroom floor and I picked them up to hang them on the door. He doesn't call me Motherfucker Hubbard for nothing. That's when the small bottle of reds fell out of the pocket. I was surprised to see it and picked the bottle up from the floor in quiet amazement. It didn't look like any of the pills had been taken as the bottle was quite full. I know downers when I see them. I'm gay and I lived in Greenwich Village. I was looking at Seconal. Real horse-sized killers. And for someone like Chris, someone who simply can't take that kind of a chemical rush anymore because his body will not tolerate it, Seconal will take you out with no chance of making it back into the real world.

"What the fuck is this, Chris?!" I yelled.

He was in the bed and looked at me. He rolled his body over with his arms so he didn't have to look at me and said that they were nothing . . . to throw them away.

"Nothing?! The hell these are nothing. You stupid shit, Chris. I knew you were depressed. I knew you were down. But you aren't the only person in the world to sometimes have a problem. What, first everyone else I know, now you? Well, it sucks!" And I hit his numb legs with my fist. And I hit them again. And again. There was no reaction. I hit his muscled shoulder. I knew he could feel me there but there was no reaction. He let me do it. I hit the lunk again. Nothing. Chris was thinking about killing himself. I could smell it like a virulent stink. Chris didn't take pills anymore. We had both stopped doing that. That had been a battle we had supposedly left in the past where it belonged. No more fucking pills. But Christopher was thinking about taking all of the pills in the bottle. Probably with liquor. I knew him like I knew every vein in his cock. "Get up, Chris!" I yelled at him. "We're going for a ride."

Bang, you're dead. The shock wasn't Vietnam. The shock

was coming back and realizing that no one cared. No one cared that some anonymous Vietnamese whore got her brains blown out. No one cared that some anonymous eighteen-year-old boy from Nebraska had eaten a rain of incoming—our incoming—the damn radios didn't work half the time. We got sprayed with red from the choppers. Anything and everything sprayed with red meant that it was enemy territory. We yelled in the radio, Hey, assholes, it's us, it's us! But our position had been sprayed with red and we ate 82 millimeter mortars for lunch.

We didn't know who he was. Or why he was there. But he got caught in the red with the rest of us. Only he bought a bunch of shrapnel in the face. If you could call it a face. It had once been a face. A boy's face. You tried not to care but you cared anyway. It just ate at your guts because he was a kid and he was beautiful and you wanted to love him he could have been your goddamn brother. The shock was in coming back to find that all anyone else cared about was their nine-to five, and their TV, and their mortgage, and their car payment, and getting laid, and getting drunk. That's all she wrote. No one wore love beads anymore. It had all been a very sick kind of joke.

You came back and you wondered if the war had been about anything. Anything at all.

The cab took us to the edge of the Manhattan side of the Brooklyn Bridge. I dragged the chair out of the back seat angrily and yelled at him to slide himself into it. The driver ignored us. He was from New York. "Get in the chair, Chris!" And he quietly swung himself in. Chris hates to be strapped in but I didn't want him going anywhere anywhere so I strapped him in. Tough shit.

LOVE ME TENDER, LOVE ME SWEET, NEVER LET ME GO . . . The sun was just beginning to bathe Manhattan in the first subtle hits of mesmerized light. A tug boat softly bellowed its moan-like cry below us in the cold water. Two

bearded long-haired faggots, one in a wheelchair, slowly made
their way to the middle of the bridge. The handgun was one that
Chris had bought when he had first moved in. He said that
we'd need it for safety. Protection. It was stupid, really. I had
hated it then and I hated it as it weighed my pocket down as I
pushed his chair to the center of the bridge.

The water passed underneath the grating of the bridge as
we stood there watching the city slowly breathe itself alive. I
took the snub-nosed gun out and handed it to him. He
wouldn't look at me. The small silver gun sat on his lap. "Go
ahead, Chris," I said. "Do it. If you're going to kill yourself
you may as well shoot me, too. Then you can shoot yourself." I
bent down and took ahold of his face firmly in my hands and I
stuck my face directly in front of his. His rock-a-bye blue eyes,
blue as polar ice in the sea on a clear cold day at noon, looked
at me with something called love. "Go ahead, Chris. Do it right
here. I fucking dare you. If everybody is hellbent on doing it
you may as well take King Shit with you." I put my finger up to
my forehead touching it. "The lot of you fuck-ups were all I
really ever had, Chris. And if you're dying then I want to die
too." Chris picked up the gun and quietly threw it into the East
River. He very softly told me to just shut the fuck up. I shut the
fuck up.

He always hates for me to see him cry.

We were laying side by side in the old oversized antique
tub. We had filled that sucker to the brim with warm water.
Chris "suffered" from a massive erection. His rage had helped.
So had crying. "Read to me, baby," he asked.

So I picked up his book of poems, poems which no one
else would ever in a million years read, and I read back to
Christopher his own thoughts. Thoughts which were new to
me. "Oh, he lets me run," I read, "in the way he looks at me in
the morning. Our bed smells with us it is our smell: two men.
He is not always at his best at this time and this is when I am

able to manipulate him easily. His eyes look at me as if I am normal just anyone. And there I am with all this power and he just gives it to me. So I lord it over him. Which is what power is for. And in his glance I am able to run like the wind running wherever it is the wind runs on such mornings. I run to him. To his tender arms. Into his kisses. His mouth is always full of such soft daddy kisses. And although I cannot run I can run for him so fast it makes even the gods laugh with jealousy. Sucking his tongue into my wet mouth. Running with his soul in my hands . . . "

I put his book down and looked at Christopher. "You have to have," I said, "the dirtiest most evil mind in the entire universe."

"I can't help it," he explained. "I love you. I have always loved you. Even in Nam. When I hated you. I loved you even when I hated you for making me live." Christopher picked up a bar of soap and gently washed my chest, his eyes never leaving my line of vision. The blues the blues. I DON'T WANNA BE YOUR TIGER CAUSE TIGERS PLAY TOO ROUGH. I DON'T WANNA BE YOUR LION CAUSE LIONS AIN'T THE KIND YOU LOVE ENOUGH. SO JUST PUT A CHAIN AROUND MY NECK AND LEAD ME ANYWHERE. OH, I JUST WANT TO BE YOUR PERSONAL TEDDY BEAR. BABY, JUST LET ME BE AROUND YOU EVERY NIGHT. I'LL RUN YOUR FINGERS THROUGH MY HAIR AND CUDDLE ME REAL TIGHT. OH LET ME BE (OH, LET HIM BE) YOUR TEDDY BEAR. I JUST WANNA BE YOUR LITTLE TEDDY BEAR . . .

I couldn't any more leave Chris than I could put a handgun to my fucking head and pull the trigger.

Part Two

THE TUNNEL RATS

—oh bitter daddy death stalks
dragons behind your eyes
in your embrace let me climb
up onto your lap to look
behind the armour your hiding place
where dragons breathe fire
and sons run rampant
sweet like sugar lips
glistening on the diabetic mouths
of all your insulin babes
death stalks even dragons
in such a place where
sons do as sons are told
where sons become the dragons
themselves where bitterness
reigns on the sweet lips of men
where armour no longer matters
where sons discover the touch
of other sons where daddy's eyes
breathe fire where far across the sea
is not far enough anywhere
anywhere—

You were afraid to die but even more than that you were afraid to die alone. Alone was the worst. You wanted to believe, you had to believe, that if you took it, if you bit a big one, that one of your buddies would at least hold you while you died. There were a lot of different *kinds* of fear. Just like there were a lot of different *kinds* of love. And hate. But the most intense ingrained type of fear was the fear of being abandoned. If you were going to die the way we saw so many of them go— armless, intestines torn apart—then you wanted to feel the warmth of another human being as you convulsed and vomited up your own death from whatever was left of your soulless belly. For as many times as you might see your friends' flesh and bowels ripped apart you thought that when it came your time that you'd go cleanly, morally, shitless like in the movies.

Somehow dying was unmanly. It wasn't winning.

It was, of course, never that simple. Or easy. I never saw any of them die so cleanly or elegantly. You never just bled a little and then died. YOU AIN'T NOTHING BUT A HOUND DOG CRYING ALL THE TIME. YOU AIN'T NEVER CAUGHT A RABBIT AND YOU AIN'T NO FRIEND OF MINE. More likely your flesh, your guts, and your shit would have been blown all over your buddy's face. Oh, he'd hold you. Whatever there was left of you. They'd scrape up your dead meat, strip you, throw you into a body bag, tag a number on you, send your mama a form letter, and be done with it. Dear Mrs. Apple Pie, little dumb Johnnycomemarchinghome just done got himself shot. You learned to count on the men you were with. There were no other options. Nobody wanted to die alone.

But in the end we all die alone.

Candy, soda, dirty pictures, boom boom dope. The sounds of Elvis singing in your head. Bang, you're dead. It was neverneverland. It wasn't really happening. It was destiny breathing down our necks. It was Vietnam. Our squad had tunnel rats. They did as they were told. No questions asked. Just shut up and get your fucking ass down into that dirt hole before you get a boot shoved up your grunt's butt, Soldier. My boot. They were boys. I hated them. I hated them because they were boys. I was supposed to keep them alive. Any way I could. You wanna live, Boy? Do as you're told and don't ask me any questions. I could not tolerate their fucking questions. I did not have answers. I did as I was told. Period. Nothing more. Nothing less. It was just what we did. We died. It's what we had been born to do. In Vietnam we tended to do it thankfully. It was neverneverland and Peter Pan was out to lunch.

WELL, THEY SAID YOU WAS HIGH-CLASS. AND THAT WAS JUST FINE. YEAH, THEY SAID YOU WAS HIGH-CLASS. AND THAT WAS JUST FINE. BUT YOU NEVER CAUGHT A RABBIT AND YOU AIN'T NO FRIEND OF MINE. I hated them. They were from Iowa. They were from Ohio. They were from Georgia. They were from Maine, Oregon, maybe they were from Michigan. I didn't much care where the fuck they were from. They were young. Young, dumb, and full of cum. And laughter. And love. Even the ones who never thought they could experience loving another man always ended up bawling their high school eyes out when their best buddy got shot. Tunnel rat was a nickname. We all had nicknames. A name either humanized you or dehumanized you. It was a war with names that weren't really names. Charley was VC. Charley Company was us. CINCPAV. CORDS. COSVN. You didn't die eyeless dead; you were KIA. Hand frags. Huey. Even Willie Peter was actually a type of white phosphorus used in grenades. Gook could be the enemy or gook could be South Vietnamese. Chink. Slant. Dink. Zip. YOU AIN'T NOTHING BUT A HOUND DOG ROCKIN' ALL THE TIME...

You were told to win their hearts and their minds. And then you were told to blow them away because they were less than human. You were told that every naked little kid in the street had a gun or a grenade. You were told that in the long run we would win. It was not a good war with idealistic morals. It was a war of death and boys. And grandma mamasans, and water buffalo, and rice paddies, and mud, and humping mountains in the heat, and heroin, and whores and soft rivers in the rain. My nickname was King Shit. Or Boss. I used to send them down into those VC spider holes, then I'd stand around uptop with a joint in my mouth, praying to fucking waiting breathless Christ that they'd eventually emerge— alive—out of the other end of the tunnel. There were a lot of tunnels. Hundreds of miles of airless, lightless, swallowing tunnels.

You could never hear a tunnel rat scream.

I loved them. I loved them more than I had ever loved anything. I loved them with my life. I called them my boys. I was establishing my authority because I had never had any. Most of them were eighteen although I suspected that one, Christopher, who else, was really seventeen. He had lied about his age. I was nineteen with a year of UCLA under my belt which made me older and wiser. And less afraid. I could not afford to be afraid although I was so afraid all of the time that it kind of sat at the base of my stomach like a twisted knot of moist cement. When they died on me I'd cry if there was time to cry. When they died it meant I had failed them. I did not want to fail them because every time I looked at them I knew that I loved them. So I kept telling myself that I hated them. That I could not afford the luxury of loving them. But there it was.

They were so goddamn beautiful.

They were the kind of boys who thought that it was somehow the duty of every woman in the world (except for their mothers) to either look like Jayne Mansfield or Raquel. One or the other. After all they were men—now—and didn't the world owe them at least that? They knew, of course, that it was a stupid thing to want. And that if your girlfriend really was the playmate of the year you might not like it much. All those guys drooling over what was yours. Yet if you were honest with yourself you knew that you wanted the guys to drool over what a piece of masculinity you really were. After all, the bottom line wasn't Vietnam. Or Jayne Mansfield. The bottom line was how big your balls were. You sat on your helmet while riding around in the choppers because you knew for a fact that if Charley could shoot your left testicle off he would. You saw other boys getting their balls shot off all the time. Charley always went for the balls. It happened. You tried not to look. You looked anyway. They'd hold their crotches and scream. It looked like bloody mush. You had to know what it looked like. You closed your eyes and tried to think of Jayne Mansfield.

When they died they died looking up to me; they were always looking up to me. I wanted to beg them not to. I wanted to get on my knees and tell them that I was as fucking terrified of it as they were. Don't look up to me! I DON'T WANNA BE YOUR TIGER CAUSE TIGERS PLAY TOO ROUGH. I DON'T WANNA BE YOUR LION CAUSE LIONS AIN'T THE KIND YOU LOVE ENOUGH... They were cornfed midwest southern supper's ready on the porch lover boy baby boomers. They were not complicated. I hated them. I hated them for who they were, what they were, and why they were who they were. I would have done anything just to keep my boys alive. Don't die on me, guy, don't die on me because I fucking can't deal with it.

I love you.

Most of the time there were four of them which made five of us. I can't remember where they were from. Four stupid asshole middle-America scared-to-shitass-death smiling jerkoffs. Not one of them was in reality stupid. It was a war of names that weren't really names, body counts that weren't really body counts, Zippo raids, and ineloquent inconsistencies that were always flawlessly consistent. I loved them and I hated them. I loved Vietnam. It was lushly beautiful. Yet I hated it. We weren't stupid! We were all stupid just for being there. They were Saturday night at the drive-in screwing some cheerleader backseat cunt into swollen pregnancy. They listened to Jim Morrison even when every single one of their fathers disapproved of Jim Morrison. Fervently. No son of mine is going to listen to that cocksucker although no father would ever use the word cocksucker. They listened anyway. They all had posters of Elvis the pelvis and Janis and the Beach Boys and Dylan and Jagger and the Greatful Dead on their bedroom walls at home wherever home was. Wherever home was there'd be a small stack of raggedy *Playboy* magazines under the bed maybe stuck between the mattresses. Nude magazine photos of Jayne Mansfield carefully hidden under your socks. Tits as pink as a Memphis Cadillac. If they believed in anything they believed that rock'n roll was probably going to be their only rhythmic salvation, and that rock itself was the symbolic release of what was left of their collectively castrated sense of conscience.

Philosophically they were confused and more than slightly hungry.

OH, BABY LET ME BE AROUND YOU EVERY NIGHT. I'LL RUN YOUR FINGERS THROUGH MY HAIR

AND CUDDLE ME REAL TIGHT. JUST PUT A CHAIN
AROUND MY NECK AND LEAD ME ANYWHERE
. . . Anywhere, anywhere. COME ON, MAMA, LET'S
ROCK. They were midnight fireworks Main Street on the
Fourth of July and everybody including Grandpa goes ahhh.
They were Friday night's bowling team. They were smalltown
lover's lane knee-deep in rubbers. They were hot rod cruising
not that any of them could in a million years score while cruising. They were classic fuck-ups. They were popcorn at the
movies. When every one of them had been seven-years-old,
every one of them had made obscene fart-noises with their
hands cupped under their boy armpits, because that's the
kind of seven-year-old they all would have been. They were
buckboy beerdrunk looking for trouble; well, they found it.
    They were Vietnam.
    They did not know why they were where they were. It was
just what you did. You never really knew what any of it was
about. They were drafted mostly. But they were the kind of
boys who had allowed themselves to be drafted; it was as if
being drafted was some kind of a badass badge or medal of
honor in and of itself. Your mama would kiss you goodbye.
Your papa would shake your hand. Your younger brother
might even cry. And your girlfriend would pledge that her
pussy and her soul would belong to you forever after. As in
eternity which is a very long time for a pussy. Let alone a soul.
    You kept your girlfriend's letters and her picutre, the one
of her at the Jersey beach, in your helmet where your sterile
compresses were supposed to be. You jerked off at night and
hoped to God if there was one that jungle rot didn't get to your
dick the way it got to your feet. You thought of her, you wondered if she really loved you, and in your bones you knew she
didn't. Not really. She wasn't going to be there when you
needed her. Never happened. Your best buddy, your fellow
grunt, now, he might love you. And if he said he loved you,
probably drunk or stoned or both, well, it didn't much matter

if he was drunk or stoned—or both—if he said he loved you he loved you. You could depend on it. You didn't want to—it was a secret—but if he said he loved you hot damn you loved him, too. Hell, she was probably sucking some collegeboy's erect dick, drinking his cum warm from his educated balls, not thinking about you, Soldier. Don't be so barefaced stupid, Boy.

OH, JUST PUT A CHAIN AROUND MY NECK AND LEAD ME ANYWHERE. They were naive. They were not college educated. Every other word was a curse word because their language was the language of the great cover-up. Even their language covered their humanity and their despair. Not one of them could read a map correctly even if their collective dumbass lives depended on it which they frequently did. They were tunnel rats. They were neverneverland. Candy, soda, dirty pictures, boom boom dope. Elvis the pelvis. They were destiny. They did not know where it was, it was anywhere anywhere, and they did n-o-t know what it was all about. If it was about anything. They were very good at what they did. They'd been trained to it. You had to respect them even if you hated them even if you loved the hell out of them because they did what nobody else wanted the fuck to do. It was beyond guts. It had nothing to do with patriotism. The tunnels were terror and the smell of human rabid stink. Death in the closed-in dark. There wasn't going to be anybody down there to hold you when you died.

My boys saw everything down there that there was to see. Five VC could hole up in one tunnel for as long as a week. Eating nothing. Drinking their own urine. Standing upright in the dirt blackness. Just knowing I was uptop ready to blow their oriental brains out if they so much as showed one hair of their VC heads. And if I couldn't budge them with grenades or smoke-bombs or machine gun fire I'd send one of my boys down there to flush the sons-of-bitches into the terminal light of day. Then there were the rats. The real rats. It was assumed that all the rats were rabid. One bit you and you had the shots. All of them. Soup-rats as big as dogs. The killing part was easy. It was the staying alive part that was hard.

Grunts. Stand at attention piss in the woods squatshit dogtag C-ration trench-foot bug-juice sweat-dripping grunts. YOU AIN'T NOTHING BUT A HOUND DOG. Boys who had been told all their lives that they had to win because winning was it. That's all she wrote. Win or die. They were scared eighteen-year-olds armed to the teeth with M-14s, M-60s, CAR-15s, M-16s, M-79 grenade launchers, 66mm LAWs, fragmentation grenades, insecticide, C-4 plastic explosives, Kool-Aid, salt tablets, and homesickness. Ammunition you carried wrapped around your chest. Homesickness you carried in your belly and in your eyes. In addition to their regulation-issued weapons each boy had a flashlight and a bayonet which were not regulation but then Vietnam wasn't fought according to regulation. A tunnel rat might need his bayonet.

The flashlights were always going out.

They were afraid of death in the tunnels; you could hear it in their nervous masculine laughter. It was okay to emerge alive with your ass in your hands from a hole, laugh about it, and tell us that you almost shit in your pants, crawling around down there. But if you'd really shit in your pants you'd hardly laugh about it. They were more afraid of their fear than they were of death. You could show another man the raw insides of your soul, you could fuck a village whore in front of your buddies, you could shit in front of a hundred naked men hoping that nobody watched, you could bare your guts and anger, but you could not show your fear.

You were not an animal you were a man.

I DON'T WANNA BE YOUR TIGER CAUSE TIGERS PLAY TOO ROUGH . . . At least you hoped you were a man. You wanted to believe it but you had doubts. You doubted your own humanity. You hoped that when it came your time that you wouldn't turn around and fucking run. You were afraid of death. But you were terrified into the depths of your liquid bowels over the possibility of confronting the naked lunatic reality of your fear. To the Vietnamese it was about madness and killing but then they had always known madness and killing. To us it was about fear. You went to Vietnam for two reasons: to see if you'd come back and to see what kind of a man you were in the face of unadulterated terror. In time you feared becoming not just an empty shell. But you could swear that when you walked you rattled like a desert snake.

YOU CAN KNOCK ME DOWN, STEP ON MY FACE, SLANDER MY NAME ALL OVER THE PLACE. BUT, MAMA, GET OFFA MY BLUE SUEDE SHOES . . . Tunnel rats were considered pogue by many which was slang for military personnel employed in rear echelon support capacities. We wiped up. Pogue was an obscenity. We were not pogue and they knew it. We were in the thick of it all of the time. Bang, you're dead. We ate incoming as if the sky had erupted with red hot Rice Krispies. Tunnel rats did not have long life spans. The only thing worse than going down into those damn spider holes was sending somebody you loved down into those damn spider holes. And the only thing worse than that was going after somebody who hadn't come out when he should have come out. So I figured that the least the US military could do for a grunty tunnel rat if he emerged from the ground in one soldierboy piece was to offer the son-of-a-bitch a joint.

I rolled mine big and thick. More than enough to go around. They were soaked in opium and they could help you forget where you were, what you had seen, what you had done. You popped outta the tunnel, you laughed, you were still alive, and you took a long nervous toke on a sweet-burning oriental baby. You put it to your lush boylips and you shared it with your buddies. These were the men you loved. You passed it around. It became a ritual. These were the men who'd hold you when you died. Sometimes it felt good just to be alive. Sometimes it didn't. They were boys and initially they had a lot to learn. It was my responsibility to show them that the only way they were going to stay alive, and return to their brothers and their mamas in anything other than a body bag, was for them to trust in no one but their fellow tunnel rats. No one. They were wet behind the ears. I wanted them to see killing because they were itching to see killing. I wanted the mystery of it to go away. Killing is anything but glamorous. It's neverneverland. Bang, you're dead. I wanted them to hate killing. I did not always get what I wanted. Not in Vietnam. Jayne Mansfield lived in a pink house, bathed in a pink tub, drank pink champagne, and had big pink tits in another life. A million miles away. We were men and we had a war to win.

Candy, soda, dirty pictures, boom boom dope. LOVE ME TENDER, LOVE ME TRUE, ALL MY DREAMS FULFILLED. FOR MY DARLING I LOVE YOU. AND I ALWAYS WILL . . .

Once during our first village search-and-destroy mop-up we caught an old mamasan who had escaped from the village detention. Her white hair was pulled back. She was small and had become entangled in the coiled razor-sharp concertina barbed wire which surrounded the thatched hooches. Most of the hooches had been marked for burning and demolition. Tunnels had been discovered under the homes. Tunnels that my boys would have to crawl around in and search. We hated taking firethrowers down there, not because we might get burned, but because a firethrower would suck up all the oxygen. You could barely breath anyway.

The old woman lay on the ground, cut and bleeding. She swore in Vietnamese and struggled to free herself from the barbs which only cut into her—worse horribly—the more she fought it. "What do we do with her?" one of my boys asked. I told him to go get a couple of the ARVNs (we called them arvins), a couple of the South Vietnamese regular troops. I wanted my boys to learn something from and about the South Vietnamese. "Du ma! Du ma!" she screamed at us. Du ma or do mommie is Vietnamese for fuck your mother. "Didi, didi Mao!" she screamed again. And again. Get the fuck away. Get away. "No VC! No VC! GI numbah one!" My boys watched them shoot her. It was their first shooting it would not be their last.

Bang, you're dead. It is that simple. You just die. You don't thrash around slowly, dramatically, the way they do in Hollywood. Not when you're shot in the head. Vietnam was not Hollywood. She begged them not to shoot her. My boys, the ones from Ohio and Iowa and Georgia, where killing was something endemic to nighttime television, where death is something that happens to your pet turtle, watched in silent neverneverland frozen fascination. She screamed at them to fuck their mothers—do mommie—and the ARVN shot her. GI numbah one. They left her body just messed up in the rolled wire, her brains oozing onto the ground. Peter Pan was fucked. Sometimes it didn't feel good to be alive.

Or worth the bother. GET OFF GET OFFA MY BLUE SUEDE SHOES . . .

"VC," one of the Arvins said. And he smiled with that smile they all had; the kind of smile where you were supposed to smile back but you didn't because the only thing you hated more than the VC were the arvins. No arvin was going to hold you when you died. The mamasan in the wire did not die needlessly. She taught my boys the biggest lesson of the war. A lesson they were going to have to learn and learn well if they wanted to survive. They were going to have to put the fact that they were in Vietnam, now, into their bellies for breakfast, lunch, and dinner. They would have to choke on the reality of it. I didn't care anything about the war. I hated the men who said we had to be there. I didn't give two cents for winning the time of day. I just wanted my team to learn how to survive.

They were going to eat Vietnam, sleep Vietnam, shoot it into their virgin Iowa cornfed veins for dessert. Just live, damn you. Win. In time they would become Vietnam. The irony, of course, is that if they lived long enough, if they got crazy enough with it, if it festered in their bellies for a good while like a pus-filled sore, they would learn to love Vietnam. She was indigo beautiful. She was horrifically ugly. She was blood, shit, and death. She was the only place in the world where no one gave a fuck.

About anything.

Peter Pan could not fly. It was all a lie. Elvis never sang about the house of the rising sun. Never happened. In time they would choose to lock themselves, wrap themselves, tightly into the enigmatic embrace of the war. They would inhabit insanity because they had become addicted to it. It was their shared insanity which kept them alive. We saw it all. We saw lots of winning. Win! Other boys from other states, Michigan, Virginia, Maine, Oregon, would sit with us in Quonset huts and bunkers. They'd show us their pictures. Everyone who had been in the field had pictures. Very few of those kinds of pictures found their way back to the States. If the brass caught you with forbidden pictures, particularly pictures of the dead, the film got confiscated. Period. The brass was always looking for pictures. The pictures were all the same. You'd sit down next to some prettyboy with rock-a-bye Nebraska eyes. First he'd show you a picture of his buddy, the one who'd stepped on a Bouncing Betty, the one who'd had his lungs blown out.

That's Jimmy or Ronnie or Bobby. Or whoever. And then he'd show you the pictures of the burning villages. On the bottom of the pile of photographs would be the images of the dead

VC. Naked corpses with their dicks cut off and stuck into their mouths and their assholes. Before and after shots of girls with grenades in their rectums. "It's war, isn't it," the boy from Michigan, Virginia, Maine, or Oregon would say. And you realized that it was not a question. You looked at his photographs. Stunned. Horrified. Fascinated. And then you were horrified all over again because you—Y–O–U—were so goddamn intrigued. You told him, Yes, kid, it's war. Yes, people do things in war.

Don't they.

Don't they. Yes, damn you. WELL, THEY SAID YOU WERE HIGH-CLASS. AND THAT WAS JUST FINE. BUT YOU NEVER CAUGHT A RABBIT AND YOU AIN'T NO FRIEND OF MINE. You couldn't take your eyes off the photographs. Oh, you didn't want to look. It made you sick. You were a nice person from Michigan, Ohio, Virginia, Oregon, wherever. You bought your clothes in a fucking mall somewhere where they played Elvis' songs on the public address system. Your daddy had taken 8mm home movies of your sweetness in the front yard. WELL, THEY SAID YOU WERE HIGH-CLASS. AND THAT WAS JUST FINE. You didn't want to see the images of death. You wanted to win this basketball game and get it over with. You didn't want to see this. But you looked anyway. The photographs grabbed you by the throat and made you breathless; so this is what it's like. You knew that the kid had done more than just snap a photograph, that he'd been part of it. Sure, he'd tell you, with that numb look they all sooner or later got when they had seen and participated in more than their fair share of it. I put the grenade in her ass. I pulled the pin. You didn't want to know that human beings could do such things to other human beings. You told yourself that you were better than that.

And then you knew that it simply wasn't so.

You didn't want to know that little kids could be blown to

bits for the sheer pleasure of it. You didn't want to know that you were as fully capable as the next man of putting a grenade up some twelve-year-old boy's butt and pulling the pin. You couldn't take your eyes off the pictures of the villagers, mostly women and children, lying in ditches with their hands locked behind their heads, dark holes in their faces. Earless. Guts everywhere. You didn't want to know. You didn't want to know how ugly another human being could get. But there it was. Neverneverland.

Candy, soda, dirty pictures, boom boom dope. Put an Elvis song in your head. Maybe Elvis could save you.

You spent hours with the kid on his bed trying to figure it all out. You wanted to win but now somehow you began to wonder. Win what? You wondered if it was really happening. You got angrier and angrier. He showed you the pictures of his girl, the ones where she smiled on the Jersey beach. He told you that he hoped that she would never know about any of—it. It. Just it. The kid with the photographs would put them away, excuse himself, and go into the latrine where you'd find Peter Pan an hour later sitting there with his pants down around his ankles, nodding out, a needle stuck into his virgin's arm. You'd pick him up in your arms like a baby, and put him to bed. Bang, you're dead. Candy, soda, dirty pictures, boom boom dope. LOVE ME TENDER, LOVE ME LONG, TAKE ME TO YOUR HEART. FOR IT'S CERTAIN THAT I BELONG AND WE'LL NEVER PART . . .

The good guys won because they were good guys and they had goodness. You were from the fifties and the sixties and you knew it to be true. You looked toward heaven when you prayed to God. The bad guys lost because they were bad guys and they were filled with badness. It was war, you were there because you were good, and the possibility that you might not win was not only unthinkable it was heresy.

And sometimes if you were new at it, if you'd never

picked up Peter Pan stoned sitting on a toilet, if you'd never felt a boyhero limp like that in your arms, you'd cry until you couldn't cry anymore.

They were rock'n roll virgins, these boys from wherever it was they were from, and if they weren't virgins they knew little about love. Not the kind of love you find in a song. They knew little of the kind of love you find between people—they knew little of this. They knew even less about making love. They were the kind of boys who didn't make love they *made* a piece of nookie. You weren't concerned with love. You concerned yourself with anatomy. They knew in their bones that love was what Alice and Ralph Kramden had on the Honeymooners. Ralph was always going to send Alice to the moon with his fist because he loved her. They also knew that the person Ralph really loved was his friend, Ed Norton. Now, this was a relationship. They were the kind of boys who didn't expect life to bring them anything more than the opportunity to perhaps drive a bus. Or work in a sewer. And they expected to live out their psychic love lives in one small cramped room. Now, that was love.

Vietnam was not about love. It was less about virginity. If we were not at any point during the fighting able to figure out what the war was about, all of us were at least able to figure out what the war was not about. It was not about love. You were an eighteen-year-old and your balls were full of yourself. You had several sexual options. You could jerk off alone which could be a stupid thing to do. You could take Jayne Mansfield out with you into the field, which was about the only place to go to be alone, we were always finding numbah one GI bodies, often headless, guys with their cocks in their hands.

You half wanted to laugh when you found them. But you didn't because you knew that you'd go into the boonies yourself to jerk off if it was at all possible. Or safe which it wasn't. Jerking off alone in the boonies was downright crazy. You could jerk off with a buddy. There was a lot of this. More than got talked about. It did not get talked about. You could get your dick sucked and getting your dick sucked wasn't queer. Sucking dick, now, that was queer. Queers were tolerated as long as they kept a lid on it. PUT A CHAIN AROUND MY NECK AND LEAD ME ANYWHERE. OH, LET ME BE (OH LET HIM BE) YOUR TEDDY BEAR. I JUST WANT TO BE YOUR LITTLE TEDDY BEAR. . . .

You could go queerboy—there were risks. It happened. You got caught and sure as the sun shines they'd send your ass where no ass should have gone. You'd get your butt kicked to the front of the line. You'd walk point through mine fields where the Bouncing Betties were as numerous and as thick as the stars on a night so bible-black you could have choked on heaven. Cocksuckers—the crime had to fit the punishment. You get caught with your dick in somebody's mouth you cleaned latrines until the cows came home. But you didn't die. You get caught with somebody else's dick in your mouth and they'd send you smack dab into a nest of VC or NVAs. That took care of the cocksuckers where a court martial wouldn't. You get caught being butt fucked and they'd just shoot the both of you and say the VC did it. Guys who got caught in the act of fucking often went up in Cobra or Huey choppers where they had a tendency to fall off. I DON'T WANNA BE YOUR TIGER CAUSE TIGERS PLAY TOO ROUGH . . .

And then there were the whores. Most whores were VC. They'd put glass up their pussies. Or they'd infect you with strains of VD that would put you behind the lines. VD so powerful you thought you'd die if you ever pissed again. You didn't have to kill a man to put him out of action. One whore could infect a lot of GIs. The whores did not always have to have pussies. The transvestites were pretty in-fucking-credible. Or you could do what a lot of virgin soldierboys from Ohio, Iowa, Georgia, Michigan, Virginia, and Maine did. It got talked about less than jerking off got talked about. A lot less. You were a soldier. You were someone with authority—an M-16. It was power. Probably more power than you'd ever had over another human being. You were eighteen-years-old and they had to do whatever it was you told them to do. You could take what you wanted. It wasn't going to make the CBS evening news. There were never any court martials for a man taking what he wanted.

None of the whores looked like Jayne Mansfield. None of them looked like Raquel. Somehow this added to the unconscious rage you carried around in your GI fuck'em belly. A woman was supposed to look like Jayne Mansfield. Or Raquel. A real man was supposed to want real tits. The Vietnamese didn't respect us. A woman was supposed to look like the playmate of the year. Even if your backhome girlfriend didn't look like the playmate of the year you wanted her to. In Vietnam the rules were so abstract you could easily convince yourself that there were no rules. You closed your eyes and pretended she was Jayne Mansfield. We all had one foot in the ideological and sexual grave even if we tried to suck it out. The foot held. You paid for a woman's services. Blackmarket fuckee fuckee. We couldn't see them as human beings. We wanted Jayne Mansfield. We wanted Raquel. And all we could get our hands on was Charley's younger sister. Charley, himself, was out there dug in waiting. Listening to his sister scream. LOVE ME TENDER, LOVE ME DEAR, TELL ME YOU ARE MINE. I'LL BE YOURS THROUGH ALL THE YEARS UNTIL THE END OF TIME . . .

My tunnel rats were some of the best grunts in the business even if two of them were fucking queers and the other two were questionable. We were all questionable. Candy, soda, dirty pictures, boom boom dope. WELL, THEY SAID YOU

WAS HIGH-CLASS . . . The universe was questionable.
Billy Boy had blue eyes, a bad mouth, and looked like he'd
just walked in off some surfers' beach in Malibu. He was
blond and beautiful. And he knew that he was blond and
beautiful. I called him Billy Boy or Geronimo because I'd seen
him parachute from a plane directly into a fire fight for the
sheer pleasure of it. He was intrigued with the adventure.
Young and cocky. Geronimo talked in his sleep. His sleep was
jerky nightmare sleep. I tried to break him of it. But there it
was. Billy Boy could be broken—any boy can be broken—but
his nightmares could not be broken. Nightmares are not boys.
Billy Boy was cat-nervous. He had a toothpick stuck in his
mouth most of the time.

    Billy was the kind of man who would eventually fail at lov-
ing. He would fail at all of his relationships in life because
nothing else in his life could live up to Vietnam. Vietnam
simply overwhelmed who and what he was. He slowly drowned
in it. I loved him. He had the most outrageous Elvis routine.
Chris stole his Elvis routine from Billy. Billy played a mean
guitar. And he really could sing the blues. Sing it, Billy.
COME ON, MAMA, LET'S ROCK! Yet he would eventually
drown in his own bitterness as if it was some kind of a blue-
sweet sustenance. Vietnam didn't kill Billy. Billy Boy saved
that for himself in a Cleveland SRO with a gun in his mouth.
After Vietnam. There was a name for it because there was a
name for everything that came out of Vietnam: Post-Traumatic
Stress Disorder. YOU CAN KNOCK ME DOWN, STEP ON
MY FACE, SLANDER MY NAME ALL OVER THE
PLACE . . .

    He was supposed to come back to the States, forget about
what he had seen, what he had participated in, he was
supposed to fit in. Quietly—no muss no fuss. Hey, baby, you
done won the ballgame. Get a job, become a file clerk, fuck
your wife on Friday night, watch the Superbowl and cheer. Put

your guitar away, Billy, listen to Elvis, get drunk—and remember. Live. But don't remind anyone that in your sleep you see images of the babies you've murdered. Shutupshutupshutup! Don't think about it. Don't suffer from Post-Traumatic Stress Disorder. Only perverts and faggots and weak baby killers suffer from PTSD. Billy Boy was only a mediocre killer. While he had a certain lust for the adventure of it he had no lust for the killing that accompanied the adventure the way a group of whores might accompany a platoon. We often found ourselves carrying his weight. Not that we minded. We didn't. If we were going to die, and we were all sure that we would, well, we wanted to do it while we were with Billy because there was never any doubt as to the fact that he would hold us and cry while we bled on him.

Not only did we not want to die alone, when we bit it we wanted someone to fucking cry. If we were going to die we wanted someone to bleed on. GET OFFA MY SHOES!

After he killed his first VC, a kid in black pajamas, a fourteen-year-old if that kid was a day, Billy Boy cried. He did not want anyone to see him cry. I sent him off into the treeline. He did his crying there. We waited. When he didn't come out I had to go in there to get him. He was out of control, shaking, sobbing, talking to God. I had to hold him and tell him that it was okay. It's okay, guy. If you hadn't killed him he would have killed you. Or us. It was a lie. I knew it was a lie. Billy knew it was a lie. The kid was unarmed. We said he was VC because to us they were all VC. And he was dead so he had to be VC. VC numbah ten. Candy, soda, dirty pictures, boom boom dope. It's okay. After that Billy Boy didn't cry when he killed them he just killed them.

James LeRoy Washington was black and big. And filled with a confused sort of misdirected hate which is why I liked him. I called him Jim Bo because somehow it fit. I also called him the Killer because that fit, too. James LeRoy Washington was from the Bronx and he did not mind killing. He did not mind it at all. Killing was like taking out the garbage. Just something that had to be done. Jim Bo was the kind of grunt who could stand the stench of a burning man. Sometimes the smell and the blackstink that poured out of the tunnels after we'd burned the hell out of whatever was down there would be enough to make most anyone else puke themselves into the Sea of Japan.

But not Jimmy Bo. Jim Bo was over it before he got off the plane which flew him to Asia. Jimmy Bo had been born to come to jaded Asia with a gun clenched between his teeth. He swore that he'd been fathered in the middle of the desert by the devil and we believed him. He was a royal fuck-up. White men laughed nervously, with anxiety stuck in their throats, and white men were always looking over their shoulders. Jim Bo laughed from his bowels like a growl and he never looked back much less over his shoulder. He was from the bottom of the social slime barrel and he knew it. He hated and he hated well. He did it honestly. Jim Bo would be the kind of man who would eventually survive the war on the sheer morality of his stubborn determination.

Jimmy loved the kids. Vietnamese kids. Gooks. Dinks. Slants. Zip kiddies. Chinks. He had a thing for them in his heart even when nobody believed that black man had ever come near a heart. He always seemed to have a gook kid riding on his shoulders. They adored him. They called him numbah one niggah GI. At first their calling him that amazed us even offended our liberal sensibilities. It shocked us. Until we realized that they were only repeating the hate they'd heard—the term numbah one niggah GI meant nothing to them. Hey, numbah one niggah GI, you got candy? You got soda? You numbah one. It was a war that imported technology, boys, guns, fuel, choppers, Kool-Aid, and rampant racism.

There were more black GIs than anyone wanted to admit. It was harder for blacks to evade the draft. It was harder for them to afford college. So they bit the draft, they chewed it, and they spit Vietnam out of their mouths like it was so much vile crud. The Vietnamese, of course, knew something about racism. In Vietnam racism was so thick you wallowed in it like it was mud. The Chinese in Cholon hated the Vietnamese. And the Vietnamese hated the Cambodians. And the Cambodians hated everybody. The Vietnamese would have been the last people on the planet to be surprised with America's unique form of fighting racism. It was a war and in war a society is going to compel those men it feels it can afford to lose to fight that war. PUT A CHAIN AROUND MY NECK AND LEAD ME ANYWHERE . . .

In the whole war Jimmy never once killed a kid.

Christopher and Taylor were crazy. Just crazy. I always thought those two were queers. Cocksuckers. It swam around in my head unconsciously before I finally put two-and-two together. One boy'd go take a leak and the other one had to go with him. They were inseparable but they never talked about it. Somewhere along the line, I have no idea where, they'd lost it. They just went nuts and started taking chances because it amused them. Taylor was a pretty little guy. He wore a red bandana around his head—he said it was lucky. You were sure he had the kind of family somewhere that had to love that boy. YOU AIN'T NOTHING BUT A HOUND DOG ROCKIN' ALL THE TIME. He was the kind of kid who had a math scholarship to some hick school in Nebraska or Texas or Missouri or Tennessee or wherever the fuck Taylor was from. Taylor had brains although I wondered if he ever used them. Taylor was the kind of boy who would smile when you needed him to. Wherever it was that Taylor was from it was the kind of place that sent you her boys because those people believed that sending you their boys to fight and die would make a difference in the world. They were wrong. They were good but they were wrong.

Frequently they were dead wrong. God himself never thanked them much for the sacrifice of their sons. Their sons . . .

Taylor's nickname was Titi which was Vietnamese for little. If I had to pick out the best of the rats it would have been Titi—his size made it possible for him to negotiate even the most cramped of tunnels. Taylor was small although you never really thought of him as being small because he had such guts. Taylor never hesitated about going down. He'd fucking volunteer. I had to make him stop volunteering everytime we came to a tunnel. "Hey, Boss," he'd say. "Let me go. I got cat eyes. I see in the dark." Taylor never talked about whatever it was he did down in the tunnels. If Titi went down into a hole it'd be a sure bet that no VC would emerge alive.

Christopher was the exact opposite. We called Chris the Ranger because in military terms Ranger meant a soldier specially trained for reconnaissance and combat missions. The gospel on the Rangers (or LURPS) was that you could always tell when a Ranger had been around. It was said that your house would be a royal mess. Your garbage cans would be in the street. And your dog would be pregnant. Chris was too damn big for most tunnels. But he was perfect for taking out whatever emerged *from* a tunnel. Chris was usually the last one I'd send into a hole. The lunk was strong and he could haul out anyone who'd gotten themselves stuck down there. Stuck usually from plain and simple fear. Sometimes you just froze. Your flashlight would go out, you couldn't go backwards, you couldn't go forwards, so you froze. I'd send Chris down to haul your ass out.

The Ranger was seventeen-years-old; even then he was a lunk. When Chris first heard the term R&R he thought they were talking about a rest room in Hawaii. Chris was in Vietnam because his father thought that that's where you went in order to become a man. A *real* man. If only we had had enough real men over there we would have won the war. Chris adored his father although that adoration was mixed with a certain amount of confused if frightened apprehension. Everytime he shot a VC or an NVA he'd write home and tell his old man about it. I half suspected Chris of sending enemy ears through the mail. Others did it. Chris was always trying to explain to his family through letters that he was okay, it was war to be sure, but so what, he was okay. We were winning. Not that his old man ever wrote to Chris. Mail came on Mondays. Big red bags of it. Everyone knew who got mail, who wrote back to whom, and whose mother knew how to bake halfway decent oatmeal cookies. Chris was the only man on our team who never once got any mail.

He always checked. He'd double check. But they never wrote to him. "My dad thinks I should learn how to live without having to be patted on the back for everything I do," he'd tell me when I was finished reading my mail from college friends at home. "If my old man were here he'd know how to win this war." The longer they didn't write to him the more he'd write to them. Chris wrote to them on the backs of C-ration wrappings. Anything he could find to write on. When we were in Saigon once during Thanksgiving Titi and I went into a store and we bought six pairs of white socks because Chris' socks were disgusting to look at. Even for us. We sent the socks to him for Christmas with a note saying it was from his folks. When the package arrived he tore it apart like a crazy person, never even noticing that the military post mark was from Saigon not Lansing, Michigan, which was where his parents lived. Chris tore open his package, pulled out his socks, and ran into our bunker because he was too ashamed to let us see him bawl his seventeen-year-old eyes out. I DON'T WANNA

BE YOUR LION CAUSE LIONS AREN'T THE KIND YOU LOVE ENOUGH . . .

If there were basketballs and baskets available at whatever base we were stuck in Chris and Taylor would be found shooting. Just shooting baskets. Over and over again. Their dog tags always bounced against their sweaty boyhero chests. Those two were forever sitting in front of the bunker writing their letters. They'd even ignore incoming. Dear Mom, Peter Pan sucks a big one. They played this game. Called it the bang, you're dead game. They'd just point a finger at somebody—bang, you're dead. And then they'd laugh. Chris and Taylor were insane. I saw them pick up a wounded soldier one time, a boy who'd stepped on a Bouncing Betty. They dragged the boy across a paddy through some thick incoming like it was nothing more than a little drizzle. There was nothing crazier than that. And they gave him to a medic. They laughed and returned to our position. Chris was an ear collector. He'd cut them off corpses providing they were corpses that he'd shot. He'd string the ears onto a fishline necklace. I made him throw it away when the damn thing turned brown and attracted maggots.

LOVE ME TENDER, LOVE ME SWEET, NEVER LET ME GO. Everyone knew that winning was only a matter of your team trying a little bit harder. We were the good guys. We had to win. Jayne Mansfield was waiting for us back home—the champagne was chilled. There were no other options.

It was not a war of heros it was a war of boys. They were my boys and I did whatever I did to keep them alive because I hated their grunt guts. I loved them because they were all that was left to me. They were all that was left to one another which is why they loved one another even when they hated who they were, where they were, and why they were where they were.

Someone had changed the rules of the game. Suddenly winning wasn't enough. We had one another. We had to have one another. Period. No questions asked. I wished they had been thirty. Or forty. Or fifty. It wouldn't have been so hard. It was their youth and their innocence that jerked me around. I did not want them to be so young. I did not ask for their innocence. They had no right. No right at all. There is nothing casual about the relationship of such men to the men who will hold them and cry when they die. There was a dark tension between us.

An intimacy that could not be discussed because it could not be fathomed. Like the horror around us it just was. Search and destroy. Win their hearts and win their minds. Mop it up.

We'd been in the field for weeks mopping up and mopping up. The more we mopped the more there was to mop. It was a sea of blood. The more blood you squeezed out of the mop the more blood there was to squeeze. We'd had a gutful of tunnel searches. We were bone tired of smelling corpses. Weeks of it without a break. If you were in the field you used to pop 15 milligram diaphetamine pills—dexies—like they were aspirin and you had a vicious headache. What you had was fatigue. So you took speed because the military told you to take speed—uppers—to fight the fatigue. Something had to. Johnnycomemarchinghome was a speed freak. Of course the irony to it like all of the ironies of Vietnam was that after awhile you liked it. You popped enough speed in the field and you could be John Wayne and then some. They spoonfed it to you. It was regulation. Everyone had a supply of pills and if you needed more there was more. More than enough to go around. The speed kept you awake so you could hump, fight, kill, stay alive. Taking speed was like taking candy. It was coming down that was such a ravenous bitch.

YOU CAN DO ANYTHING YOU WANT TO DO. BUT GET OFF, GET OFFA MY BLUE SUEDE SHOES. When you came down from the amphetamine sometimes you'd beg somebody who loved you to blow your brains out and just get it over with because you ached so bad. If you were on a LRRP, and you were in a village, you'd want to shoot anything that walked and breathed. Hey, coming down you saw boogies in every tree. Coming down from speed is the meanest thing a human body can go through. Even your sweat stinks with it. Coming down from the speed they gave you, pumped into you, was easier if you smoked boom boom dope. Or maybe you shot what we called Asian-Mary-Jane—heroin—because it took the screaming edge off the dexy.

Speed was the worst.

We had syrettes and needles in our medic's bag. Billy Boy bought our smack from a Saigon whore. There were whores. And then there were the Saigon whores. Plenty goodtime, GI. I saw the needle that first time go into his prettyboy vein clean-blue and virginal. There is nothing worse than a virgin so I figured that if I couldn't beat them I might as well join them. The killing had become secondary. It was being so zapped-out tired all of the time that got to us. It wasn't the heroin that numbed us. Peter Pan was already numb by then.

If we couldn't win on their terms perhaps we could win on terms of our own—of our own invention.

BABY, LET ME BE AROUND YOU EVERY NIGHT. I'LL RUN YOUR FINGERS THROUGH MY HAIR AND CUDDLE ME REAL TIGHT . . . We lived one day at a time. One hour at a time. One minute at a time. We saw other GIs kill children. And we saw children kill other GIs. I no longer cared. We passed the needle around. Always remember to crumple your empty beer cans. It becomes a habit. An empty beer can makes a perfect grenade casing. The sharp pieces of aluminum can go right through you when they go flying. And we sat in a field, a rice paddy, watching the latest village burn itself oil-black into oblivion, which is where we wished we were. Stoned to the gills heroinhigh and virginal. Coming down from speed and the taste of blood. Listening to their screams and their rage. We were tired of their rage we had our own. Watching an occasional villager run for it. We machine-gunned a pregnant water buffalo until we split the sucker open with it's stinking guts, its bellowing, and its rage.

It wasn't really happening. Everyone believed in fairies. Eighteen-year-old boys from Ohio and Iowa and Georgia don't run around killing old women and babies. Burning villages to the ground. Boys from Ohio and Iowa and Georgia do not fuck with Asian whores or suck dick; they marry nice girls from New Jersey with big tits and nylons and aprons and babies and Corvettes. It was not Route 66. Never happened. Boys from Ohio and Iowa and Gerogia do not love each other because they are all that is left of what they know. None of it was real. Candy, soda, dirty pictures, boom boom dope. Elvis screaming his guts out on a Las Vegas stage. It was destiny breathing down our tunnel rat necks. Bang, you're dead.

Sit down watch the sunset warm your speedy soul with its tropical indigo beauty.

It was neverneverland gone hysterical psychotic and Peter Pan was a scared adolescent in black pajamas. We were all very very scared. We weren't winnning. We tried. We tried hard. With sweat and technology. And they just laughed at us. They refused to let us win. They didn't play by the rules. We were the good guys. It wasn't supposed to be like that. It wasn't Elvis grinding out the jailhouse rock. It was bitchdeath sticking her wet war tongue down our breathless boyhero throats. It was being bentover virgin dry-fucked by some anonymous manic cock. It was bigger than we were. And badder. And more twisted. YOU HAVE MADE MY LIFE COMPLETE

AND I LOVE YOU SO.

And so wrong the enormity of it raped anything that dared get too fucking close.

They briefed us in one of those small tin-roof shack-like hooches that surrounded Ton Son Nhut. Everytime a jet took off it'd shake the hell out of the hooch. There was the inevitable incoming. They usually missed anything of importance. Occasionally a stray bullet would strike the tin on the roof and you'd feel yourself ducking instinctively. We were going to Cambodia in a fleet of Cobras. Nobody said it would be Cambodia. You'd have to have dogshit for brains to not have figured it out. A U-2 had downed and we were going in to retrieve the goddamn black box. It was not going to be tea with the queen mother.

It was some of the most remote territory we had ever seen. It was some of the most savage fighting we had ever experienced. The Cambodian guerrillas we'd picked up outside of Phnom Penh took the worst of it. It was hand-to-hand. We showed the Cambodians how to mix soap flakes with gasoline. The mixture not only burned it stuck to you while it burned. We called it homemade napalm because that's what it was. Every other three feet was a punji trap. Punji was sharp bamboo that'd snap into your leg like your flesh was cheese. Metal detectors weren't shit against punji. It was slow going. The tunnel rats brought up the rear which meant they were saving us for last—the best part was yet to come.

We inflicted a lot more damage than we took. It meant nothing. There were less than two hundred of us and there were thousands of them. We left 81mm mortar launchers connected to timers around the perimeter and when the whole shebang went off just before daylight the VC thought they had us by the balls. But we were gone. They were fighting a bunch of timing mechanisms. The jungle sucked us up. It began to rain. Monsoon is officially from April to October. It was December and monsoon was supposed to be over. Somebody neglected to tell it to the monsoon. It rained like Niagara Falls for three solid days of hacking through the brush.

We slept curled up onto and into each other under our ponchos. I was curled up next to Billy Boy in the jungle blackness. I don't think anybody really slept like that. You half-slept. You ached. My hands were burning with blisters and I could hardly carry my gun. We lay sort of all around each other, two men to each poncho, trying to stay dry, trying to stay sane. Trying to stay out of each other's breath. Trying not to touch. Trying not to let your dick squeeze against his ass. Trying not to feel good about it if you did. I never saw it rain so jungle hard. Chris and Taylor lay under a poncho just across from us. "What is it with them?" Billy said.

"Shut up, Billy. Go to sleep."

"I can't sleep. Who can sleep in this?" Billy lit a joint and we both deeply inhaled it under the poncho, savoring it, hoping that it'd take some of the edge off. "I think they're queers."

"I said shut up."

"Boss, do you think I look like Elvis?"

"Not even close." Billy snarled and curled his lip all badass-like.

"You think they're queers, Boss?"

"No."

"I'm queer." Billy laughed.

"Sure. And I'm Ho Chi Minh."

"I need to kiss something. Somebody."

"Save it for a whore."

"I don't want to save it." LOVE ME TENDER, LOVE ME SWEET, NEVER LET ME GO. YOU HAVE MADE MY LIFE COMPLETE AND I LOVE YOU SO. LOVE ME TENDER, LOVE ME TRUE, ALL MY DREAMS FULFILLED. FOR MY DARLING I LOVE YOU. AND I ALWAYS WILL.

"Ever notice how all the whores have gum in their mouth? I want it now. Right fucking here. I think I'm a fucking queer, too." I said nothing. He just looked at me with those silly eighteen-year-old eyes. "I want to die. I can't go another step."

"Fuck you, Billy. Just fuck you."

"Do you think Elvis ever sang House of the Rising Sun, Boss?"

"Never happened."

"I feel like blowing my head off right here under this wet poncho. I want somebody to fuck me before I die." Billy put the barrel of his gun in his mouth and looked at me. I took another drag of dope and breathed it out into his face.

"So then do it. I'm not going to stop you. You wanna do it? Then do it." The sound of the rain was so loud you couldn't hear anything outside of the poncho. Billy pulled the trigger. Click. Click. Click. His gun jammed. Ask any grunt. M-16s weren't worth a pile of KP garbage. He laughed. And I kissed him. I lay back onto the soaked ground and I kissed him. He moaned softly and put his bitter marijuana tongue into my mouth. No one could see us. It rained. And I kissed him.

"I'm not really queer, you know," he said.

"I know." He fell asleep with his face buried into the flack jacket on my chest.

LOVE ME TENDER, LOVE ME DEAR, TELL ME YOU ARE MINE. I'LL BE YOURS THROUGH ALL THE YEARS UNTIL THE END OF TIME. The hardest part were the hills. They were small mountains, really. And your grunt's back could be piled down with seventy pounds of shit and ammo that had to be humped up. Just fucking up. Normally we had those goddamn heavy C-4 radios that had to be humped along with everything else. But this was Cambodia and there were no radios. This was Cambodia and we weren't really there. We were figments of our own imaginations. We didn't officially exist. AND DON'T STEP ON MY BLUE SUEDE SHOES. This was Cambodia and we had to hack it through. Tree by tree. Rock by rock. Stream by stream. Our machetes broke. We had to wrap our hands in towels for the hacking because our hands bled like stuck pigs. And there it was. Wreckage. All over the mountain. The fuselage had broke in two. The box was gone. . . . CRYING ALL THE TIME. YOU AIN'T NEVER CAUGHT A RABBIT YOU AIN'T NO FRIEND OF MINE. Thirty men dead. My ass was tired and wet. Jungle rot trenchfoot was crawling up my leg and any day, now, it was gonna make my dick fall off. My tunnel rats were exhausted beyond endurance. And some officer is telling me that the fucking black box we'd busted our nuts to get was gone. "VC must have gotten here first," he said.

"So fuck them," I said. "You go out there, you find one, you put a knife next to his testicles, and you tell him that if he doesn't show you exactly where that idiot fucking box is, you'll cut his sweet little balls off one at a time. It's simple." Nothing that simple was ever that simple. We didn't have to find them because they found us. Mixed in with the rain that was drenching us came a barrage of incoming so furious that it threatened to make the rain look like a sunny day at Buckingham Palace. They pounded the shit out of us—they had artillery. It was big boy time in neverneverland.

It was like being baptized all over again. We had to dig in and sand-bag it. Every grunt carried empty bags that could be filled with dirt. We sent a contingent of the Cambodians around to the other side of the hill. The guerrillas circled, climbed over the hill, and dropped a river of concussion grenades and rockets down the throats of the VC. But these weren't any VC. They were NVA and they were hard core. They did not go down easy. They tended to fight to the death versus allowing themselves to be captured. Out of over one hundred dead NVAs we reeled in one sixteen-year-old boy who looked like he just might lose his arm if somebody didn't stick some antibiotics and morphine into him and soon.

We didn't have to cut his balls off. We told him we'd just

leave him there to die if he didn't tell us where the black box was. You talkee talkee? Me no talkee talkee. You talkee talkee? Somebody put a bayonet into his wound and twisted it. Me talkee talkee. An NVA base camp was one day's march from where we were. They'd be expecting that our butts had been blown into the South China Sea. It was night and we attacked. Somewhere there'd be that fucking box. I knew where it was. I'd known all along like it was a bad taste at the back of my throat. Old cum I couldn't swallow. I knew why we'd been near the end of the detail throughout the mission. We saw some of the NVAs run into the jungle. The rest of them got sucked up into the ground.

The earth just ate them.

Geronimo took one tunnel. Titi took another. Ranger jumped into a third, the largest one. And Jimmy Bo, the Killer, grabbed a firethrower and eased himself down into the fourth and final hole. It was a maze. Damn fucking war. Candy, soda, dirty pictures, boom boom dope. Damn it all to death and fuck. I stood there, uptop, because that's what I did. Black smoke poured out from one of the holes liquidthick and sick with flesh. "You hear anything?" a G3 CO asked me. Black combat jungle make-up covered his face. Made him look like a Haitian voodoo out for a night's juju walk through hell. I always refused to wear the make-up. It was too fucking theatrical. Somehow that junk on your face turned the whole thing into some kind of a charade.

"Sure," I said, "I hear screaming. You can't hear it?"

"I don't hear a thing." I lit a big joint. A very big joint. It was what I did. I blew the smoke into his painted face.

"You want a toke?"

"You wanna get busted, soldier?"

"Go screw yourself, fucking asshole." He came at me. "You take one more step toward me and I'll pull this pin." I held up a grenade, walked over to the CO, and put it into his face. "Me no fuckee fuckee." NVAs started pouring out of the holes. The CO left. He had boys to shoot. Why bother with me. NVA were dropping like flies. Bullets zipped everywhere. Guns belched. Killer came out. Billy Boy came out. Chris came out. Everyone took a toke. Taylor did not come out. We waited. No Titi. Billy looked at the ground. Killer looked at the ground and sighed. I looked at Chris. He was crying. I put the joint to his boylips. "Be careful, Chris. Be real careful."

COME ON, MAMA, LET'S ROCK! Chris disappeared into Titi's hole. Nothing. We waited. Killer loaded the M-60 with the fifteen pounds of ammunition he wore strapped across his sweating black chest and flipped off the safety. North Vietnamese RPG rockets started going off, exploding everywhere, illuminating the whole area like it was a hot day in June. We waited. NVA poked their heads out of Chris' hole. Jimmy Bo, Jimmy Bo from the Bronx, pressed his thick black finger to the trigger of the machine gun and killed them as they emerged. Each body flew at least twenty feet into the air. Chris came out carrying Taylor's head in his arms.

"I think he'll be okay, Boss," Chris said. "Here, you fix him, Boss, you fix him." I took the head. Chris disappeared into the hole for the rest of Taylor.

"It's his fucking *head*, man!" Billy said. "Oh, God! It's his fucking head! I can't stand it. I can't fucking stand it!" Billy Boy took the M-60 from Jim and shot at the now dead bodies laying on the ground. As the shots hit home the corpses of the North Vietnamese bounced up and rolled another fifteen feet.

Chris hauled out the rest of Titi and then dived back into the hole. I was still standing there, holding the head, trying to decide whether to throw up my guts or cry when Chris came out of the hole with a black box in his hands and threw it to Billy like it was a football on the fifty yard line. Chris then took the head from me and tried connecting it to Taylor's torso. His hands were covered in blood. For what seemed like forever we just stood there, surrounded by gunfire and incoming, listening to Chris jabber. "Put it on, man," he kept saying. "You gotta put it back on. I gotta fix you, Titi. I gotta fix you." Jimmy Bo had to wrap his big bear arms around Chris to restrain him. To make him stop. The veins on the sides of Chris' neck bulged, he looked up, and he screamed.

"We gotta move, Boss," Jimmy said. "When they realized we're what? A hundred men to their thousand? They'll be back down here so fast it'll be like flies on a carcass. Ours."

So we moved. We left Taylor and his head. And we moved ass. It was two days and two nights of hacking our way out of there. I handed over the black box to the CO. "I ought to bust you for dope right here," he said.

"Then do it, you shitbag. Then do it." He just stood there with his precious black box in his hands.

The four of us slept dick-to-butt under two ponchos in the goddamn rain. If they wanted to bust us for smoking dope, well, then let them. Nobody said shit to us. We smoked ourselves into a silent rage. We hauled ourselves aboard a Cobra and it lifted us out of there as if it were an angel with whirly wings. In the whole two days getting out of there Chris never uttered word one. Not a sound. His emptiness hurt. I DON'T WANNA BE YOUR TIGER CAUSE TIGERS PLAY TOO ROUGH. "Something wrong with your man over there?" the Cobra chopper pilot asked. Chris was sitting in the corner of the chopper rocking back and forth. Just rocking. Just shooting baskets. Over and over again...

"No," I said over the noise of the helicopter. "He's just a little tired, that's all. He's just a little tired." We were all a little tired. They gave us one week of R&R. Jim Bo and Billy pulled Hawaii. Chris and I pulled Hong Kong. Chris slowly pulled out of it. "Good thing," I said to him in the bird on the way to Hong Kong. "Or I was going to have to put you into psychiatric." We shared a room at the Hong Kong Hilton. They had toilet paper. And soap. And hot water. And a fucking tub. I had to make Chris get out of the tub. "Give me a turn, you asshole. I got trenchfoot to soak off." My dick was still there. Two Chinese guys came up to our room with suits. The suits felt like they belonged to another universe. They'd give you a suit in the hopes that the next day you'd come around to their shop and buy one for thirty bucks. We did. There we were. Walking around Hong Kong in three piece suits and jungle boots. Five-hundred dollars dogtag rich. And alive. It was an amazing sight seeing all those people. Nobody had a gun and we felt naked without ours. No Bouncing Betties. No body bags in the corners discreetly stashed—just in case. We ate steaks until the steaks were coming out of our ears. And baked potatoes with sour cream and chives.

I DON'T WANNA BE YOUR LION CAUSE LIONS AIN'T THE KIND YOU LOVE ENOUGH. "Here's to Titi," Chris said, lifting his glass. "He died alone."

"Here's to Titi," I said. I was angry and I hurt. I hurt for Chris. I hurt for Taylor. But most of all I hurt for me.

"Here's to Elvis the pelvis," Chris said.

"Here's to Elvis, man. May rock'n roll never die."

"Don't let me die alone," Chris said. "Promise me I won't die alone."

I promised. I had made the promise to every one of them not knowing, really, whether I could follow through on my end of the deal. According to the rules of the game a promise is a promise. It was the kind of pact that boys make. Boys who cut themselves with knives, hold their cuts together, and mix their blood. It was that kind of an agreement. I could not let them die alone. It had very little—perhaps nothing—to do with the war. It was the kind of promise that would transcend the limits of any war. We were bloodbrothers, now. We had mixed our cuts and held them together. Although we were not boys we were men. And we would hold each other to our promises to the end of our days on this planet. Through war, peace, brotherhood, or total destruction. I was not to let them die alone.

Our plan was to find some whores, take them drinking, go back to our room and fuck the whores. Hey, Joe! Fifty bucks. Plenty goodtime. But we knew that we wouldn't really do it. We didn't know why we wouldn't do it. We never admitted that we knew we wouldn't do it. We just knew. We drank ourselves nearly blind, went back to the hotel, and slept in that huge luxurious bed together. It was the first time I had ever slept with Christopher or any other man for that matter—knowingly. On purpose. Because I wanted to. Because I had to. Because I needed to feel him next to me just breathing. I kept my underwear on because I knew that I was walking on some very unexplored territory here. At least for me. Chris was naked and soft. And beautiful. I got a hardon and I held him. I guess I was a cocksucker.

And he cried his guts out on me until I cried mine out on him.

We did not know why. And we never talked about it. Candy, soda, dirty pictures, boom boom dope. Rat holes and death. LOVE ME TENDER, LOVE ME TRUE, ALL MY DREAMS FULFILLED. FOR MY DARLING I LOVE YOU AND I ALWAYS WILL. I still have the dreams. Billy and I talked long distance just before he did it—put the gun in his mouth. He asked me to hold him while he died. They all asked me to hold them while they died. I said no and then I said okay. No one knew what it was about. If it was about anything.

Mamasan. Incoming. Bang, you're dead. Boys with picture books and needles in their arms. Just boys with rock-a-bye eyes as frigid blue as polar ice on a clear cold day at noon. Iowa boys. Ohio boys. Boys from places with supper on the table. They were tunnel rats. Do as you're told. Don't ask questions. No one has the answers. Villagers in ditches. C-rations.

Bouncing Betty. Dogtags. Heat tabs. Morphine and smack. Soft rivers in the rain. Nights as bible-black as a starless universe. Ponchos. Body bags. He died alone. Hold me, Chris, just hold me. Fifty bucks? Plenty goodtime, soldier. You numbah one GI. None of it was really happening it never happened. You held Peter Pan in your heroin arms but he died anyway. Candy, soda, dirty pictures, boom boom dope. It's his fucking HEAD, man! LOVE ME TENDER, LOVE ME LONG, TAKE ME TO YOUR HEART. It was Neverneverland.

It was Vietnam.

Part Three

SONS AND LOVERS

—metaphoric boy princes playing soldier
knee-deep in ideological viscera
fresh from daddy's soft kiss against your childboy neck
becoming one with the saturated wetdream
where even the rain reigns orange
bloodred smelling of genetic synergism
where even ideology hides its chromosomes
metaphoric sperm making quantic leaps
dream-to-dream son-to-son kiss-to-kiss
the sky has turned the earth to moon
and our babes from between our legs
into syndromes
where boy princes are anything but metaphoric
and sons are infertile
and agents are orange responsibilities
futureless and virginal
where even the rain is dry
insecticide
where our babes twirl and spin
where justice is as dry as the dunes
where sons procreate nothing
the final humiliation
reign of blood
rain of orange
rain of terror
reign anywhere anywhere—

IT'S ONE FOR THE MONEY, TWO FOR THE SHOW, THREE TO GET READY, NOW, GO-CAT-GO. GET OFF. AND DON'T STEP ON MY BLUE SUEDE SHOES. YOU CAN DO ANYTHING BUT GET OFFA MY BLUE SUEDE SHOES. YOU CAN KNOCK ME DOWN, STEP ON MY FACE, SLANDER MY NAME ALL OVER THE PLACE. BURN MY HOUSE, STEAL MY CAR, DRINK MY LIQUOR FROM AN OLD FRUIT JAR. BUT, HONEY, GET OFFA THEM BLUE SUEDE SHOES! The psycho-ward at the Bronx VA Hospital is on the sixth floor. There are bars on the windows. But if you look between the bars there's a nice un-obstructed view of the Harlem River. Which is why no one bothers much to look out of the windows. The sixth floor has its share of inmates. The sixth floor also has its share of rules.

The psycho-ward at the Bronx VA Hospital is a somewhat cheerless place. Most of the men there dress in bathrobes. Pajamas with your dick hanging out. My dick was always hanging out of my PJs. I hated that. Don't look at it—it's my dick. And I can't help it if it hangs out of the damn PJs. Oh, the nurses tried to pretend that they didn't look at our dicks. We tried covering our dicks with our hands. But the nurses were always looking. They were nurses. It's what nurses do—they look. Everyone looked. That's why you were there. For people to look at. And there you were with your dick hanging out through the hole in the damn PJs.

WELL, THEY SAID YOU WERE HIGH-CLASS. AND

THAT WAS JUST FINE. WELL, THEY SAID YOU WERE HIGH-CLASS. AND THAT WAS JUST FINE. BUT YOU AIN'T NEVER CAUGHT A RABBIT AND YOU AIN'T NO FRIEND OF MINE. Most of the men there danced the Vietnam shuffle. You danced it in the hallway. You danced it in the showers. You danced it in your sleep. You danced it with an enema in your belly.

You came back from Vietnam, you went nuts, if you were sane enough to go nuts, and the first thing they did was give you an enema. They held you down, they spread your butt crack, and they violated you. You might scream bloody murder that you were crazy—it was your brain that needed an enema—your gut didn't need an enema but everyone got an enema.

You were back.

You danced the shuffle shuffle with orderlies, strong-armed handsome neighborhood virginboys dressed in white, on either side of you. Dance dance—shuffle shuffle. The bathrobes were how you separated the real crazies from the temporary crazies. The real crazies had store bought bathrobes from Macy's and Gimbel's and Sears. Robes from mothers and wives and girlfriends. The vets themselves, their mothers, their wives, and their girlfriends all knew that the men in the nice robes would be staying on the sixth floor of the Bronx VA Hospital for awhile. Probably a long while.

Maybe forever.

No one ever wore any blue suede shoes on the sixth floor. Never happened.

Dance and shuffle. Dance and shuffle. Did you have a bowel movement today? Hey, soldier, don't feel too sorry for yourself. You wanna see an ostomy bag, you dumb mother-fucker? Place is full of dumb motherfuckers. Hey, soldier, you get sprayed with agent orange? No? You're lucky. Makes your balls shrivel right up like hard raisins stuck up into your groin—cum looks like brown tar. Hey, soldier, put your dick back into your PJs. Everyone can see it. Everyone is looking. And laughing. Thorazine cocktails turned the back of your neck into slowly melting ice.

COME ON, MAMA, LET'S ROCK! You may as well have nice bathrobes. Forever is a long time. Even for a hard core. Buying you a nice robe was the least your nice mother, or your nice wife, or your nice girlfriend, or the nice nurse who changed your ostomy bag, could do. After all, you were too sick to look at your ostomy bag, it made you vomit, that wasn't you down there, it was someone else. You no longer recognized who you were. Buying you a nice bathrobe at least made the nice mothers, the nice girlfriends, and the nice nurses who changed the ostomy bags, feel better about the fact that you shit through your stomach, and maybe, just maybe, you were crazy for a reason. You needed decent PJs, the kind where you didn't have to deal with the humiliation because it was absolutely impossible to humiliate you anymore ever again. Shuffle shuffle. Maybe she bought you some slippers, too. They never let you keep the belt portion of the nice robes. You could use this thing to hang yourself. Hanging yourself was against the rules. Hanging yourself was beyond humiliation. Nice guys could always find a way to hang themselves. It was the assholes who lived.

The temporary crazies—the only "kind of" but definitely crazy crazies—wore VA issue bathrobes. Thin with gray stripes. Cheap and institutional. When the VA ran out of these we had to wear those little cotton gowns where your butt hung out and your balls rubbed between your legs. It was worse than being buck naked. At least when you're naked you're not trying to hide anything with your own inadequacies. Our VA issued PJs absorbed coffee stains and cigarette burns well. They were not from Macy's. They looked as if they might have been leftover uniform stock from a German concentration camp. Auschwitz haute couture. The temporary crazies wore VA issue bathrobes because no one cared what a temporary crazy might look like.

They looked like shit. The hard-core crazies looked shaved and showered. Their dicks never hung out of their pajamas—this was one of the few things that did not demean them. The hard cores all had agendas. Urgently important things to do. Secret places to go. Imaginary people to meet. WELL. THEY SAID YOU WERE HIGH-CLASS. AND THAT WAS JUST FINE. Many of them had wars to win. The hard cores were presidents and rock stars and God. Many became generals since the generals they knew when they were sane had somehow terribly failed them. So they just submitted their own psychic resumes and took over the vacant military positions. Mental ostomy bags and all.

There were a lot of generals. The temporaries cried. Sometimes they cried a lot. The hard cores never cried. They were all cried out. Their emotional entrails were as dry as the dirt-cracked floor of the Mojave Desert at the end of August. Badly in need of rain. Hard cores laughed a lot. Usually at private jokes. Or at commercials on the day room's TV. Or at those hard cores unfortunate enough to wear ostomy bags on their brains. Hard cores would bite big chunks of flesh out of their arms and their wrists. They'd spit out a mouthful of blood and veins onto the spotless floor. This, too, was against the rules. They'd pound heads on the pea-green wall, and laugh while the staff tried to make them stop please stop. We all wanted them to stop.

There was something about the hard cores that was untouchable.

You touched one and the contact would leave third degree burns on your soul. PUT A CHAIN AROUND MY NECK AND LEAD ME ANYWHERE. OH, LET ME BE (OH, LET HIM BE) YOUR TEDDY BEAR. The hard cores all lived somewhere else. Wherever it was it was a place that the rest of us tried very hard not to visit.

The voices they heard in their hard-core heads did their crying for them. The hard cores all had voices. Do you hear voices today? Do you hear voices today? It was the number one question. Everyone asked you over and over if you were hearing voices. They asked you at breakfast. They asked you in the art room. They asked you while you were in bed with the covers pulled up over your head. Sweating. Forgetting. Doing the Vietnam shuffle shuffle. Dance dance. They asked you while you sat in the john.

The minute you started hearing voices somebody went out and bought you a very nice robe. And new pajamas so your dick didn't stick out. The strong-arm boy orderlies would smile and walk you down the hall, one boy on each side, hey, you had escorts. They weren't afraid to touch you. You wanted them to touch you. You wouldn't admit it—but if you were a hard core you wanted them to touch you. Dance dance. Shuffle and rock. You didn't have to deal with the pain of crying if your private voices were willing to go through it for you. Voices were many times tolerable where the pain from crying was not.

John Wayne didn't have voices. John Wayne was a man. God only knows what the fuck we were. We were much too busy dancing the shuffle shuffle to hear the music. And our blue suede shoes done got dragged through the psychological mud and all we could do was cover our dicks with our hands and somehow pretend that we were human beings not animals. WELL, YOU NEVER CAUGHT A RABBIT AND YOU AIN'T NO FRIEND OF MINE . . .

The temporary crazies got the good drugs. Stuff like valium and librium. Maybe elavil or adapin if you were depressed. If you were too crazy, or too paranoid ("they" might want to poison you), to swallow your meds, you could always be held down while someone slid in a melting suppository—we called them butt-bullets. There was electroshock if you urinated on yourself. The men who urinated on themselves while they slept hated their wetness. It confused them. It embarrassed them—to have to be cleaned up like that. YOU CAN KNOCK ME DOWN, STEP ON MY FACE, SLANDER MY NAME ALL OVER THE PLACE . . .

The orderlies told you, hey, it's okay, it happens. But you did not want it to happen. Not to you. And you'd wake up in the morning frozen with some kind of postmodern fear, post-urinated fear, postmasculine disorder; frozen in your own surreal pee. Your pee stank because you had so many drugs in your system. Your insides were rotting. You wet the bed and you hated it. You hated what and who you were because you had lost control of your own life. The more you tightened up trying to regain control the more your bladder emptied itself while you slept. You did battle in your dreams. This pissing on who you were, what you had become, perplexed you. It hurt. It was humiliating beyond anything another man could do to you. You were your own worst enemy. WELL, THEY SAID YOU WERE HIGH-CLASS . . .

Everyone pretended that they didn't know that you had turned into a bed-wetter. But they knew. We all knew. There were a lot of jokes on the sixth floor of the Bronx VA Hospital. All the usual wise-cracks. I DON'T WANNA BE YOUR TIGER CAUSE TIGERS PLAY TOO ROUGH. But you never joked about the men who pissed on themselves. It was off limits. Dance dance. The electroshock shuffle put an end to most of your confusion and most of your unconscious pissing. The electroshock shuffle reached down into your unconscious and simply burned the hell out of it. Zap. Convulse. Stick your tongue out. Bite down on this. Juice the bastard. End of confusion. You stopped wetting the bed.

The hard cores went for more extrapolated complex cotton-in-the-mouth modalities. Shuffle, jump, turn, spin, do the

twist. The hard cores got phenothiazenes.Thorazinc. Stela-
zine. Sinequan. Haldol. Nardil. Compazine. Lithium. Mel-
laril. Dalmane. Ativan. Equinil. Anything that'd make the
voices go away. The hard cores had so many butt-bullets that
sometimes they literally left a trail of dripping drug-drool as
they walked down the hall shuffle shuffle. It just dripped down
their legs. You had to be careful when you walked down the
hall because you could slip on the compazine puddles. You GI
numbah one crazy.

The hard cores rarely got electroshock because they
weren't considered worth the time or the trouble. Turn out the
light when you leave the room, please. The hard cores sat in
the dark a lot. The hard cores were always throwing ashtrays
through the TV screen in the day room. They thought the ashtrays were grenades. So the staff took the ashtrays away until
the hard cores promised scout's honor not to do it again.
Dance dance.

Only a hard core had no honor. None of the voices in his
head were the voices of John Wayne. Not one. The kid who
kept wrecking televisions on my floor would promise not to and
then he'd do it again. He'd slap himself across the face. I
never saw anyone smack themselves as hard as that kid did.
Smack! Right across the face. Why did you do that? You're
bad! Smacksmack! He would verbally berate himself up one
side and down the other. And he'd keep hitting himself until
welts formed on his skin and they had to tie his hands with re-
straints. They took him away. When a hard core got taken away
he usually never came back. No one knew where the hard cores
who got taken away went. They tied you down to a stretcher and
took you away. Maybe they pushed you off the roof.

You felt abandoned and alone.

The sixth floor was referred to as The Zoo. The guys in
The Zoo didn't get awards for bravery, guys with compazine
bullets in their assholes, guys who wet on themselves do not get

congressional medals of honor, although we all got a letter from the Governor of the State of New York welcoming us back home. Welcome back, jerks. When your mind snaps you don't bleed right away. Usually when your mind snaps you save the bleeding for later because you don't snap—click—just like that. Going crazy is a process. It takes time.

The guy next to me used to sleep under his bed. Curled like a baby. Fetal-warm around his one blanket on the floor. The darkness under his bed comforted him. He had made some kind of peace with darkness. It made sense to him. Hey, man, you don't need to sleep under your bed. This is America. You're home, now. Nobody's coming in here with a grenade—there aren't any mortars. Buddy. Calm down. They'd drag him out from under there, screaming, terrified, and they'd tie him to his bed because he was home, now. Safe. He had his letter from the Governor of the State of New York. And sleeping under your bed was against the rules.

Welcome back, motherfuckers.

I was a temporary motherfucker. I did not have a nice bathrobe, a nice girlfriend, a nice mother, or a nice wife. I was not a hard core. Although I would have been a hard core— about as hard core as you could get—if it hadn't been for Christopher. Chris was on the third floor of the Bronx VA Hospital with the paraplegics and the stubs. The stubs were the amputees. Chris would come up to visit me and do wheelies in his new chair. The wheelies left rubber marks on the spotless floor and the staff would get pissed about the marks.

Doing wheelies was against the rules. Chris had to promise not to do any more wheelies or they weren't going to let him visit me in The Zoo's day room anymore. "Man, you gotta get out of here," he said to me. "Your dick is sticking through your PJs, Boss. Jesus, I don't know which floor is the worst, you know. This one where they got all these locks. Or downstairs with us cripples and stubs."

Chris' back was all bandaged up where they'd opened
him to see what they could see. His spinal chord had been
damaged when the bullet had gone through him and he would
be confined to the chair for the rest of his life. His hips were
black and blue from all the pain shots. It looked like I would be
getting out before Chris. "They're going to let me go pretty
soon," I told him. "But first they want to make sure that I don't
drool or masturbate in public." I was trying to be funny. Chris
looked out the window.

"There's this kid down the hall from me," he said. "Lost
both arms. I saw them changing his bandages. Oh, man. We
were kidding around, you know, and this guy asks me to jerk
him off. I didn't know what to do. 'I'd ask a nurse, you know,'
he says. 'Or somebody. But I can't.' Jesus. So I hardly know
this guy. I don't know him at all. I'm just trying to be friendly
a little bit. You know how it is."

"I know how you are."

"I don't know why he hit on me. But he did. I didn't tell
him I would. I didn't say I wouldn't either."

"What did you do?"

"I told him I'd think about it."

"What are you going to do?"

"You got any cream up here?" I laughed. I hadn't really
laughed in a while. At least not bitterly. "You think he's
queer?"

"No, I think he just wants to cum."

I got Christopher some cream I had in my room. He
winked at me, did a wheelie, and left. I was due for another
psychiatric exit exam. When they let you go they wanted to
know that you at least knew who you were. WELL, THEY
SAID YOU WERE HIGH-CLASS. AND THAT WAS JUST
FINE. WELL, THEY SAID YOU WERE HIGH-CLASS.
AND THAT WAS JUST FINE. BUT YOU NEVER CAUGHT
A RABBIT AND YOU AIN'T NO FRIEND OF MINE. You

were also supposed to know what day it was. So you went to social workers who asked questions. They knew who you were. And they knew what day it was.

It didn't matter whether or not you had the answers to the questions. What mattered was that you didn't upset the social workers. Most of us believed that it was probably just one social worker who used twenty different names. All the social workers looked alike and they asked the same questions. Do you know your name? Do you know what day it is? Do you hear voices? What are you going to do when you leave the hospital? My name is General William Westmoreland. It's Sunday and my voices are in church. When I grow up I want to be Elvis Presley.

Her desk was piled with papers. She wore glasses and had a poster on the wall that said something about this being the first day of the rest of her life. "Name, please."

"King Shit."

"Is this going to be one of *those* interviews?" she asked. She looked at my dick which was somewhat inevitably sticking through the hole in my pajamas.

"I can cover it with my hand if it makes you more comfortable," I said. "I blame the VA. They could at least get us some decent pajamas so our dicks don't stick out."

"This is a hospital."

"I didn't know."

"And in the hospital sometimes these things happen," she said. She was trying not to look but she looked anyway. I put my hand over my dick.

"Do you have a cigarette," I asked.

"There's no smoking in here. What day is it."

"All the days are the same. I honestly don't know. Does that make me crazy?"

"Do you hear voices today?" I lit a cigarette. "Lighters are forbidden on the ward. Where did you get that?"

"My voices gave it to me. I am always hearing the voice of Elvis Presley." YOU AIN'T NOTHING BUT A HOUND DOG CRYING ALL THE TIME. YOU AIN'T NOTHING BUT A HOUND DOG CRYING ALL THE TIME. YOU AIN'T NEVER CAUGHT A RABBIT AND YOU AIN'T NO FRIEND OF MINE. She rolled her eyes.

"What are you going to do when you leave the hospital?"

"I'm going to buy a pair of blue suede shoes and find a gay bar and I'm going to buy a drink. Maybe two drinks."

She looked up at me. "Are you a homosexual?"

"No, I'm a faggot who likes loud shoes, high-class hound dogs, teddy bears, and my dick is always falling out of the hole in these fucking cheap VA pajamas. Does that make me crazy?"

She sighed and surveyed the ocean of papers and forms on her desk. "It says here that during the evacuation of Saigon you refused to leave. Why?"

"I liked Saigon. I thought it was pretty."

"It says here that they had to force you onto a chopper, that you had to be forced to leave Vietnam."

"I was temporarily deranged."

"It says here that you were disoriented."

"I was disoriented. I'm sorry. Really, I am. Let me piss and apologize to you all over the place. Give me an enema. I am in total disgrace, okay? For years I was told that I had to be in Vietnam, that it was . . . right. You weren't there. You don't know. What do you want me to do? Say that I'm sorry I lost my mind until I bleed on you? I'm putting people, and babies, and friends, and my best buddy who's just had a bullet go into him, onto choppers. Everything that walks wants to get on a chopper. You numbah one GI! You let me on chopper. Everyone is screaming at me. At me! Well, fuck them. The whole world has been fucking itself in the ass for years and I'm supposed to stand there and say, 'You can go. But you have to stay. You can get on board. But your wife can't. Do you have a pass?' I mean, you think that I was insane? You had to be there. You weren't there. You can't ever know. I numbah one GI. Well, fuck that shit. Parts of Cholon and Bien Hoa are burning. Have you ever seen a city burn? It's an amazing sight. You ought to see it sometime. I'd been sane, you know, for years with it. I'd force myself to hold myself together. No matter what. I do whatever I have to to keep from going nuts. To keep from falling apart. Boys I *loved* get blown up in my face, okay, and I say to myself, 'Now, don't get upset. Don't get upset. Don't get *fucking upset!*' And then suddenly it all just ends. And it hit me."

"What hit you?"

"That the whole thing hadn't been *for* anything. That I'd been holding myself together for all those years for nothing. That I'd seen my friends fucking die for nothing. That I'd killed people for nothing. Have you ever killed anyone?"

"I'm not the issue here. The issue here is what to do with you now."

"That's where all of you are wrong. The issue is that *none of it* was for anything. I don't *care* what you *do* with me. Now or ever. Maybe I just need to be crazy for a while and play with my dick through the hole in my pajamas. I'm tired of holding myself together, okay? Sure, I lost it. At the last minute I really did lose my mind. I was one of the last ones there. I stood there, you know, on the roof of this building. I could see the choppers coming to get me. There were only a few of us left. I turned around the other way and I just looked at Saigon. It was burning in the distance. It was still war. War was all I knew. Hell sucks, right? It wasn't so much that I didn't want to leave as it was that I didn't fucking know how."

"Listen, King Shit. Or whoever you are. I'm the one who decides whether you get to leave here or not. Okay? Now, what do you plan to do *after* you buy the shoes and after you have two drinks in a gay bar?"

"Then I'm going to find another gay bar. Watch my lips.

A *thirsty* gay bar. And I'm going to buy another two drinks."

"This isn't getting anywhere."

"Well, what do you want me to say? When I leave the hospital I'm going to become Elvis the pelvis and live happily ever after. How's that?"

"What about a job?"

"I'd rather be Elvis Presley."

"Somebody else already has that job."

"Then I think I'll just be gay. It's something I've been putting off. I don't want a job."

"Being gay isn't a job."

"Trust me."

"If I decide to let you go will you go to group counseling once a week?"

"Religiously," I lied.

"The school board is hiring custodians." She wrote something down on a piece of paper and handed me the paper. "This is your interview appointment."

"You want me to be a janitor?"

"It's a job."

"It sucks."

"You can leave the hospital tomorrow. They'll give you some meds before you go. Good luck."

"Am I cured?"

"We call it Post-Traumatic Stress Disorder."

"I was in Vietnam four weeks ago. What's Post-Traumatic Stress Disorder?"

"It's what you have. I mean had."

"Am I cured?"

"Learn to adjust. Buy a new pair of pajamas. It'll help."

"I've been adjusting for years. In war. What if I don't want to fucking adjust anymore?"

She sighed and took off her glasses. "Do you or do you not want to get the fuck out of here, soldier?"

"Yes."

"Then adjust."

"I'll adjust."

"Then you're cured." AND DON'T STEP ON MY BLUE SUEDE SHOES!

"I think maybe I need electroshock."

"Stick your tongue in a wall socket. Do you know where to apply for food stamps?"

"What are food stamps? Are they like green stamps?"

"They're like money only you can't buy things like dog food or booze with them."

"Do bartenders take them? I don't have a dog."

"Bartenders won't take them."

"I don't need any."

"Are you going to be okay out there?" She was serious. I looked out the window. "I don't know. I want to care. But I don't know how. Maybe I can learn."

"I hope so," she said.

"They all wanted me to hold them when they died."

"You're going to have to learn how to hold yourself."

I was right. They were wrong. It hadn't been about a damn thing. PUT A CHAIN AROUND MY NECK AND LEAD ME ANYWHERE. OH, LET ME BE (OH, LET HIM BE) YOUR TEDDY BEAR. I JUST WANT TO BE YOUR LITTLE TEDDY BEAR . . .

It wasn't much of an apartment, really, but it wasn't the psycho-ward. It wasn't The Zoo. I wasn't even tempted to put my tongue into a wall socket. Another man's mouth might have been nice. But wall sockets weren't my style. And my dick didn't hang out of my pants. The rules were mine which meant there weren't any. It wasn't the Bronx. It wasn't in the street in the rain. And it wasn't the subway. I knew several vets who were living in Central Park. They spent their days sitting around with one another, smoking weed, and panhandling. Change for coffee. LOVE ME TENDER, LOVE ME TRUE, ALL MY DREAMS FULFILLED . . .

You didn't want to feel sorry for them. After all they were where they were because they wanted to be there. It was a matter of choice. You had to know something about their experience to realize that in some respects they were not at all where they were because they wanted to be there. They were immobilized. Frozen. Numb. They wanted to reach down into who they used to be and care. But they weren't who they used to be. They didn't care. They profoundly believed that what they'd been through didn't mean anything; that what they were going through now didn't mean anything, either.

Most of them weren't lucky enough to look and act really crazy. Crazy enough or immobilized enough to be hospitalized. The thought of being held down and having someone slip a compazine butt-bullet into your squirming rectum was off limits even to their somewhat strained sense of imagination. Yet, ironically, most of them were smart enough to know that being hospitalized in all likelihood might not mean anything more than living on the edge meant.

One edge can be about as good as another.

GET THE FUCK OFFA MY BLUE SUEDE SHOES! I knew some vets who preferred the subway. I used to sleep or what at least passed for sleep with all of my clothes on in bed because I didn't see or feel any need to change them. Why bother? I found an Elvis poster, Elvis when he was still afraid and in awe. Prettyboy Elvis. Sultry with those rock-a-bye eyes. Elvis when he was tender, innocent, and turning the world upside down. Country boy Elvis. And I tacked it onto my wall. It was my one and only decoration. I'd just lay there for literally days on end, watching the roaches crawl around, drinking until I passed out. I was unable to shake the pregnant sense of numbness that sat at the base of my brain.

Nothing felt right.

Eventually I tried cleaning up my act. I told myself that what I was feeling was self-pity. And only weak people felt self-pity. I went to a few gay bars because I was sure I was maybe probably I was scared to death that I was maybe probably definitely at least a little bit gay. I wanted to be with men. But the gay men I met lived in another time zone. Another universe. Another space. Certainly, they had a very difficult time relating to who I was as I had a very difficult time relating to who they were. WELL, THEY SAID YOU WERE HIGH-CLASS. AND THAT WAS JUST FINE. WELL, THEY SAID YOU WERE HIGH-CLASS. AND THAT WAS JUST FINE. BUT YOU NEVER CAUGHT A RABBIT AND YOU AIN'T NO FRIEND OF MINE. I was arrogant and the walls between us were real. I didn't feel connected to their scene. You were either one of them or you weren't. I went into it with the expectation that I would be embraced—the gay ghetto—which was a somewhat stupid thing to have wished for. I DON'T WANNA BE YOUR LION CAUSE LIONS AIN'T THE KIND YOU LOVE ENOUGH. There was a total lack of any kind of brotherhood.

You were a piece of meat.

The gay men I knew who I discussed this with disagreed with my assessment vehemently. They said I wasn't making enough of an effort at being gay like they were gay. And if I'd only try harder. It was a very closed subculture. Their lives seemed to revolve around sex which is fine but then what. There was this permeating unavoidable sense of loneliness to the men I was meeting that contrasted significantly to all the sex they seemed to be having. I was quite used to being surrounded by people obsessed with sex. And sex. Sex and more sex. Sex was contact. Suck off get sucked off.

Vietnam had sucked me off every breathing minute of every day for a long time. I wanted sex in my new life to mean

something. I'LL BE YOURS THROUGH ALL THE YEARS
UNTIL THE END OF TIME. LOVE ME TENDER, LOVE ME
TRUE . . .

It still didn't mean anything. Maybe it was beautiful and
liberating and raw and powerful to them. But it seemed compulsive and not at all very liberated to me. I didn't feel any
more connected to them and what they were about than I felt
connected to people with families. And wives. And girlfriends
with nylons and tits. And pictures at the Jersey beach. And
whatever the fuck they were about. I was a loner. It fit. I
DON'T WANT TO BE YOUR TIGER CAUSE TIGERS PLAY
TOO ROUGH. I DON'T WANT TO BE YOUR LION CAUSE
LIONS AIN'T THE KIND YOU LOVE ENOUGH . . .

I wanted sex to mean something and then I felt . . .
guilty . . . about wanting it to mean something. I don't know
what. Just something. Anything. Sex in subway bathrooms.
Sex in bars. Sex in parks. I had to be extremely abnormal—a
freak—nobody else seemed to want it to mean anything whatsoever. I'd look around at the men who surrounded me. Where
you expected to feel a sense of, hey, we're in this together,
there was none of that. Nothing. It seemed as if they were using
their sexuality in much the same way the guys in Nam had used
theirs. As a weapon. As a vehicle to confirm who they were
only none of them seemed to know who they were. The guys in
Nam didn't know who they were, either. Or why they were
where they were. You were just there. Nothing more nothing
less. You breathed in you breathed out you fucked. You got
fucked.

You fucked yourself.

I used to wonder what it would take to bring these men
together? I knew that men tended to come together only in
times of horror. And death. And I wanted life to be more than
that. I knew that sexuality and sex actually had very little to do
with it. Death was not new to me. I knew that men bonded in

the face of death. I used to wonder why these men never seemed able to reach out and touch the connections they all had wanted—never happened. They were afraid. I'd walk into gay bars, drink, try to talk to someone. Anyone. But I was just there. I felt stupid next to most of them. Just stupid. I'd talk about Elvis, how much I liked him, they thought I was o-u-t of my friggin' mind. Which I suppose I was. They thought I was stupid because I guess I was stupid. I'd go home with men but they all seemed to want the physical part of it to be rough—after all they were men. I DON'T WANNA BE YOUR TIGER . . .

I was too afraid to just ask anyone to simply hold me.

Hold me all night. LOVE ME TENDER, LOVE ME LONG, TAKE ME TO YOUR HEART. FOR IT'S CERTAIN THAT I BELONG. AND WE'LL NEVER PART. Just hold me, please. Let me sleep with my head on your chest. I didn't have the guts to ask. The rough part of it, the parts where they had to prove to me that they were men, I endured, I let them twist my tits. I smacked them around when they asked to be smacked around. Whatever. But no one wanted to hold me. The more guys you tricked with the more desirable or masculine you had to be. Supposedly. In Nam the men were always fucking whores. It was the same game with the same rules.

Different players.

You used someone and they used you. In Nam the more whores you screwed the more you became a man. Sex confirmed your identity. As did killing. In Nam both sex and killing became compulsive. It wasn't the psychological dynamics of gay sex that scared me as much as it was the obsession with the unavoidable killing anonymity that surrounded me like so much New York attitude. I was bone tired, weary of, and I deeply distrusted any mass subculture obsession. Obsessions were supposed to have hard uncompromising centers, and they were supposed to be about something. They were not supposed to be illusions. I wondered if the gay men I was meeting were *about* anything. Is that all there is, my friend. It was another shuffle shuffle. Break out the booze. Have a ball. I refused to buy a telephone answering machine. "Where are you from?" It was an inevitable question. Everyone wants to know where everyone else is from. You can't relate to a person unless you know where he's from. Maybe he's from anywhere. Anywhere. Or nowhere. "I'm from California," I'd say. At least it was the truth. Or it was at least close to the truth. I was from California but I did not feel as though I were from California. It was three-thousand and a hundred million miles away. California was another country in another universe. California was sun, surf, beaches, golden hills. This was dark, gray, the new me. I felt as if I were in reality—my reality—from Vietnam. I couldn't get that place out of my head. LOVE ME TENDER, LOVE ME TRUE, ALL MY DREAMS FULFILLED . . .If I closed my eyes I could see it. Candy, soda, dirty pictures, boom boom dope. Elvis in my head. Dead boys and whores. I could taste it. I ate in Vietnamese restaurants. It was okay to eat rice with your fingers. Nobody cared. And I was still numbah one GI. The only way I could really sleep was to put my old rotting rain poncho on and sleep in that. I could smell the fires, the monsoon, Billy, Titi, Jim, and Chris. But they weren't there to hold me.

I pretended I was from Memphis.

I met a man who said he wanted me. Everything about it was good. This was a good man. Nevertheless I knew that I was wrong for him. I had to ask. I had to know. It was important.

"What did you do during the war?" I asked.

"I protested," he said. "I didn't have to fight. I was in college. And I felt that the war was wrong. Most of the people I knew felt that way. We did our part."

"What part?"

"We marched on Washington. It was a big demonstration."

"I was over there. Vietnam. We heard about the demonstrations."

"What did you think about them?"

"Think? Nobody there thought about anything. You did what you were told. And you felt. You tried not to think. You tried not to feel, too. But mostly it was impossible. We felt that the demonstrators were right. But that they didn't know what they were right about. Or how right they were. We hated them. It's easy to demonstrate."

"It wasn't easy."

"What we felt was that you guys all thought that you were all better than us. That we were baby killers. And you were the good guys. But you had to be there to understand that it was all much more complex than that. It was this place where everything was gray. The issues there just weren't black and white, you know, clear cut. So what are you going to do when it's an eight-year-old who you're seventy-five percent sure is carrying a cache of grenades in that bag of rice slung over his shoulder? Are you going to confront him? Or her? You're playing moral odds and nothing and nobody is right and nothing and nobody is wrong. You survive and you get the fuck out. You had to be there to understand on a gut level that there are no good guys. Not anywhere. Anywhere. There are no bad guys. There are people. We are all related. You had to be there."

"You didn't have to be there," he said.

I smiled. I kissed him. He looked confused. "You had to be there," I said. And I left him. I never saw him again. PUT A CHAIN AROUND MY NECK AND LEAD ME ANYWHERE. OH, LET ME BE (OH, LET HIM BE) YOUR TEDDY BEAR. I kept tearing at the chains. Everytime I'd rip one off from around my sweating lily-white American throat someone always seemed capable, maybe because I allowed them this power, of putting another one, another set of choke chains, around my stupid throat when I wasn't looking. When my guard was down. Ironically, the only person I have ever melted into, on a level where there were no symbolic chains involved in what took place between us, where we merged because we wanted to merge, was with a Vietnamese man who I became somewhat involved with during the war—somewhat.

We fucked. There were no chains. I had gone through the whole thing around sleeping with Chris in Hong Kong. In my not-so-protective underwear. And I had never slept with a man before. Like that. Bare, without my not-so-protective underwear. So when Chris and I returned to Saigon it wasn't exactly an accident that I met Kai—his name was Kai. And he lived in a small apartment above a bar in Cholon. At the time I had this burning in my belly for anyone who was Vietnamese—I hated them. But Kai changed all of that. Dramatically. Not only did Kai change the way in which I started seeing the Vietnamese but he was the right man in the right place at the right time. And I started seeing who I was in a different way as well. In the universe man is one of the few organisms who is absolutely capable of changing the way in which he experiences the world when the way in which he experiences the world simply doesn't work for the organism anymore.

I wanted to experience loving a man. In the middle of men-killing-men, in the middle of being forced to eat shit, I wanted to know on a very intense level what it was like to love another man. It was anything but heroic. It was selfish and introspective and obsessed and arrogant and love-me-tender. So he did. I just picked him up because I was ready to be picked up. We met. On the Chinese streets of Cholon. At night. In a bar because I wanted to be picked up in a bar. So there he was and there I was. There were no chains around my neck. I could shut the war out. It didn't exist. He was this soft sleek brown

totally erotic creature under me, naked, compliant, and mad.
Kai could speak little English and I could speak only a
little Vietnamese. He was my age and he was an arvin deserter.
So there I was with an arvin in his bed. Making love to the enemy. To someone I wanted to hate. He was a male. And he was
the enemy. But there we were. And he was just a man, like
other men, and he was beautiful. And his sense of dignity was
awesome. It permeated who he was. Kai cared for me. This
amazed who I was. He was small but masculine. Dark and soft.
He allowed me to dominate him, at least sexually, without giving up any of his masculinity. I made love to another man. We
didn't communicate on a level that was verbally oriented—it
was physical. Yet Kai made the same emotional sounds—
basic—the same moans that all men make when they are making love with another human being. His tongue was as sweet as
it was intoxicated.

So I took him.

And then in the end I found myself in his immaculate
apartment waiting for him to come home because he always
came home. Listening to the clock tick. Realizing that I was
only a visitor, a guest, in this place. That this was his place.
That there was a great deal of dignity to it as well as there was to
him. Because he was who he was. Even though he was poor, a
deserter, he waited on tables in a Saigon cafe. Always waiting
for the day when he might be discovered as having deserted the
ARVN. Although Saigon was filled with men who had at some
point become cognizant of the fact that this war made no sense.
That killing their own people was going against the tide. That,
now, it served the purposes of a select few in their society. But
it was wrong. It was wrong for us and it was wrong for them. So
they deserted and they lived.

I found myself waiting for him. Feeling him around me
because this was his space. His things. His brush in the bathroom had his sleek long black hair in it. And his smell. His

slippers had been carefully placed under the bed—our bed. Just so. The overhead fan cooled the room. Sounds from the street drifted in, muted, just like they did when I was in bed with him. Next to him wanting me to take him. I waited. It grew dark. But I waited. Only he never came back. Although I waited. Patiently. There were no chains around my neck. I waited and I waited. When I realized that something was badly wrong, that he was in all likelihood not coming back—ever—I stripped, climbed into his bed, put his pillow, the pillow that smelled of my strong Kai, between my legs and I held him to me for one last time.

I never saw him again.

With a few good words from the VA I landed that job as a school custodian. I had experience cleaning up. I was good at it. I was a janitor. It actually wasn't all that bad. I could pick up shit after high school students. BURN MY HOUSE, STEAL MY CAR, DRINK MY LIQUOR FROM AN OLD FRUIT JAR. HONEY, YOU CAN DO ANYTHING YOU WANNA DO. BUT GET OFF, GET OFFA MY BLUE SUEDE SHOES. Nobody hassled me. I needed a job where nobody hassled me. It passed the time and paid the rent. It was Billy who put his foot up my butt. He called me from Cleveland. "I still don't understand why you're in Cleveland," I said to him on the phone. "Why didn't you go home?" Home for Billy as it was for me was California.

"For the same reasons you're not there, asshole. You tell me? Why didn't you go back?"

"I don't know. I don't know if I will ever go back there. I'm not really sure I ever want to see it again."

"Yeah," he said. "I want to remember it the way it was before the war. It's probably changed, you know; California pussy. Everything's changed. All the girls I know are married by now, anyway. Most of them probably have ten kids each. I'd probably fall off my own surfboard, man. I guess I don't want to see any of the changes. How's Chris?"

"He's fine. I guess. Sometimes I pick him up on a day pass and we'll get drunk together." There was a long silence. "Are you okay, Boss?" I was crying. I did not know why. "Yeah, I'm fine. I miss you. I miss Chris. I—I can't sleep." "Don't cry, Boss. I can't stand it when you cry. You ain't nothing but an old hound dog, man." "God, I hate the crying part, you know." "I know. You're just a soft fag, Boss. You always were. You saved my fucking life, what, how many times, Boss. I love you." "I love you, too," "Why don't you go get him? Just fucking go get him. I don't understand why the two of you aren't together. You're both fags. You've both always been fags." "And then what? He's in a fucking wheelchair, Billy." "What? I'm a goddamn cripple myself. Look at me! I can't even find a job. What? You're telling me you can't go get Chris or be with Chris because he's a cripple? Fuck that, Boss. We're all cripples. You need him. He needs you. I'm going to call him. I don't care what it costs. Fucking phone booth. Go get Chris, Boss. He needs you. Not the goddamn VA. I'm calling Chris. Goddamn fags, anyway. I'm in Vietnam with two goddamn faggots. I love two fucking queers. Shit."

I knew that Chris would call. "Billy called me."

"I know."

"Why is he in Cleveland?"

"I don't know."

"Fucking asshole." There was another long silence. "Are we queer or what?"

"I don't know."

"I'm doing a wheelie in the hall by the pay phone."

"You'll mark up the hall again."

"Fuck the VA, man. I saw this new guy's stub today. All raw, you know. The whole place is crawling with stubs this week. They're putting in a new rehab lab. I can't stay here."

"You wanna live with me, Chris?"

"I think I'm queer. I used to have sex with Titi."

"I know."

"You knew? Well, why didn't you ever say anything, Boss?"

"Don't call me Boss anymore. I'm not anybody's friggin' asshole boss. Okay!"

"Okay."

"What did you want me to say? 'Ranger, are you sucking numbah one GI's dick?' I didn't care."

"Like hell you say."

"You can suck all the dicks in China for all I care, Chris. Why should I care?"

"Because you love me, that's why. And now you're crying again. You're always crying."

"There must be a thousand guys out there, Boss. They'd climb all over each other to fuck your ass."

"I just want somebody to hold me, that's all."

"Jesus, I guess we're queers. Elvis the pelvis queers. I never thought I'd grow up to be a fucking queer." Another silence. I felt as though disconnected pieces of me were floating around. "I can't even *walk*, Boss! I wet my damn pants! I can't get it up! I'm a cripple. *Don't you know that?!* What's wrong with you, man? You don't want some fag cripple. Fuck you, Boss. Just fuck you. Taylor's dead, man. He's just dead." Chris was crying. I did not know why.

"Let me hold you."

"Hold me, Boss. You used to hold me when I was scared. You promised me, man."

"I'm—I'm holding you right now. I can feel you in my arms, Chris. I'm with you."

"I'm scared."

"Of what, man?"

"I don't know. Taylor's dead. I don't know. Of everything."

"We'll live together."

"You don't want me. Not like this. How can I ask you to
want me when I don't want me?"

"Pack your bags, you asshole. I'll be there in the morning."

"I love you, you faggot. Boss, you're a faggot."

"I know." I moved him in the next day.

YOU AIN'T NOTHING BUT A HOUND DOG CRYING ALL
THE TIME. We named her Boom Boom because she'd emit
exploding grenade sounds whenever we drove her. She was a
1965 spraypainted VW bus. She was red and blue and purple
and yellow and silver but mostly she was rust. We bought her
from six hippie-types who lived upstairs. They needed the
money for dope. She was a steal. We never could get all the
marijuana seeds out of that van. They were everywhere. She
had something of a personality. "I think she's originally from
California," I said to Chris as we checked her out for the first
time. It was snowing and New York was cold. Chris' chair kept
getting stuck in the gray slush that passed for snow.

"How can you tell?"

"I don't know. She just reminds me of someone who
probably used to live in California. Look at this..." There was
an old Beach Boys tape in the glove compartment. I put it into
the tape player. OH, BARBRA AAAAAN. OH, BARBRA
AAAAAN. YOU GOT ME ROCKIN' AND A ROLLING
ROCKIN' AND A REELING, BARBRA ANN—BA—BA
BARBRA ANN...

"That's disgusting," he said. "I'm gonna throw up."

"That is not disgusting. It's art."

"Who says it's art?"

"I say it's art."

"You're from California. What the fuck do you know?"
BA BA BA—BA BARBRA ANN. BA BA BA—BA
BARBRA ANN...
"I thought that hippies liked Steven Stills?" Chris had
long hair. From hippies he knew nothing. Chris was from
Michigan. "In Michigan we liked Mitch Ryder. Every she-
devil wore a blue dress. A blue dress..."
Chris was bouncing around. "I've never heard you sing
before."
"I sing all the time. But not the Beach Boys give me a
break."
"In the retired glove compartment of every old hippie
van, Chris, lurks at least one slightly musty Beach Boys tape."
YOU GOT ME ROCKIN' AND A ROLLING ROCKIN' AND
A REELING BARBRA ANN BA BA . . .
We couldn't decide whether to visit California or Michigan. I bought two wooden planks from a hardware store so that I
could pull his chair up into Boom Boom. We took out the pas-
senger's seat so that he could park his chair in the front until
one day I slammed on the brakes in heavy traffic. Chris went
flying. So we had to put the front seat back in. He was rather
good about getting himself out of the chair and into various different kinds of seats. We used to drive up to the Cloisters at
night where we could see the lights from downtown and the
George Washington Bridge. And we'd neck.
"I feel like a schoolgirl out on a date," I told him.
"You are a schoolgirl out on a date. Don't fight it just kiss
me, you fool."
I laughed whenever his beard got to be too much. It took
me a long time to learn how to get used to kissing a man with a
beard. We did a lot of kissing. "Well, what's it going to be,
Chris? Michigan or California?" It would soon be Christmas
and we'd been talking about either visiting my mother in California which isn't what I wanted to do. Or we could visit his
family in Michigan which isn't what he wanted to do. "You

wanna flip a coin?"

"Flip a coin. Only if we have to go to Michigan do I have to go along?"

"Yes."

"Flip the coin." It was Michigan. "Shit."

"I thought you loved your family?"

"You have to know something before you can love it, Boss. I don't know them anymore."

"Call them. You never call them."

"I forget the number."

"You used to write to them every day from Nam, Chris. Sometimes twice a day."

"People do strange things in war, don't they. Hell sucks, remember?"

"You're not seventeen-years-old anymore. You can handle it."

"Yeah, maybe they'll love my new chair, right? Or maybe they'll love the fact that their son is queer? Are you sure you want to do this?"

"We can play the Beach Boys on the way to Michigan. I bought a new tape."

"You didn't."

"I did."

WENT TO A DANCE LOOKING FOR ROMANCE. SAW BARBRA ANN SO I THOUGHT I'D TAKE A CHANCE. BARBRA ANN BA BA BA BARBRA ANN. YOU GOT ME ROCKIN' AND A ROLLING ROCKIN' AND A REELING BARBRA ANN. BA BA BA BARBRA ANN. TRIED BETTY SUE, TRIED BETTY LOU, TRIED MARY LOU BUT I KNEW IT WOULDN'T DO. BARBRA ANN BA BA BA BARBRA ANN. BARBRA ANN BARBRA ANN . . .

We weren't really sure if Boom Boom could make it to Michigan. But she was relentless. She'd gasp and belch and explode for a while and then she'd run as smooth as a dry martini. YOU GOT ME ROCKIN' AND A ROLLING ROCKIN'

AND A REELING BARBRA ANN.

"Did you know any girls," he asked me as we were going through Ohio.

"What do you mean, did I know any girls? Of course I knew girls. I'm from California."

Chris laughed. "They invented homosexuality in California, you know. It's where all the weirdos are from."

"I am not a weirdo." He laughed.

"You listen to this music and you're telling me you're no weirdo? My father takes one look at you, Boss, he's going to say, 'Yup, weirdo. My son lives with a California fag.'"

"My son lives with a fag?"

"That's what he'll say. Only he'll say California fag. You'll see."

"How about my son *is* a fag?"

"No. Now, if we lived in California *then* he'd say, 'Yup, my son's a fag.' But we don't so he won't."

TRIED BETTY SUE, TRIED BETTY LOU, TRIED MARY LOU BUT I KNEW IT WOULDN'T DO. BARBRA ANN BA BA . . .

"What girls did you know, Mr. Wise Guy?" I asked.

"I knew Donna Jean Satterfield. We were engaged."

"What happened?"

"Vietnam happened." Chris went into his 'father imitation' and started shaking his finger at me. "Okay, Mister. My father used to call me Mister. Okay, Mister. There's a war going on and you're going over there to fight it. No son of mine is gonna sit on his ass when his country needs every kid it can get. It'll make you into a man. You know what a man is, boy? Yes, Sir. A man fights for his country, Sir. A man fucks pussy, Sir. A man does what he's told. Sir! Fuck you! Sir! She was a nice girl, actually."

"Who?"

"Donna Jean. She never wrote to me. Not even once. I heard she married some guy who knocked her up."

"I was going to marry Rhonda," I said.

"Rhonda? What kind of name is Rhonda?"

"Don't ask."

SO I THOUGHT I'D TAKE A CHANCE. BARBRA
ANN BA BA . . .

"Sex is weird. Don't you think sex is weird, Boss?"

I looked at him. "What's weird about it?"

"What was Rhonda like."

"After the second grade I lost track of her." WENT TO A
DANCE LOOKING FOR ROMANCE . . .

"I never made it with a girl. I guess I'm a weirdo. Let's
move to California."

"You're much too bizarre for California, Chris. They'd
kick you the fuck out."

BARBRA ANN. BARBRA ANN. YOU GOT ME ROC-
KIN' AND A ROLLING . . .

"Everyone in Nam was into whores, man. Sometimes I
felt so sorry for them, you know, the whores. I used to know this
whore. Some asshole killed her. She was this really nice girl. It
didn't make any sense. She was sixteen-years-old. I was one
year older than she was. We talked. It was all we did. She'd
say, 'GI, you want fuckee fuckee?' I'd say nah. She'd say,
'Me fuckee me no suckee me go pee pee me be right back.'"
Chris laughed and laughed. "I loved the way she talked. You
know what, Boss?"

"What?"

"I loved her. I think she was the only girl I ever really
loved. I didn't want to have sex with her. I just wanted to be
with someone who wasn't about the killing, you know, it was
like I couldn't wash my hands of the killing. Remember Titi?"
I just looked over at him. "Remember how Titi was always
washing his hands? He could never get them clean." Chris
paused. "It was the killing."

"I know."

"She had the nicest little hands, Boss. They were always

clean. She had this baby. It was half-black half-Vietnamese. She didn't care about what color it was. It was her baby. Her mamasan took care of it. One day we went to her village together. Just her and me. I met her mamasan. I saw her kid. We had this C-ration picnic, you know, out by this rice paddy. It was beautiful, Boss. Just the three of us and the C-rations. And then about a month later I'm back up there and the whole village is gone. Just gone. It's been burned to the fucking ground. There'd been a zippo raid. We killed them. We just killed all those people, Boss."

"I know."

"That was when I wrote my old man my last letter. I told them about what had happened. After that I stopped writing to them. They never wrote to me. Once I got some socks."

"What did you tell them?"

"You mean that last time?"

"Yeah."

There was a long silence. We left Ohio and entered Michigan. The sky was gray. The air was frigid. The heater only half-worked and we could see our breath in the van. "I told them about the girl. I told them about how she'd been killed. I told them about how her village had been leveled to the ground. I can just hear my old man right now. Gook lover. My son's a goddamn gook faggot lover. I told him that I hated him. I told him I hated what I was doing. Where I was. And, you know, none of that would have bothered him. Not him. Not at all. You know what would have really bothered my old man?"

"What?"

"I told him that he was wrong."

BARBRA AAAAAN. OH, BARBRA AAAAAN . . .

"And the moral of the story is that I haven't talked to them since."

"Not at all? You haven't had any contact with them at all?"

"Not at all."

"What about . . . ?"

"They know about the chair if that's what you mean. Oh, I guess the service probably told them I'd been wounded. I've talked to my sister a couple of times. Gloria's a real case. She's got her own problems, you know, two kids, a jerk for a husband. She said that when Dad found out about me getting hit and all that he felt it must have been my own goddamn stupid fault. They know I'm a cripple. Gloria told them. But they don't know that I'm a fag. I don't talk to them." Chris rifled through the glove compartment. "Those hippies leave us any marijuana, Boss?"

YOU GOT ME ROCKIN' AND A ROLLING ROCKIN' AND A REELING BARBRA ANN—BA BA—BA BARBRA ANN...

WELL, THEY SAID YOU WAS HIGH-CLASS. AND THAT WAS JUST FINE. WELL, THEY SAID YOU WAS HIGH-CLASS. AND THAT WAS JUST FINE. BUT YOU NEVER CAUGHT A RABBIT AND YOU AIN'T NO FRIEND OF MINE. Lansing, Michigan is a factory town. A car-making town. A jailhouse rock town. It sits on the banks of the Grand River the way a dead fish rots alongside a slow-moving polluted stream. Lansing kind of insolently snarls at you as though it were somehow an insignificant hoodlum who'd been expelled from snotty school for smoking reefer in the snotty bathroom. Even the air seemed trapped. Chris wanted to drive around before we went to his family's house. Here's where I went to high school. Here's where I worked at a burger joint it'd been a burger joint then. Now it was a shopping mall. Here's the Olds plant. Everyone works at Olds. Everyone? Everyone. You've never seen so many color TVs in so many homes in your life.

"I have a dream!" Chris orated. "I have a dream! I dream of a society where every white American family has a color TV in the loo. I have a dream! I dream of a society where a man's children will be judged not on the color of their skin but on the content of their credit cards I have a dream!" Chris was quiet for a minute. "Lansing is a dream come true. Malcolm X was born and raised here. Most people don't know that. It's true. His father was murdered here. Lansing helped mold Malcolm X into the gentle religious man of God that he was. His real name was Malcolm Little."

"What were you expecting, Chris?"

"I wonder if he still sneaks booze into his coffee thermos?"

"Say what?"

"He carries this black metal lunch pail. I'll bet he carries the same lunch pail. He's carried it, now, for over twenty years, you know. Can you imagine? Carrying the same lunch pail with the same thermos and the same liquor and the same lunch for over twenty years to the same job? I wonder if she wears the same coat?"

"I doubt it," I said.

"He'd tell her every winter. Get a new coat. Here's some money. Get a coat. She's always worn the same cloth coat. I know she still has that coat. It's gray because gray lasts she says. Gray wears well. And don't we know it." Chris laughed softly. "Gray is the official color of Lansing. She'd take his money and she'd buy us Christmas presents. Never a coat for herself. I never saw her in anything but that goddamn gray coat. If I see that coat I swear I'll puke."

"No, you won't."

"Yes, I will I'll puke if I see that fucking coat. Don't park in the drive."

"Where do I park then, pray tell?"

"Park down the street. Don't park in the drive. My father will have a stroke if he sees this van."

"He'll live."

"No, he won't. My father almost had a heart attack the night Elvis came on the Ed Sullivan show. Seriously. My father almost died. He thought that Elvis had been sent over by the communists. The only thing worse than a communist is a homosexual communist. I don't think my father ever really met a card-carrying communist in his entire life. Although God knows he's met a homosexual. Me. His own flesh and blood. I lived under his roof. I remember. His hands will reach up to his head, his eyes will roll back, he'll pound his face. And he'll die if he sees this van. It's a communist's van for sure. Probably a homosexual communist. And then he'll have a stroke. And then he'll die. My sister will weep. My brother will probably rejoice . . ."

"What brother."

"I have a brother."

"Why don't you tell me things?"

"And if my father has a stroke when he sees this van we'll have to stay for the funeral. Do you have any idea what a funeral is like in this town? Christmas is depressing in this town. You can imagine what funerals are like. They prop you up in an Oldsmobile, probably one that you helped make, and then they drive you and it into the Grand River where the carp eat your flesh. It's true."

"Sure."

"You'll see." I parked down the street. His parents were very nice. His father was small and bent. His mother was tired. His sister was on her way. There was a younger brother I didn't even know existed.

"So you do have a brother!"

"Yeah, sure. He's not bad for your average asshole. He even likes Elvis the pelvis."

I saw them through my eyes. Try as I might I could not see them through my lover's eyes. Listening to Chris you got the impression that his father was this towering imposing authority figure. An unforgiving horrible giant made from solid steel. John Wayne and then some. He was a broken little man with a lunch box, a mortgage that was close to being paid off, and one not-very-new color TV. He stood on his porch, watching me wheel his son, the returning Vietnam vet, up the sidewalk, tears in his confused father's eyes. Hands shoved too deeply down into his pockets. Fists clenched. He tried to smile. It was Christmas. It was a scene every person who had been to Nam had envisioned in his head. What was it going to be like when you walked up that sidewalk to what had once been your home. Even if you couldn't walk you still had the vision. COME ON, MAMA, LET'S ROCK. Chris' father didn't want to cry. But he cried. They hugged and their hugging was as intense and as painful as it was fierce and moving. I found tears welling up in my own eyes.

LOVE ME TENDER, LOVE ME SWEET, NEVER LET ME GO.

"And this must be your friend," his mother said. "Well, you boys come right on in here this instant cause there's food on the table we didn't know when you'd get here it's an awfully long ride and I've been keeping this food warm and I'll bet you could use a drink well we didn't know where you were I know you've gotta be hungry Gloria made Christmas cookies Chris always liked those . . ." Her nervous chatter stopped abruptly. She took a deep breath and a long slow look at the new son who had been wheeled into her kitchen. The one who didn't walk anymore. The one who no longer played football. The one who wouldn't be fathering any babies. She knew in her head what it was going to be like; what he would seem like sitting there when he finally after all this time—arrived. She'd told herself about a zillion times that she'd just pretend he was normal. It'd be for the best—back home from a day at school. Fresh and hungry out of football practice. Hi, Mom! What's for supper? A cold healthy blush to his cheeks. Her son. He

would still be her son. She tried. She made a real determined
stab at it. She gave it everything she had. But the issues were
bigger than she was. She failed. She dropped a piece of china
which shattered on the kitchen floor. No one moved or said
anything.

"Oh, Mama," Chris said.

She bent down to him, hugged his head to her bosom, ran
her fingers through his hair. She kissed her son. She clung to
him.

"I'm so sorry, Mama."

"Be still," she said. "Be still."

"Well," Chris said to everyone, "this is it." And he did a
wheelie in his chair in the middle of his mother's kitchen.
"You get used to it after a while. The chair grows on you."
Everyone tried to smile. His brother, a kid who looked exactly
like Chris, maybe ten years younger, bit his lip, and ran from
the room. "Mike!" Chris yelled after his brother.

"Let him go," his father said, "He doesn't want anyone to
see him upset."

"You mean cry, Daddy," Chris said. "It's okay if he
cries."

"Not in front of Daddy, it's not," his sister said. "It's
good to see you, Chris." She bent down and kissed him. "War
is hell, honey, at least the ones around here are, but you didn't
have to stay away so long. I bet your friend can use that drink. I
know I need one. A double." I liked her immediately. In fact, I
liked her a lot. She was one year older than Chris. She had
three small children that she introduced to me. She had an incorrigible honesty that was her way of disarming you, putting
you at ease, as much as it was her way of dealing with her life.
She was tough, there was an exterior, and under the exterior
there was more exterior. Her children were excited by Christmas because they were children. And it was Christmas. She'd
roll her eyes and say, "Motherhood. It's the pits." I laughed.

"It's okay," she said. "After the last one I had my tubes tied."

"Gloria," her mother said. "You don't have to tell everyone."

"Oh, I don't mind, Mama. There's nothing wrong with having your tubes tied. Sometimes I think I'll wear a sign, you know, it'll say: tubes tied horny woman have orgasm will travel." She turned to me. "Donna Jean Satterfield, Chris' ex, well, kind of his ex, they were engaged, well, she had *her* tubes tied. About time. Let me tell you. Donna Jean's got more kids than a cat has kittens." She handed me my drink and spoke as if we were co-conspirators. "I have some dynamite maui wowie out in the car, honey, if you're interested. You know, later."

"Sure."

"Don't tell Daddy, though. He'd have a stroke on us and probably die. Did Chris ever tell you about the time Daddy saw Elvis Presley on the Ed Sullivan show? Daddy has to be the only person in the universe who thought that Ed Sullivan was a pinko."

"I think that Chris mentioned it."

"Daddy had a stroke, you know, at the time. An actual *man* moving his hips. And we all know what that means whatever it means. Well, let me tell you this whole town was shocked to its Irish core. Can you imagine what my father would do if he knew I smoked maui wowie? By the pound?"

"My lips are sealed."

"Not for long they won't be. Not for long." And she laughed. NEVER LET ME GO. YOU HAVE MADE MY LIFE COMPLETE AND I LOVE YOU SO. "Christopher, you little rat. You never told me your roommate was so handsome. Now, here I am my own husband gone moose hunting at Christmas. Can you believe it? Moose hunting. Give me a break." Gloria took a long sip of her drink.

"Gloria, why is Chuck moose hunting," Chris asked.

"He's pussy hunting if you ask me," she said.

"Gloria," her father said. "I think you've had enough to drink."

"Well, I think I've only just begun . . . Daddy. Cheers!"

Their boyhero had returned home. They bit their lips and pretended that he was the same, that they were the same, that nothing had changed since he had left them. Virginal and unbroken. Johnnycomemarchinghome. We went into the living room and Chris' brother, Mike, came downstairs slowly. "Come here," Chris said. Mike just looked at the floor. "I said come here. I want to look at you. You're a young man. I can hardly believe I'm looking at you, Mikey." Mike reached his hand out as if to shake his brother's hand. He was stiff, formal, intimidated, and hurt. Chris wanted more than a handshake. He took hold of his brother's hand and pulled the boy to him. "Look at me. It's me."

"It's *not* you!"

"It's *me*, Mikey! It's me! Christopher! Don't shut me out." Chris took the boy's face in his hands and kissed him.

"We always were this really emotional gushy family," Gloria observed. "Personally, I blame Daddy."

"For what?" I asked.

"For everything that ever went wrong. Ever."

"Everything?"

"Everything."

Mike and Chris were crying. Gloria and I were drinking. Chris' parents were in the kitchen making Christmas dinner. It was one of those families that sat around a big table and ate turkey because they were a family. And it was Christmas. Christopher played Santa Claus. "And this is for you," he said, handing his mother a large box that was from Bergdorf Goodman. They do not have a Bergdorf Goodman in Lansing. I had wheeled him through Macy's but no. Macy's wasn't good enough. So then I wheeled him through Saks but no. Saks didn't have what he was looking for. So then I wheeled him through Bloomingdales for Christ's sake but no. Bloomingdales wouldn't do. My feet were weary but Bloomingdales simply would not do.

"Oh, that's okay," he'd said. "I'll wheel myself over to Lord and Taylor." And he gave me his best I'm suffering through these Christmas crowds what with this slush in the street and you want me to wheel over to Lord and Taylor all by myself look. "I can do it."

"Shut up," I said. And I wheeled him over to Lord and Taylor but no. Lord and Taylor wouldn't do. "Look, it's late. We'll go to Bergdorf's, Chris, but that's it. After that I dump you into the East River." Bergdorf Goodman had what he wanted. It was expensive but they didn't have a fucking Bergdorf Goodman's in Lansing.

"What good is SSI if you can't go to Bergdorf Goodman?" he'd said.

"Oh, Mother," Gloria said. "It's beautiful. What a beautiful coat. Jesus! I hated that thing she always wears! The dump look 1955. Now it won't be an embarrassment to be seen with you, Mama."

"Gray wears well, Gloria." her mother said.

"Yeah, it matches the air." Gloria whispered to me. "I need some maui wowie, you wanna maui with my wowie about right now, Soldier?"

"Why not?"

Gloria and I kind of snuck out to her car in the garage while Chris related to the rest of the family all about Vietnam and what had happened the day he'd been shot. "I can't hear any more Nam stories," Gloria said. "My husband was there. He's still there I think."

"It can take a while to adjust."

"A while? Are you serious. A while? Honey, it's going to

take that man a loooong while." Gloria lit a joint. "Marijuana makes me horny? You ever get horny, Soldier?"

"My dick got shot off."

"Stop."

"It's true. All I have is a little stub. You wanna see it? I'm walking point and one day—Blam!—they shot my dick off."

"Stop. I don't believe you." Gloria laughed and laughed. LOVE ME TENDER, LOVE ME LONG, TAKE ME TO YOUR HEART. FOR IT'S CERTAIN THAT I BELONG AND WE'LL NEVER PART. There I was in some godforsaken factory town in the middle of nowhere in a garage in a 1967 Chevy Impala with the windows rolled up smoking boom boom reefer with a madwoman. It's fucking Christmas. I'm stoned. And my lover's sister wants to see my equipment. "Show me!"

"I'm shy."

"I'll just bet you are." She laughed again, crawled into the back seat, and sort of sprawled out, kicking her heels off. She passed me another joint. Gloria had a lot of joints. They were all perfectly rolled. "He's changed. But he's the same Christopher. When we were in high school he'd moon my girlfriends. It outraged me. I'd get really pissed off about it. 'Daddy, Christopher is showing his butt to the girls. It's making me sick.' So then Daddy would get on him, you know, about mooning. All the guys were into mooning. We'd drive to the drive-in and everyone would moon everyone else. One night I didn't even know Chris was at the drive-in. He was with Donna Jean. And I mooned them. There I am mooning my own brother. Only I didn't realize that it was him because they were in her car. Well, you can imagine. I wanted to die. He threatened to tell Daddy that I was mooning people at the drive-in. You ever been to a drive-in?"

"We don't have drive-ins in California."

"They sure as hell had lots of drive-ins when I was there," she said. "Drive-ins for days. They *invented* drive-ins in California. I'll bet you're one of those weirdos, aren't you?"

"There are a few things in life that were not invented in California."

"Name one."

"Diaper buckets were invented in New Jersey."

"That's true," she said. "I forgot about diaper buckets."

"Disposable diapers were invented in California," I explained. "I am not a weirdo. When were you in California?"

"That was my runaway period. I'd graduated from high school. Daddy said I had two options. 'Gloria, you can go into the WACS.' Heaven forbid. 'Or you can find a husband.' Which would have been worse than the WACS or the WAVES or whatever it was Daddy had planned for me. So Gloria said to Gloria, 'Gloria,' she said, 'why don't you just go to California and live with the weirdos and smoke marijuana until the earthquake comes?' So I did. Only I moved to Haight Ashbury where I burned my brain cells out on LSD when I lived in the New Buffalo Commune, you had to be there, and Daddy had to come get me. Now, that was a sight to see. Daddy in Haight Ashbury at the New Buffalo Commune. You had to be there. Daddy was somewhat less than amused. So he brought me back home. You know, kind of dragged me by the hair. I'd been totally ruined in California. Daddy didn't think too much of the New Buffalo Commune. Communists for days. Real communists not the Michigan kind of communists. California communists. And then there were the homosexuals. Well, Daddy didn't stay too long in San Francisco. I think it was the world's shortest visit to the West Coast. Fifteen minutes. The WACS or the WAVES or whoever they were didn't want me. So I met Chuck and I got pregnant. You'll never guess where..."

"Where you met Chuck or where you got pregnant?"

"Both."

"Where?"

"At the drive-in. Isn't life sublime? Is my brother a fag?"

"Why don't you ask him?"

"Because I'm asking you. I've always thought maybe Chris might be a fag, you know."

"I can't speak for Chris."

"Like hell."

"What makes you think he might be gay?"

"Gay! Gay? Everyone from around here says fag. Or faggot."

"I'm not from around here. I'm from California, remember? I grew up with the weirdos, and the communists, and we all say gay not fag, only I find myself using that word probably too much. I happen to be straight."

"Yeah, and I'm Connie Francis. Oh, my God, my brother's a fag. I knew it! I just knew it."

"You don't know anything. None of you know Chris anymore. He's really gone through a lot."

"Honey, we've *all* gone through a lot." She laughed again. "Hey, don't get me wrong! If he wants to be a...if he wants to be gay that's just fine with me. I am very very good at keeping secrets, you know. Ask anyone. Shit!" She laughed hilariously.

"What's so funny, Gloria?"

"All the handsome ones are gay! I suppose you're gay, too? No, don't tell me. I don't want to know. Yes, I do. I'm dying to know. Tell me."

"It's none of your business."

"That's what they all say. Ha! All the handsome ones. Why is it that all the good-looking ones turn out to be fags? You tell me. I was seeing this guy in high school, Morris Stevens, really good-looking. Honey, the man was a knock-out. Had all the girls salivating after him. It was disgusting. You should have seen us making drooling fools out of ourselves. Morris Stevens could have had any girl in that school. And then some. And then one day on the front page of the paper everyone in town, and I mean everyone, reads that a certain Morris Stevens had been arrested for commiting certain unnatural acts in a certain park at the edge of town. If you can imagine. Well, that was the end of Morris Stevens."

"What happened."

"Well, we all heard that he'd been put into a mental institution, you know, he had problems. Or something. We all tried to get old Morris to moon us at the drive in. But he never did. Old Morris was too busy elsewhere."

"I love Christopher very much."

"Welcome to the family."

"Thank you."

"Tell me. Why . . . ?"

"Does why matter?"

"I guess it doesn't." She sighed. "He needs someone, doesn't he? I mean, I'm not sure Chris could make it on his own."

"You're wrong. He is very independent."

"I don't mean his legs or lack of legs. I mean he's always needed someone. You know, some kids are just like that. I wasn't like that. Not really. At least not back when I knew Chris. I didn't *need* anyone. I had myself. But Chris always needed the guys. His buddies. And Chris always needed his father. Only I don't think Daddy knew how to be there for him. I think Chris scared the hell out of Daddy actually."

"Some kids are like that."

"Michael is just like Chris. I don't mean gay. I don't think Mikey is gay. But he's one of those kids who just needs someone. I've tried. First I tried to be there for Chris. But I was too young. I was just finding out how exciting adulthood could be. He needed me but I was never there for him. And now there's Mikey but I've got three kids of my own. I want to be there for him but I've lost hold. It's too late. Of course he adores Chris. Have you been upstairs? Have you seen his room?"

"No."

"Pictures of Chris everywhere. Michael needs Christopher but I'm not sure he knows how to reach out to him. We're not too good at that around here." She smiled. "We're real good at bottling things up. I knew that Michael was going to have a hard time coping with the new Chris. And now Chris is gay . . . "

"Maybe he's always been gay, Gloria. Why didn't anyone write to Chris in Vietnam. Nobody ever wrote to him."

"Oh, it's more complicated than that. I think that Daddy knows about Chris. I really do. I think that Daddy has always been really afraid of the fact that Chris might be gay. He was always pushing Christopher to be something that he wasn't. When Chris was in high school he was on the football team—he's a lunk if you haven't noticed—only none of us were allowed to go to any of Chris' games. 'He has to learn to do things on his own. For himself,' my father would say. 'Not for us. Christopher has to learn to be a man.' By the time Chris was overseas I was in California discovering acid, mu tea, and the Jefferson Airplane. Michael and Mother I think would have written to Chris but it's much more difficult going up against my father than you think. Besides, my mother has spent most of her life waiting on my father's every whim. She's made fearing him into an art form. 'The military,' my father used to say, 'will turn that boy into a man if anything can.' God, I'm glad Chris is gay and lives somewhere else. Hell, I'd live somewhere else if I didn't have three kids to think about. Maybe Chris can *do* something with his life. But not here. Never here. It'd only kill him here. Just like it was before he left. Well, if I can't have you I'm glad Chris can." She was silent for a short while. "You know what they used to call me?"

"What?"

"They used to call me the acid princess." She laughed again. "Now they just call me the reefer queen. I'm the fucking reefer queen. Whatever that is. I have been demoted in life. Welcome to Lansing."

The car was full of smoke. We could hardly see in front of ourselves. There was a knock at the door. It was Chris. "Open the door, you drug freaks." he said to us. "The doors are locked."

"Of course the doors are locked we're smoking marijuana go away," Gloria said to him.

"I'll moon you if you don't unlock the door." Chris said. And we both laughed. Gloria let him in.

"You're pretty good at sliding in and out of that thing, aren't you, Brother," she said and she handed him a lit joint. Gloria slid into Chris' chair, herself, took a tour around the garage, did a wheelie, laughed, and got back into the car.

"I'm ashamed of both of you," Chris said as he exhaled. "Smoking evil weed in the garage on Christmas. What *will* Daddy say? I smell a communist plot."

"Probably the same thing that he said ten years ago. *Bums!* I've raised *Bums* for children." Both Chris and Gloria laughed uproariously. "I tried seducing your friend, here," she said. "To no fucking avail. He swears on a stack of bibles that he's no fag, Chris."

"He lies. I'm always having to fight him off." It was my turn to laugh.

"Yeah, with a stick."

"Remember Morris Stevens, Gloria?" Chris asked. "I wonder whatever happened to good old Morris the queer."

"He moved to California after they let him out of the institution. At least Morris made it o-u-t of here. After I heard that he was gone I seriously considered having myself institutionalized but then who'd wait on Chucky-poo hand and foot night and day?" Gloria sighed. "The worst part of it is that sometimes I really do think I love him, Chris. And besides they let Morris o-u-t. They'd never let me past the rubber room, right? Michael needs you, Chris. He needs you real bad. Things here . . . things here are not good for Michael right now."

"How's that?"

"What, I have to spell it out? He's seventeen-years-old and the man we call our father has Michael totally convinced that Michael is shit and that the only thing he's going to be able to do with his life is work in that goddamn plant. You know, the one where Daddy works and where my husband works and where every man in this town works, Chris? What, you don't remember what it's like to live here! Give me a break. You might be gay but I didn't know it affected the memory cells."

"I remember."

"I keep thinking that he could do something with his life. He's smart, you know. He should go on to college. But nobody encourages him. If it was good enough for us it's good enough for our kids. You know how it is." Gloria looked down at her boobs. She pushed them up. "Do you think I look like Raquel?" she asked. "I keep thinking that I'd be happier, you know, if I could just look a little more like Raquel. Do you like my tits?"

"Jayne Mansfield sat in my lap," I said.

Gloria laughed. "You're kidding?"

"No, it's true. She did. I was in San Francisco and she was doing *Gentlemen Prefer Blondes*, you know, onstage. And when she sings the song about diamonds are a girl's best friend she'd come out into the audience and sit on guys' laps. I was fourteen-years-old. She had big tits."

"Did they get you—you know."

"I was embarrassed. She hurt my leg."

It was Chris' turn to laugh. "Gloria, I'm gay," Chris said.

"I know. Waddaya want, Chris, a marching band and a parade down Michigan Avenue?"

"I don't know that Michael can deal with it."

"It would be nice," she said, "if just once in his little insignificant shitty life somebody would give the kid the benefit of the doubt. But I won't tell him my lips are sealed." Gloria turned to me. "I always was very good about keeping secrets. Ask anybody."

The inside of the locked car was getting pretty wicked. There was another knock on the door. "Okay, you three. I know you're in there." It was Mike.

"Go away," Gloria said, "You're too young to know about marijuana. Shoo! Shoo!"

"Open the door."

"Should we open the door?" she asked Chris.

"I think he's too young to know about such things," Chris said. Gloria laughed.

"I've got some tapes," Mike said. "Anybody wanna listen to Grace Slick?"

"Who's Grace Slick?" Chris asked.

"Oh, man," Gloria observed, "you really are behind the times."

"Open the door. Let me in."

"He'll asphyxiate himself on the secondary smoke," I said.

"Shoo shoo! We're all too old in here to listen to Grace Slick. You got any Simon and Garfunkle, kid?"

"I got lots of Simon and Garfunkle. I got Lawrence Welk, too. I've got the Stones, man. I got Elvis. Come on, Gloria, open the door. Let me in, too. *Please!*"

"He was in diapers when I used to listen to Mick Jagger," Christopher observed.

"You, young man," Gloria said through a small crack at the top of a window, "were in diapers when we used to listen to

Mick Jagger. How d-a-r-e you bring that old rock and roller's tapes into this garage and remind us of how o-l-d we are. Go away. You got any Kingston Trio?"

"There are limits, Gloria."

"The child is talking to me, his older sister, about limits. Shoo, be gone with you before my other witch sister drops a house on you and your tapes."

"You don't have a witch sister," Mike said. He wanted to join the party. "I'm it. I'm all that's left. You two never did let me in anyway. Fuck both of you, man."

Gloria was a merciless tease. She did not let up. "You, young man, how dare you say fuck to me. A lady. I should wash your vile teenager motherfucker mouth out with soap."

Chris opened the door. Michael got into the front seat and put a tape into the tape player. AND HERE'S TO YOU MRS. ROBINSON, JESUS LOVES YOU MORE THAN YOU WILL KNOW. WOOO WOOO WOOO. GOD BLESS YOU PLEASE MRS. ROBINSON, HEAVEN HOLDS A PLACE FOR THOSE WHO PRAY. HEYHEYHEY, HEYHEYHEY . . .

"Michael, guess what!" Gloria said.

"What."

"These two are fags." WE'D LIKE TO KNOW A LITTLE BIT ABOUT YOU FOR OUR FANS. WE'D LIKE TO HELP YOU LEARN TO HELP YOURSELF . . .

Chris turned to me. "When I was sixteen, Gloria, here, used to extort blackmail from me. In return for keeping her mouth shut about the fact that she knew I was having Donna Jean do my homework assignments I was required to keep my sister, the reefer queen or the acid princess or whatever she was then, supplied with marijuana or she'd blab to Daddy. Gloria is great with keeping secrets as long as there's something in it for Gloria."

"You mixed it with oregano, you twerp, admit it."

"I admit it." LOOK AROUND YOU ALL YOU SEE ARE

SYMPATHETIC EYES. STROLL AROUND THE GROUNDS UNTIL YOU FEEL AT HOME . . .

"Are you . . . gay . . . Chris?" Michael asked. Chris turned up the tape player. AND HERE'S TO YOU MRS. ROBINSON, JESUS LOVES YOU MORE THAN YOU WILL KNOW. WOOO WOOO WOOO. GOD BLESS YOU PLEASE MRS. ROBINSON, HEAVEN HOLDS A PLACE FOR THOSE WHO PRAY. HEYHEYHEY HEYHEYHEY . . .

"Have a joint, Michael," I said. "This isn't a family of bums. It's a family of pot-heads."

"I'm gay, Michael," Chris said.

"No shit, man."

"No shit." HIDE IT IN A HIDING PLACE WHERE NO ONE EVER GOES. PUT IT IN THE PANTRY WITH YOUR CUPCAKES . . .

"I think we're *all* misfits. I blame Daddy," Gloria said.

"You would," Michael said to her. IT'S A LITTLE SE-CRET JUST THE ROBINSONS' AFFAIR. MOST OF ALL YOU'VE GOT TO HIDE IT FROM THE KIDS. KUKUKACHOO MRS. ROBINSON . .

"Does it bother you?" Chris asked.

"What, that you might be gay?"

"I *am* gay."

"No. Why should it bother me? Personally, I don't think I'd like another man's dick in my mouth. I've thought about it. But I don't think I'd like it. But if you like it, well, then it's your thing."

Gloria started howling from the back seat. I thought that she might die from the laughter. "When all is said and done," she said. "I mean, when you boil everything down to the bottom line, honey, it always comes back to s-e-x, now, doesn't it? Either you like a dick in your mouth or you don't. It's that simple. Only nothing is that simple. Mikey, darling, sweet heart, baby, I like a nice big dick in my mouth from time to

time and it doesn't make me gay. I don't think." GOD BLESS
YOU PLEASE MRS. ROBINSON. HEAVEN HOLDS A
PLACE FOR THOSE WHO PRAY . . ."Am I stoned or is it
Christmas? Where are my kids?"

"Mom's got them."

"Three cheers for motherhood."

"You mean grandmotherhood," Michael said. "Mom always has her kids."

"I am an unfit mother."

"The reefer queen," Chris said. SITTING ON A SOFA
ON A SUNDAY AFTERNOON. GOING TO THE CANDI-
DATES DEBATE. LAUGH ABOUT IT SHOUT ABOUT IT
WHEN YOU GOT TO CHOOSE . . .

"Do you think Jagger's gay?" Michael asked me.

"No. I think he's rich not gay. There's a difference.
Trust me. I'm from California. We know about these things."

"This is true," Gloria observed, exhaling. EVERY WAY
YOU LOOK AT IT YOU LOSE. WHERE HAVE YOU GONE
JOE DIMAGGIO, OUR NATION TURNS ITS LONELY
EYES TO YOU . . .

"I'm glad it doesn't bother you, Mikey," Chris said.

"Waddaya want, Chris? A marching band and a parade
down Michigan Avenue?"

"That's what I said," Gloria laughed. WHAT'S THAT
YOU SAY MRS. ROBINSON, JOLTIN' JOE HAS LEFT
AND GONE AWAY. HEYHEYHEY HEYHEYHEY . . .

"Is it catching?" Michael asked.

"Is what catching?" Chris said.

"He wants to know if he'll catch it," Gloria observed. "Is
it contagious?"

"Only if I grab you like this . . ." Chris put Michael into
a one-arm headlock. "Us fags are real weak types, you know."
Chris changed the tape with his free arm.

"Oh, here comes the Lawrence Welk," Gloria smiled.

WHEN YOU'RE WEARY, FEELING SMALL. WHEN
TEARS ARE IN YOUR EYES, I'LL DRIVE THEM ALL . . .
"Let me go." Michael whimpered.
"Brutality!" Gloria laughed.
"Chris, you're hurting my neck. Let go of me!"
"Oh, my God. Now I'm gonna have two queers for
brothers."
"I'm no queer! Chris let go!"
"Say uncle."
"Never." I'M ON YOUR SIDE—OH—WHEN TIMES
GET ROUGH AND FRIENDS JUST CAN'T BE FOUND . . .
"Say Christopher, you'll always be my brother even if
you are a queer."
"Let me go!"
"Say it."
Michael's seventeen-year-old fist found its way to his
brother's nose. He hit him and he hit him hard. Gloria and I
were in the backseat. We said nothing and we didn't move.
Michael hit Chris in the face again. And again. He climbed on
top of Chris in the front seat and grabbed ahold of his older
brother's shirt. He shook Christopher as if he were in a rage
because he was in a rage. I reached out to stop him. "No,"
Gloria said. "They have to do this." LIKE A BRIDGE OVER
TROUBLED WATER I WILL LAY ME DOWN. LIKE A
BRIDGE OVER TROUBLED WATER I WILL LAY ME
DOWN . . .
"You left me you son-of-a-bitch!" Michael yelled. And he
slapped Christopher viciously across his face. "Just like that. I
worshipped you, you fucker! I heard about you being shot. And
I wanted to go to you. And Daddy says no. It's always no. No!
No! No! I could never stand up to him. Not without you. And I
needed you. I needed you, Christopher. Do you know how
many fucking times I needed you? I hate you! I hate you! I hate
you! I hate your guts. Look at you! What did they do to you? I

don't understand. You just left me like that. The fucking hero!
Go fight your fucking war. I had to stay and fight *him*!" Michael
was crying. WHEN YOU'RE DOWN AND OUT. WHEN
YOU'RE ON THE STREET. WHEN EVENING FALLS SO
HARD I WILL COMFORT YOU . . .

"I just love Christmas, don't you?" Gloria said to me.
I'LL TAKE YOUR PART. OH, WHEN DARKNESS
COMES. AND PAIN IS ALL AROUND LIKE A BRIDGE
OVER TROUBLED WATER I WILL LAY ME DOWN. SAIL
ON SILVER BIRD . . .

"All I wanted was for you to come back in one piece,"
Michael said to his brother. "I don't care if you're gay or purple or a hero or a coward or anything. I just want to be your
brother. That's all I've ever wanted, Chris. Why haven't you
ever been able to hear that?" SAIL ON HIGH. YOUR TIME
HAS COME TO SHINE. ALL YOUR DREAMS ALONG
THEIR WAY . . .

"Because he won't listen," Gloria said. She leaned for-
ward and gave Chris a couple of hits on the arm of her own.
"Never fuck with a family of pot-heads," she said to me.
"We'll beat the crap out of you."

"I want to see your scars," Michael said.

"Why," Chris asked. Chris was always very shy about his
scars. They weren't pretty. The bullet that hit him had gone
into his back, shattered his spinal cord, and emerged out of his
belly. It had missed several vital organs by a fraction of an
inch. But it left a hole in him the size of an orange. And then
there were the surgical scars. From the middle of his waist
down Chris looked like a crossword puzzle. If he hadn't been
hit while he was getting onto a chopper he would certainly have
died. Chris got hit. And the chopper took off. There was a
medic onboard. They took him directly to the ship's hospital
when his chopper landed on the aircraft carrier it was evacuat-
ing people to. Chris was lucky. Damn lucky. SEE HOW THEY

SHINE. OH, WHEN YOU NEED A FRIEND . . .

"Because I'm your brother and I want to see, that's why."

Michael lifted Chris' shirt out of his older brother's pants. Gloria leaned forward. "Oh, my God," she said. I WILL EASE YOUR MIND . . .

"I'm sorry, Chris." Michael's hand touched the scar on his brother's abdomen. "I didn't mean it when I said I hated you. I don't hate you."

"I know, Mikey."

"I wish I could have been there for you. I keep telling myself not to listen to him. He keeps telling me not to be like my fuckup brother. But I don't think you're a fuckup."

"We're *all* fuckups, Michael," Gloria asked. "Or don't you listen to the way he talks about *all* of us?"

"Hey," Chris said, sitting up. "Nobody's fucking up, here. I'm sorry I stayed away so long, okay? I needed to be away from—this town—for a while. I knew I couldn't get better here."

"You can say that again," Gloria said.

"But nobody's fucking up as long as we have each other, okay!" No one said anything. "Okay, Gloria?"

"Okay."

"Okay, Michael?"

"Okay." WHEN TEARS ARE IN YOUR EYES I WILL DRIVE THEM ALL—OUT. I'M ON YOUR SIDE . . . We were stoned, drained, and out of tune. We sang along anyway. Michael and Chris got out of the car, went outside, and shot baskets. Just shooting baskets. Over and over again. Gloria and I stayed in the car and talked about kids, big tits, orgasms, equal rights for women, and happiness.

"I don't look much like Raquel, do I?" she sighed.

"Not really. Maybe if I squint."

"I used to be quite a cheerleader, you know."

"I'm sure you were."

"They told us that if we were all good little cheerleaders that in the end everything would turn out okay. But cheerleading wasn't enough. Not really. So we all wanted to be Raquel Welch. If our tits were big enough then everything would be okay. Jesus, no matter what we did it was never enough. Your biggest ambition in life was to become so popular that every guy in school wanted to take you out. And then every guy took you out and—wonder of wonders—it wasn't enough. I wanted more."

"You have nice children, Gloria."

"I love them. Really, I do."

"I know."

"It's not enough."

"What do you want, Gloria? It's not easy."

"I want more. I want more for Gloria. I want to be more than a nice little mother and the reefer queen. Is that too much to ask from Christmas?"

"Yes."

"Why?"

"Jayne Mansfield sat on my lap once."

"Was she happy? I need to know."

"I didn't know her well. The spotlight made her hair look funny. Not real."

"Did she seem happy? I mean, she sat on your lap not mine. I want to know if she seemed happy."

"Her eyes seemed sad."

"Was she plastic and ugly and too made up and cheap? I knew it."

"Not at all. She seemed vulnerable and she was very very beautiful. Kind of like an angel, you know. In pink."

"Then why was she sad?"

"I didn't ask her. She just looked like she was going through the motions. Like, well, this was what she was expected to do. This was what people wanted her to be like. This sex goddess. Or whatever it was that she was. She was just a woman playing Jayne Mansfield. And she was sad. I think she wanted Jayne Mansfield to be more."

"I don't believe it," Gloria said.

"You don't believe what? That she wanted more? That it wasn't enough?"

"No. I'm glad she was sad. It makes me feel better. Maybe we had something in common. Maybe both of us have always just been playing parts. Maybe we both wanted more. Every Christmas I keep expecting Santa Claus to come to town. Particularly if I've been good that year. And this year I've been so goddamn good it surprises even me. I'm not exactly young anymore and I keep expecting Santa Claus to bring me whatever it was that Jayne Mansfield supposedly had. You know, happiness. And every year that he doesn't I get a little more bitter. A little more sick of myself. He sees you when you're sleeping. He sees you when you're awake. He knows when you've been bad or good so be good for goodness sake.

"I don't feel like being good anymore. It's all a crock. I've done what they've wanted me to do. I married the man they wanted me to marry. I had my children. I did my duty. I still don't look like Jayne Mansfield. As a matter of fact, my chances of looking like that seem to be diminishing with every passing Christmas. I have been good for goodness sake to the point of nausea. Honey, that SOB done put coal in my stocking." Gloria laughed.

"Yes, Virginia," I said. "There is a Santa Claus."

"Yeah, sure. Maybe he goes to Jayne Mansfield's house but he don't come to mine. I've about had it, you know. Gloria is about ready to go out there and put some goodies into her own stocking. Not somebody else's stocking. *My* stocking! I'm tired of waiting around for that fat little sucker to show his face. I done tried it everyone else's way. It's about time that Gloria started living for Gloria." She paused. "Tits aren't everything, you know."

"I know." We both laughed.

It was Christmas. SAIL ON SILVER BIRD. SAIL ON HIGH. YOUR TIME HAS COME TO SHINE. ALL YOUR DREAMS ALONG THEIR WAY. SEE HOW THEY SHINE . . .

There is a house in New Orleans they call the rising sun. Legend has it that it's ruined many a nasty boy. And I sure as fuck felt like one. Gloria eventually took her kids, her 1967 Chevy Impala, the rest of her marijuana, and a whole lot of turkey wrapped in aluminum foil, home. Wherever home was. Wherever home was Chris and I were invited over anytime. Just please come on over. Don't call. Just come. We kissed her and stood there in the snow watching her car go down the street. She was a terrible driver. Her car with its half-bald tires slid on the ice.

Evening seemed to seduce the town. Green, blue, and red electrical Christmas decorations were beginning to blink on in the small front yards of the old factory homes. Lights were strung around picture windows. The homes there were somehow like the people who lived in them. Solid. Borderline beaten. Ancient but not quite rundown. Yet. Proud almost sad. A Santa Claus face lit up—Santa looked lonely. He smiled silently in the window of the home next door.

Chris and I were alone in the living room watching television when the phone rang. Chris was asleep. It was somebody else's house and I didn't answer the phone because I don't answer other people's phones. Chris' mom came in from the kitchen and told me that there was a phone call for Chris or me—either one—which surprised me briefly. But then I remembered that we'd told the guys that we'd be going to Michigan. We had made this pact to contact each other at

Christmas. It seemed appropriate. Billy said he might go back
and see his mom in California. Jimmy Bo was living in New
Mexico with his Vietnamese wife. Jimmy was doing very well
working as a contractor, and he seemed very pleased with the
prospect of building his own house. He kept telling us to come
to New Mexico on the phone. We said, sure, but we could not
really see ourselves in New Mexico. Jim and his wife were
planning on spending Christmas with Jim's family in the
Bronx. It was Jimmy.

"Hey, white trash! Merry Christmas, you mother. How
goes it in Michigan?"

"Hey yourself," I said. "Are you in the Bronx?"

"Yeah, we're here. Quong Lee says hello. Say hello,
Quong Lee . . . " Quong Lee said hello.

"How's Quong Lee like American numbah one holiday?"

Jimmy laughed. "Quong Lee likey Santa Claus. Santa
Claus numbah one GI!"

We both laughed. "Chris is sound asleep."

"Sleeping it off, eh?"

"War is hell."

"Hey, Boss, listen . . . "

"What?"

"I talked to Billy."

"Did he make it to California?"

"No, Boss, he didn't make it to California. I don't know
how to put this?"

"Put what? Spit it out, Killer."

"He's not doing too well."

"This isn't news. Hell sucks, remember? Why didn't he
make it to California?"

"I don't know, Boss. He's always full of excuses. If you
ask me he's full of shit, man. He sounds real bad. Real bad,
Boss. Maybe you can call him. Talk some sense into him. I
don't know."

"This is turning out to be one helluva Christmas, Jim."

"War is hell, Boss."

"What's wrong with him, anyway?"

"It's Christmas. Some folks they just get funny, you know, at Christmas. Hey, man, I told him he wasn't alone. I told him he could come here if he wanted to. I told him he could go up to Michigan with you guys if he wanted to. I don't know what his fucking problem is. Don't ask me, Boss. I'm not a goddamn psychiatrist. Maybe that's what he needs. A shrink. I don't know. He just talks nothing, you know, nothing he says makes any sense anymore. Nothing. I think Geronimo has reached the end of his rope, Boss. I'm sorry."

"If one more person says they're sorry today I'm going to fucking scream, Jimmy."

"That bad, eh?"

"Maybe I should call him? I'll call the idiot."

"It's a pay phone somewhere, Boss."

"Give me the number. And Jimmy..."

"Yeah, Boss?"

"Merry Christmas you numbah one son-of-a-bitch."

Jimmy laughed the way he always laughed; low, deep, and growling with strength.

LOVE ME TENDER, LOVE ME LONG, TAKE ME TO YOUR HEART. FOR IT'S CERTAIN THAT I BELONG AND WE'LL NEVER PART. LOVE ME TENDER, LOVE ME TRUE, ALL MY DREAMS FULFILLED. FOR MY DARLING I LOVE YOU AND I ALWAYS WILL. LOVE ME TENDER, LOVE ME DEAR, TELL ME YOU ARE MINE. I'LL BE YOURS THROUGH ALL THE YEARS TILL THE END OF TIME. It'd been Billy's song. One of many. But this one was special. When he sang it he meant it. Billy was one of those silly souls who wanted whatever love he could find in his life to last all of his life. If it didn't last, if it wasn't a commitment, then at least to Billy it wasn't love. It was something else. Billy didn't know what it was but it wasn't love. So when this straight silly boy with his songs and his simplicity told me he loved me he meant it.

"Boss! It's you, Boss. How you doing, you mother?"

"Merry Christmas, Geronimo."

"Merry Christmas, Boss. How's Ranger? You guys in Michigan?"

"We're here. Why the fuck aren't you in California, Billy?"

"I don't know, Boss. I didn't make it. How's Christmas, Boss? I'm so glad you guys are together. Fucking fags."

"Christmas is fine, man. How's your Christmas doing? I love you, man."

"It's cold. Assholes turned my heat off."

"You know, Billy, I'm getting really tired of waiting around for you to get your act together. What the fuck is it going to take anyway? You tell me."

"Do you have nightmares, Boss? Do you sleep?"

"Listen. Listen to me! I really am getting better. And you wanna know something? I've got Chris. I'm not doing it alone. Billy, you've gotta get some fucking help. It gets better. I know. But you've gotta give it a chance. You can't stay isolated, man. You gotta find something or somebody. You gotta do some of the reaching, man, because if you stay alone it'll feed on you. It'll start gnawing at your guts. It'll eat you from the inside. You can't do it all by yourself."

"I've been trying. I'm just so tired. I can't sleep."

"I know. Talk to me. It's Boss."

"They had a turkey, you know, down at the Salvation Army. I was going to go. I'm real tired, Boss. I called my mom."

"How's your mom?"

There was a long silence. "I'm cold. It's not working anymore, Boss. I've tried. Really I have. I can't even sing anymore, man. I've got the shakes but I've got to do it this time. I tried but I got scared, you know, but I got to do it this time. It's just so cold. I'm—I'm so glad it's you."

I felt empty and angry and sad and furious. And bitter. "Damn you. Chris tried once. I wouldn't let him. I can't handle this. I refuse to deal with this. Do you know what it feels like to keep having to handle this in my life? It's shit. Don't do this to me. Please. I'm begging you, Billy. Jesus, I can't believe it's Christmas. Hey, man! It's Christmas!"

"Remember that time you let me sleep with my head on you, Boss? Remember in the fucking rain?"

"I try not to."

"You promised."

"That was a long time ago, man."

"You promised to hold me."

"I can't."

"Hold me."

"I can't."

"I don't want to die alone."

"I can't. I love you. I can't go through this. I just want it to END."

"Yeah, well, that's what I want, too."

"Don't, man. Just don't. Not like this."

"I love you, you faggot."

"Don't. Hey, man, we'll come down there. We'll come to Cleveland. We'll leave tonight."

"Tell Ranger that I love him, too. Okay?"

"Okay. Don't."

"And Jimmy. Tell Jimmy, too. Numbah one niggah GI. I love him, too. Okay?"

"Sure, man. Don't okay? Oh, God, please no. No! I—I loved you you you stupid stupid bastard."

I try not to remember the rest of it. I don't know how long I just sat there with the phone frozen in front of my face. Chris slept. The TV blared. There is a house in New Orleans they call the rising sun. LOVE ME TENDER, LOVE ME SWEET, NEVER LET ME GO. Candy, soda, dirty pictures, boom boom dope. Elvis. It was Christmas. "Come on! Wake up! I want to take you guys over to Johnson's. I want to show off the conquering hero, here." It was Chris' dad. And Johnson's was a factory bar. Chris' dad's factory bar. Most bars were closed. It was Christmas. But I was informed that Johnson's would be jumping because it was Johnson's and Johnson's never closed. Particularly not at Christmas. "I want Chris to see my friends!"

Johnson's was located in an old brick building which had one small neon sign: Johnson's. I was too numb and too dumb to do anything else. So I drove Boom Boom to Johnson's. I did not want to go there but I went to Johnson's. "Are you okay," Chris asked.

"Sure, I'm fine. Buy me a drink, okay." I didn't know what to tell him about Billy.

Chris' dad wanted to buy drinks for everyone. And then Chris' dad's friends wanted to buy more drinks for everyone. This is Bob and Vern and Joe and Harry and Ed and Phil. Bob and Vern and Joe and Harry and Ed and Phil all drank Christmas boilermakers. I was in a prime mood for Christmas boilermakers myself. A boilermaker is a shot of whiskey that sits in the bottom of a glass of beer. A Christmas boilermaker contains a shot of schnapps. "Now Europe, that was a war," Bob said. "I was in Italy. That was a *real* war."

"Here's to Italy," I said. And we drank to Italy.

"Here's to winning once in a while," Bob said. And we drank to winning once in a while

"Yeah," Bob said, "you didn't see any of us coming back and crying or sniveling about how nobody loved us, that's for damn sure! We kicked the crap out of the Germans, didn't we boys? We knew how to win. They don't know how to win anymore, that's all." I saw Chris' eyes take a long slow look at

Bob. Whoever the fuck Bob was. It was his, oh, my God, am I really in here I might kill somebody look. Bob slapped Chris on the back like he was an old friend of the family which he was. "You did good, Boy. You got hit. But at least you can be proud of what you did over there. Fucking gooks."

"I am not proud of what I did over there." Chris said it very softly. It was almost a whisper. Bob did not seem to hear him. Bob still had his hand on Chris' back.

"Hey, you guys remember fucking Italian whores?" Bob's old alcoholic water-red eyes lit up. The other men smiled. "Now, they were *whores*. Don't think I could ever put it into a gook pussy!" Bob laughed. The other men laughed. "But old Chris, here, probably can't get it up for nothing anyway." More laughter. It was a regular house of humor.

"Get your filthy hands off of me," Chris said. It wasn't what he said so much as it was the controlled soft way that he said it. His eyes looked right into Bob's. They weren't the Christopher eyes that I knew. They were his Vietnam eyes. They were cold and they hated. "I said get your hands off of me. I don't want slime touching me. You don't know anything about it. Hey, you ignorant shit-hot asshole, you ever see a twelve-year-old girl's skin burn right off of her, dissolve down to her bones in fucking front of you because of the napalm? You ever see a body just burst into flames, man? You ever see that, Bob? You aren't good enough to spit on me." It was an open invitation.

"Is that right, smart asshole?" Bob said. Bob took a mouthful of beer and spit it directly into Chris' face. "You're not shit to me."

"I wish you hadn't done that," I said.

"This is my fight, Boss," Chris said. Beer and whiskey dripped down his face.

"Like hell it is." By this time the whole bar had quieted. Irish eyes were upon us. None of them were smiling.

"Let's just go," Chris' dad said. "You never did know when to keep you goddamn mouth shut, did you, Chris?"

"Shut the fuck up," I said. I had had a bellyful of it. I had had a bellyful of Christmas. I had had a bellyful of Bob and the rest of them. The world was nothing more than a bunch of whores to these men and I was sick to death of them. There is a house in New Orleans they call the rising sun. LOVE ME TENDER, LOVE ME TRUE, ALL MY DREAMS FULFILLED. Candy, soda, dirty pictures, boom boom dope. Elvis. Elvis. They didn't know anything about it. They wanted us to fight their goddamn war and then they spit on us. On *us*! It's been the ruin of many a poor boy. And I'm sure as fuck not one. I went after Bob but Vern and Harry were in my way. I wanted Bob. I wanted his guts. Vern and Harry got their heads knocked together. Wham! They sounded like two empty coconuts. I grabbed Bob, pushed him up against the wall, and beat the bloody shit out of him. The man is throwing up on me and I'm still beating him. I was banging his head against the wall like it was mush when Chris pulled me off the man.

"Come on, we gotta get out of here. We never should have come here. Boss—*Stop!*" I got Chris into Boom Boom and we'd left the parking lot by the time two police cruisers pulled up in front of Johnson's. It wouldn't have been the first bar fight in there. It certainly wouldn't be the last. So Mama tell your children not to do what I have done and done and done. And done again. "We should never have come," Chris kept saying. His father had driven himself to the bar and had disappeared. "Let's just go back to New York, man. I should never have come here. Let's go over to my sister's. Gloria will put us up for the night. I don't even want to see my old man. I don't even want to look at him."

Gloria lived in a house not too unlike the house Chris' parents lived in. Chris got on the phone and called his brother. Yes, their dad had shown up. Drunk as a Christmas skunk.

Yes, Mama had cried. Yes, Daddy was mad as a plucked rooster in a cockfight. Yes, his dad had said that Chris had had no right to humiliate him. No right at all. Yes, Michael would bring our stuff over to Gloria's. We'd spend the night at Gloria's and head back to New York in the morning. Or the afternoon. "It is," Gloria pointed out, "almost morning now."

Gloria was rolling one of her famous joints when the phone rang. It was Chris' father. Chris answered the phone. "Look," Chris said, "I'm sorry. I'm sorry I came here. But nobody is going to spit on us. Not you. Not Bob. Not anybody." Chris was trying real hard to hold himself in check. He was choking up. He took in a deep breath. "We did not mean to humiliate you. Humiliating you is the last thing I wanted to do. But that's not the issue, Daddy. Don't you hang up on me, you bastard! You're the one who called me! I didn't call you. I listened to you. Now, you're going to listen to me.

"I love you, Daddy. I have always loved you. But I can't be like you because I'm not like you. I tried. I tried when I lived here. I tried in Vietnam, Daddy. I'm me. I'm not you. I tried doing things the way you would have done things. It doesn't *fit*, man. Are you listening, Daddy? I'm me. I'm just a man, Daddy. Just like you are. We're just men. We're not God, Daddy. It took me years, do you understand, fucking years, to understand this. That I don't have to be like you. That I'm good. Me. Just me. That I did what I had to do, Dad. I didn't want to be there. You wanted me to be there. Nobody in this family has ever been able to say no to you. Well, now I'm saying it. No—I'm not going to be some kind of an empty shell walking around in somebody else's image. Your shadow. It's your shadow that's been killing me. For one thing I can't walk. I'm broken, Daddy. Hey, people break. They really do. Men break, Daddy."

Chris paused and listened. "I'm sorry you feel that way. Really, I am. But I'm not responsible for you feeling that you failed with me. I don't care what you feel. If you won't let me just be me then I have to do it on my own. And, Daddy, that takes more strength than you will ever know about. Ever. Goodbye, Dad. I love you."

"I think," Gloria said, "that it's going to be one of *those* holidays. I just love Christmas, don't you?" I didn't want to tell Chris about Billy. When it rains it pours and it was pouring like Vietnam poured hot incoming at us constantly. But I could remember Chris just sitting there in the middle of incoming writing his letters. Letters that never got answered. Until that night. "We have to stop in Cleveland," I said.

"Cleveland?" Chris said. He just looked at me as if I had all the answers. I didn't have any of the answers. All I had was pain and fucking rage. And numbness. "Why Cleveland?"

"Because I said we have to go to Cleveland, that's all. And that's final. So just get off my back about it."

"Why Cleveland, Boss?"

I curled up with a small pillow on Gloria's couch. "I don't want to talk to anybody."

"It's Billy, isn't it. What's with Billy?" I ignored him. The three of us smoked a joint and Michael arrived with our bags.

Gloria looked very motherly in her pink robe and her curlers. Kind of like Jayne Mansfield if I squinted. "Christmas is my favorite holiday." Gloria said. "Why if we keep up all the crises—one crisis after the other—before you know it it'll be the new year. And what would the new year be without a new crisis? Or two? Michael, sit down. Have a toke. Have a crisis. The reefer queen strikes again."

Michael sat down. "Dad is PISSED! Whew! I've never seen the old man that creamed before. Let me shake the hand of the man who did it." Michael shook my hand. He was seventeen-years-old. And virginal. And gorgeous. And vulnerable. And strong. I saw Chris in him. I saw Billy in him. Candy, soda, dirty pictures, boom boom dope. I asked Gloria if she had any old records. COME ON, MAMA, LET'S ROCK!

"Does a bear shit in the woods?"

"Elvis?"

"I'll have to dig, honey."

Chris put his head in his hands. He started crying. He shook with his crying. I was all cried out for one Christmas. I was running on empty. Michael didn't understand why his brother was crying. Michael was a virgin and he'd never been to Memphis. "Someone we were very close to died today," I tried to explain.

"I'm sorry," Michael said.

"Yeah, so are we, kid. So are we." YOU CAN KNOCK ME DOWN, STEP ON MY FACE, SLANDER MY NAME ALL OVER THE PLACE. BUT, HONEY, LAY OFFA MY BLUE SUEDE SHOES.

It was almost morning. Chris fell asleep on the floor with his head on his brother's lap. Michael was also on the floor sort of half-propped up half-asleep on a large beanbag thing. War was hell. And hell sucks a big one. I fell asleep on the couch with my head on the small pillow which was on Gloria's lap. She ran her fingers through my hair. She kept telling me that it was going to be okay. "I have enough dope in this house to get us all through the next fifty years." BURN MY HOUSE, STEAL MY CAR, DRINK MY LIQUOR FROM AN OLD FRUIT JAR, BUT GET OFF, GET OFFA MY BLUE SUEDE SHOES

It was snowing outside. While people slept I stood in the living room and looked out of Gloria's picture window into the Michigan morning darkness—remembering—when I was small, and it snowed California Sierra snow we used to run outside and eat the snowflakes. There was no taste. But the crazy feel of a snowflake landing on your boyvirgin's tongue was one of the most intriguing sensations in the world. We'd run around eating nighttime snowflakes, knowing that in daylight we'd make the world's best snowman with our daddy's pipe, our daddy's hat, our daddy's gloves, our daddy's coat. When we woke up it was Michigan and it wasn't Christmas anymore.

As we left the brooding factory town huge white plumes of steam emanated from the GM factory that sat next to the Grand River. Like so much discharge. Like drainage. Like an infection. Like clouds of thick lust. The steam drifted over the city languidly and wrapped itself around the buildings with its lush lips and laughed. Chris directed me over the river, we crossed a bridge, it was not the way we had come in. FOR MY DARLING I LOVE YOU AND I ALWAYS WILL . . .

"Pull in here," he said. The sign on the old wooden building was covered with a fine black carbon-like soot: VFW Hall, Lansing. I stopped the van. "Help me get out, Mikey," Chris asked. I wasn't sure where he was going or what he was going to do. I sat in Boom Boom and drank coffee from a Styrofoam cup. The coffee tasted as if it'd been made in a morgue somewhere. Michael helped Christopher out of the van.

"Hey, man," I said. "Let's just get the fuck out of here. Do you mind, Chris?"

"I'll be right back, babe."

At first I thought he was on his way into the building. Christopher wheeled himself over to the flag pole in front of the building. He was not going in. I burned my mouth on the coffee. "Damn." Chris lowered the somewhat raggedy-ass American flag which was flying in front of the Lansing, Michigan VFW hall to half mast and secured the flag's rope.

As we pulled away Chris said to himself as much as to Michael or me, "I think we have paid enough. Enough." And we left Lansing. We left it with its belch and its flag and its pain. LOVE ME TENDER, LOVE ME DEAR, TELL ME

YOU ARE MINE. I'LL BE YOURS THROUGH ALL THE
YEARS UNTIL THE END OF TIME.

Forever.

It is impossible to cry in Cleveland. No human being ever
cried there. People breathe in Cleveland. They eat in Cleveland. They fuck, shit, and give birth in Cleveland. They bury
their dead. But they do not cry in Cleveland. Did we know the
victim? Yes. Could we identify him? Yes. Did he have any
family? Yes. Could we reach them? Yes. Yes. Yes. It was a
small dirty transient hotel with a black and white TV in the
lobby. The old elevator didn't work. The TV in the lobby was
surrounded by silent sunken men, dressed mostly in over-
coats, involved in the process of giving up. Did we want to take
his things? Somebody had to take his things. Could we pay his
back rent? No. Somebody had to pay his back rent. No.
They'd cut his heat but he had refused to move. Move where?
And the sheriff didn't do evictions on Christmas. They let us
into his room. "He didn't have much, did he?" Michael observed.

"We'll give it to his mom when she arrives," Chris said.
On the small dresser there was a picture of Billy, Jim, myself,
Chris, and Titi sitting around a Chinook. We had our arms
around each other and we were smiling. We were shirtless
which was stupid. I was always yelling at them to wear their
flack jackets. Guys were always getting greased because they
weren't wearing their flack jackets. In the picture we are shirtless—including me. Everyone had an ammunition belt
wrapped around his chest. "I wonder who took this?"

"I don't remember," I said.

"There's a note," Michael said. "Do you want to read it?"
Michael stood there with the piece of paper in his hand.

"What can it say that hasn't been said?" I asked.

"Why would anyone want to off himself," Michael asked.
"I guess he was insane. It's cold in here."

"The word is kill, Michael," Chris said. "Say kill."

"Why?"

"Just say it."

"Why would anyone want to kill himself."

"I went into a spider hole once to get him," Chris said. "Remember that time, Boss?"

"No. Not really. I try not to. Everyone keeps trying to get me to remember. But I try not to. I really do. And the more I try not to remember the more I remember."

"He was froze down there."

"Froze?" Michael asked.

"With fear, Mikey," Chris explained. "With fear. We were all afraid."

"Not you, Chris," Michael said.

"Not me? Hell, boy! I was the one who was the most afraid. I was just too fucking stupid to show it." Michael sat down on the unmade bed and studied the note that neither Chris nor I wanted to read. "I went down into the hole. I grabbed his damn feet. And I pulled the little son-of-a-bitch outta there backwards."

"Yeah," I said. "I think I do remember that. He was in the middle of the tunnel and he just gave up."

"There wasn't anybody here to go into the hole and grab him, was there, Boss?" Chris said very quietly.

"You couldn't go into every hole, Chris," I said. "Maybe a few. But if he decided to give up it was his decision. We couldn't have done anything. If it hadn't been in this place it would've been in another place; a place just like this one. Some other hole. We told him a thousand times, man, that we loved him. It wasn't enough. I don't know what more you can do. You hold your hand out to someone. Sometimes they just have to take it for it to mean anything. Sometimes they don't. Sometimes they can't. But whether they won't or they can't you stand there with your fucking hand out because it's all you can do. You can't grab them by the heels every time and drag them out of the hole backwards because it just doesn't work that way."

"It just makes me so shit-hot mad," Chris said. "I had somebody there for me when I needed them—you, Boss—why didn't Billy have that?"

"Sometimes all you can do is stand at the top of the tunnel, hope to waiting breathless Christ that they'll come out in one piece, and when they do you offer them a joint, and you hug them. You laugh about it. About the fact that you're both alive. And then you find the next hole. You don't know who's going down into it. You wait for volunteers. Somebody will always volunteer for trouble. Some of us froze down there. Some of us got killed down there. I don't know, Chris, Michael. Don't ask me to explain what went on here. I used to think I had all the answers. Now, I don't have any answers. All I have is me. If it's not enough I can't help that or be responsible for it."

"All I know," Chris said, "is that everyone I ever cared for ends up like this."

I looked out of the window, the window Billy must have looked out of at least a thousand times. I wondered what he saw in this place. It was a nothing place. It was nowhere. There was nothing to see. It was empty of life but full of the living. "He died in Vietnam. He didn't die out there by that pay phone with the mess on the fucking wall. That wasn't the Billy I knew. The Billy I knew was this silly eighteen-year-old kid from California with blond hair, a ton of girlfriends, a guitar, a love for Elvis Presley, a surfboard stored somewhere in his garage, and a bunch of men—including me—who cared for him. I loved him. I used to let him sleep on my chest in the rain. But now he's gone and I'll clean up the mess because somehow it's partly my mess." I paused.

"I don't know how. But it is. Then I'll go home and when

I think about him," I said, "I'll think about the Billy I knew. Geronimo who used to jump from planes because it thrilled the hell out of him. Geronimo who used to sing songs about a New Orleans whorehouse. Geronimo who used to love me tender love me sweet. Geronimo who used to slick back his hair and pretend he was the greatest singer on the face of the earth because to him he really was. We can't bring him back any more than we could have made him want to live. I'm all cried out. I want to go home and let Michael do all the cooking because I'm sick of mine."

"I can't cook."

"If you're coming with us you'll learn," Christopher said. And he laughed. We sat there in Billy's freezing cold room with our coats on, sitting on his bed, Billy's old guitar on my lap, his duffle bag on the floor, his dirty laundry everywhere. His smell, his memory, and we laughed. His mother arrived from California and claimed him from the City of Cleveland. She let me keep the picture and the guitar although I cannot play the guitar. The four of us sat in an airport coffeeshop waiting for her return flight to be announced, chainsmoking, talking, trying to make what little sense there was in it out of it. She was tanned and somewhat stunned. I DON'T WANT TO BE YOUR TIGER CAUSE TIGERS PLAY TOO ROUGH.

"He talked a lot about you," she said to me. "I tried to get him to come out, you know, home. But he wouldn't. I got the feeling that he didn't want me to see him the way he was. He always sounded okay on the phone." She paused. She looked at me squarely in the eye. "Why?"

"I don't know."

"Was it my fault? I need to know."

"No."

"He used to love to sing."

"I know."

"He used to just break out into the craziest songs."

"Yeah, that was one of the best things about him. He loved Elvis."

"God, what am I going to do with all those records? Do you want them?"

"No."

"If you ever come to California will you come see me? I'd really like that. I couldn't get him to come home. He was back from the war. But I couldn't get him to come home. I don't know why he was here or what he was doing here. If you ever come to California would you come visit me? I'd really like someone, one of you, to come see where he lived. The ocean is very beautiful. He didn't have to go to Vietnam. He wanted to."

"Sure, I'll call you," I said. "Every time I see a kid on a surfboard I'll think about him." They called her flight. She put her cigarette out, kissed Chris and I, and told us to call her if we were ever in California. She headed towards her gate, but abruptly turned around, and walked back to us.

"How old are you?" she asked Michael.

"Seventeen."

She looked at Chris and I. "If he gives you any problems don't hesitate to kick his ass. That's where I went wrong, you know. I never did kick that boy's ass. They think they know everything. They're seventeen and they think they know it all. Well, they don't! Not by a long shot, they don't." She looked at Michael. "You ever been on a surfboard?"

Chris laughed. "He's never seen the ocean. He's never even been out of Michigan."

She bit her lip and looked at Michael right in the eye with that look she had. "I've got an extra surfboard. You want it it's yours. Well, do you want it?"

Michael didn't know what to say. He looked at Chris. "I don't know. Do they surf in New York?"

"Hey, man," Chris said, "we surf in New York all the

time. Every morning I get up I ask the Boss, here, is the surf up? If the surf's up I get outta this chair, here, and I run down to the fucking beach. Hell, yes, we surf in New York. Hang ten, man."

She smiled. "You're very lucky. Do you know that, young man?"

"How's that?" Michael did not think of himself as lucky.

She looked at Chris. "Can you kick his ass?"

"I can try."

"And if he can't I can," I said.

"Good," she said. And she disappeared into the crowded airport.

"What was that all about?" Michael asked.

"Kicking ass, I think," Chris said.

The three of us drove home—to New York. Michael had never seen anything quite like it. Jimmy Bo from the Bronx came over to see us. Jimmy Bo from the Bronx, the Killer, took the news of Billy very badly. Jimmy Bo from the Bronx made us promise to keep in touch with him. We promised. And he made us promise again so we promised again. Jimmy Bo from the fucking Bronx knotted up his big black hands, put his hamburger fists into his eyes, and bawled. Once there had been five of us. Now there were three. Hell sucks.

Michael moved into our apartment and into our lives. It was not very convenient living with a seventeen-year-old who was trying to put his life together. ONE FOR THE MONEY TWO FOR THE SHOW LOVE ME TENDER LOVE ME SWEET NEVER LET ME GO. But then we were all trying to do that. We insisted that he finish school. Etcetera. Chris checked his homework. Etcetera. He complained that we were stricter than his folks. Etcetera. Michael was not above stepping out of line. And we frequently found ourselves having to kick his ass. I never thought of myself as anyone's surrogate parent or older brother. But there it was. You stand there with your hand held out. It's all you can do. Sometimes they take it. Sometimes they won't. Or can't. Michael could and did. COME ON, MAMA, LET'S ROCK.

Six months after Michael moved in a delivery truck dropped off a surfboard.

Part Four

BURSTS OF FIRE

—dancing at the glitterball
shuffle shuffle
in and out of this place
my mental wards anywhere
anywhere my prison walls
over-and-over they call us chronic
to a cruel inner isolation
for boysoldier's small idiosyncracies
up the elevator again anywhere
with that strong boy-in-white
he's back he's back
listen to them whisper
up and down the spotless hall
sing the praises of the lord
sing the praises of the ward
the inmates here are all so tame
we've lost the right to prove we're sane
whose pony arms will tranquilize me
dirty little promises for being good
I promise scout's honor
shuffle shuffle
they want me to urinate
in this tinkle bottle
to analyze the soldier sea
and took my clothes
to rob my death
to drink my foamy pee
can't move my arms or legs
to escape this madness
these straps
drag me dancing
well past bursts of fire
fire behind daddy's eyes
past laughing manic soldierboy beds
where soldierboys sleep soundly
down to the glitterball
dancing shuffle shuffle
dreams
anywhere anywhere—

Billy used to sleep bare-assed inside our bunker at Khe Sanh. Most grunts slept with their boots on. But not Billy. It was one of those little inconsistencies which would dig themselves into the war and then walk around—stark raving naked—inside of your mindcrazies twenty years after it all happened. I can still see him like that. Breathing. It was the small things that burned impressions on your brain. I saw piles of dead human bodies. During the fighting in Hue I once walked through a whole street of corpses piled on top of one another like so much garbage but it made no vivid impression. Although if I try I can remember the flies.

The horror of it was too massive to breathe in.

Vietnam was a series of small vivid impressions. I distinctly remember a young Marine, a kid from Kansas City named Patrick, we were friends, and I remember his dog. Some of the grunts had dogs. It was a stupid thing to do. A-gainst regulation. There had to be a regulation against grunts having dogs. It didn't make sense. The dog was a stray. Patrick was attached to the animal—he loved it. As a joke a couple of the men from his company hung the dog from its neck with wire in the middle of Patrick's bunker. The kid wept as if this stray dog had been his closest friend. Piles and piles of human bodies meant nothing to me. It was a war. Yet the image of one dumb kid and his stray dog will remain engraved on my consciousness forever.

Sleeping bare-assed—it was a small mad thing that made no sense. Sleeping unprotected out in the open like that. A grunt never knew when he might have to run for it. You never knew what was going to happen next. Particularly in Khe Sanh. But there it was. There Billy was. Naked and tempting. Sometimes I had to wonder if I was the only faggot in Vietnam. Not that I was a faggot. I'd lay there in the dark and stare at him sleeping beside me—naked. And beautiful.

It would drive me crazy because I wanted him. Indeed, I had him, although it was never sexual. We were about as intimate as two men could get. I never had his cock in my mouth. Yet I held his soul and his dreams in my hands. I caught him jerking off lots of times. He'd just laugh. Jerking off helped. COME ON, MAMA, LET'S ROCK. The blues the blues.

Billy was so crazy that while he jerked off he'd sing. Elvis, of course. Who else. BABY LET ME BE AROUND YOU EVERY NIGHT. I'LL RUN YOUR FINGERS THROUGH MY HAIR AND CUDDLE ME REAL TIGHT. Rock'n roll and jerking off helped keep you crazy which kept you sane. One night I couldn't sleep. Even opium refused to numb me. There was a lull in the fighting. OH, LET ME BE (OH, LET HIM BE) YOUR TEDDY BEAR.

We hadn't been hit with mortars in about three days. And there he was buck naked next to me softly singing his Elvis fantasies. I DON'T WANT TO BE YOUR TIGER . . . The bunker stunk. It smelled of sweat, death, blood, malaria, male crud, oil, piss, and cigarettes. I sat up and lit a cigarette but it tasted like insecticide. My sweat was dexy sweat. Speed juice. Backwater poison. Crotch rot hung—thick—in the air. At the other end of the bunker two red tips from two cigarettes glowed in the dark. I put my flack jacket on and went outside. The air outside was no different and there was no relief. But I was alone. Some men did their crying when they were alone.

Sometimes you just had to be alone.

About twenty yards in front of our bunker in Khe Sanh was what we called the trench. It was simply a trench-hole dug into the ground where two grunts kept watch. They were supposed to be watching for anything that came in outside of the perimeter through the rolled concertina wire. The wire was razor sharp and had a tendency to turn anything that got mixed up in it into oriental mincemeat. It was close to three in the morning and the moon hung heavy above Khe Sanh as if it were bloated with a nectareous mellowed sense of suffocation. I walked silently over to the trench and the two grunts in it were hardly keeping watch. They were making love. In Vietnam we called it fucking. Yet that image in my mind has nothing to do with fucking.

They were making love. After the war I discussed that moment with a few veterans, and I found out that I wasn't the only one who had witnessed such a moment, that others had stumbled upon such scenes. They were rare but they happened. It was one of those small moments that got branded onto your mental bag of forget-me-nots. LOVE ME TENDER, LOVE ME TRUE. I will never lose the image of it. Here we were—*men*—and we were there to kill. We weren't there to pacify. We weren't there to win hearts or minds.

We weren't there to sing like Elvis.

We weren't there to stop communism. We were there to kill people. Period. That's all she wrote. And there I was looking down into a hole dug into the earth watching two eighteen-year-old boys making love. I hated Vietnam but I loved her ironies, her contrasts. They never knew I was there. Watching. Hypnotized. I knew both of them. You never would have guessed. I can't say that they were faggots. That word—faggot—it was like the word charley or dink or slope or zip or chink or wasted or greased or whore or anything that could push you out of the reach of who you were as a human being.

They were making love. In the middle of this horror there

was this amazing scene of tenderness. And need. And passion. And brotherhood. You needed your brother to love you, to hold you, even if you didn't know you needed it you still needed it. Even if the man holding you, loving you, wasn't your brother you still needed it. I looked up at the hills where I knew there were thousands of North Vietnamese and I wondered if any of them were making love. I wondered if any of them were connected. Somehow. I wanted to jump into the trench with those boys. I wanted to embrace them. I wanted to rip my clothes off and . . . make love . . . with those two confused hopeless stinking souls in that earth hole.

I wanted someone to kiss me the way they were kissing. I wanted to dance. I wanted to sing just like Elvis the pelvis. I wanted to cry and scream and laugh. They were making love. ONE FOR THE MONEY, TWO FOR THE SHOW, THREE TO GET READY, NOW GO-CAT-GO. HEY MAMA! GET OFFA MY BLUE SUEDE SHOES. DO ANYTHING YOU WANNA DO. BUT MAMA, GET OFFA MY BLUE SUEDE SHOES. I went back into the bunker with its stink and its collective sense of fear and frustration. Who would die tomorrow? I looked at my team and thought about how much I loved these men. Billy, naked and crazy with his Elvis imitations. Titi, small and fearless. Jimmy Bo, black and gentle. Christopher, big and handsome. More handsome than the stars. I crawled onto Jimmy Bo's rack, made him move over, and lay next to him. "Oh, Boss," he sighed. His arm wrapped itself around me, held me, and I slept the dreamless guiltless sleep of a titty-sucking baby. WELL, THEY SAID YOU WERE HIGH-CLASS. WELL, THAT WAS JUST FINE. WELL, THEY SAID YOU WERE HIGH-CLASS. AND THAT WAS JUST FINE. BUT YOU AIN'T NEVER CAUGHT A RABBIT AND YOU AIN'T NO FRIEND OF MINE . . .

We called him Lima Zulu and he was forever walking on my

blue suede shoes. Lima Zulu'd put my blue suede shoes into his snarling mouth and chew on them until they were all chewed up. That was what he was good at, it was what he did; he walked and chewed on anyone and anything that got in his way. Officially LZ was international phonetic alphabet for landing zone. Lima Zulu—nobody wanted to land anywhere within his range, his reach, or his zone. He was always scratching his balls. His balls seemed to itch. Perpetually. It was as if he had this extraordinary need to let the world know that he had balls the size of grapefruits. As if anyone cared. He'd stand there, playing with himself, and you weren't supposed to notice. Although you were, indeed, supposed to notice. In fact, if you didn't pay homage to the man's testicles, Lima Zulu could make your life a living hell. Not only did he have big balls but he had power. And he knew how to use it. Lima Zulu was not all that much older than we were. Maybe he was twenty-seven. No way he was thirty.

He did not like Elvis.

He was a captain. And he was a mean-suckled son-of-a-bitch. Lima Zulu had this bad habit of grinding his teeth. If you were in the jungle with him, and it was cool-midnight, silent, only the trees breathing, you could always hear Lima Zulu grinding his teeth. He did it in his sleep. Lima Zulu was the kind of man who'd wrap his fear in the soft center of his masculinity by pretending that he was the most badass mama in Vietnam.

He wasn't.

In fact, what he was was simply irritating. He grated on you. He wore you down like sandpaper only while he did it he didn't know he was doing it. You grew to hate his guts. He did everything a man can do to lose the respect of the other men around him. "I'll never ask you to do anything I wouldn't be prepared to do myself," he'd say. If he said it once he said it a thousand times. Over and over. It became a joke. What was insulting about him saying it wasn't what he said. It was that he thought we were stupid enough to believe it. It demeaned us. Yet under the John Wayne bullshit there was a man. Just another man. A man with beliefs and hates. A man afraid of the boogies in the dark because we are all afraid of the things we do not know or understand.

Like our own humanity.

Lima Zulu was the kind of man who not only stepped on your feet, but he'd go out of his way to put the full weight of his being smack dab into your face. He'd grind it in. He'd spit in your mouth if you gave him the slightest opportunity. We kept trying to look for the fact that he was just another man. One of us. But he was never one of us. We kept telling ourselves that Lima Zulu wasn't a bad man in a bad war, he was simply a man in a bad war. Until you got to know him. And then you hated him more than you had hated him before.

Not only did he like the killing and the gasoline smell of napalm burning flesh, but he demanded that you like it as well. You knew that he lived in Atlanta, Georgia, and that he had a wife and two little girls. He was as southern as a southerner can get. He'd even show you pictures of his little girls all dressed up for the camera and full of clean virginal sweetness. You wanted to believe that Lima Zulu wasn't all bad. Then you went out on a patrol with him. You came back with Lima Zulu sitting inside your throat like a twisting fist. You wanted to like him but you hated him. The man was evil.

"I'm going to kill that sombitch someday," Killer would say.

You hated to go out into the field with Lima Zulu. He was a John Wayne wet-dream come to life. A raving nightmare. A maniac. He was so fuckingass afraid. He'd always insist that everything that walked, talked, breathed, or balked had to go. Period. It didn't matter. I saw that man kill water buffalo, villagers' ducks, puppies, chickens, and human beings. I saw him shoot four-year-olds in the head and laugh because he really did think it was funny. It didn't matter to Lima Zulu. Search and destroy to him meant destroy and destroy. When Lima Zulu finished with a hamlet or a ville you might never know that people had once lived and breathed on that spot for the past two thousand years. He wiped it off the face of the earth. He left the planet wasted, burned, and cratered. Lima Zulu made the world look like it was the face of Mars.

We used to pray that he'd stay back at our base camp. "That sombitch must be asshole deep in paper work today," Jimmy Bo would say. "I ain't seen nothing die in five minutes." And we'd laugh. Five minutes was usually an exaggeration.

Lima Zulu and Jimmy Bo were always having confrontations. We were in a small ville between Khe Sanh and Langvei with Lima Zulu when the Captain gave Jimmy Bo a direct order. "Hey, Boy," Lima Zulu said. (I swear he gritted his teeth while he said it.) "Come over here." Lima Zulu was standing over the body of a male adolescent who had an AK-47 in his arms. The boy was dead as well he should have been. Jimmy Bo did as he was told. The Captain had five words for Jimmy: negra, nigger, boy, coon, or spade. Words that tried to rob Jimmy of his humanity which wasn't possible because Jim's humanity was entrenched. It wasn't going anywhere. It wasn't something Lima Zulu could relate to because Jim's humanity was something he was born with—it could not be penetrated. It could not be taken away from him. Not even by the Captain. Lima Zulu was the last man in the universe who was going to get a piece of it.

The fact that it wasn't possible to rob Jim of who he was is what made Lima Zulu grit his teeth: negra, nigger, boy, coon, or spade. Lima Zulu never hesitated to throw his hate into Jim's face. Jim never batted an eye. "Nigger, cut out the heart of this here charley then you feed that heart to them dogs over there." Lima Zulu pointed to a pathetic pack of dogs that were just waiting for us to leave the ville.

"Beg the Captain's pardon?" Jimmy said. "Am I hearing that you want me to cut out this VC's heart and feed it to them dogs, Sir?"

"That's what I said, Boy. Are you deaf or are you just a stupid negra?"

Jimmy looked at the Captain as though the man were a lunatic and laughed and laughed. "That crazy motherfucker wants me to cut out a VC heart and feed it to the damn dogs, Boss! Ha!" Jim turned around and yelled at Lima Zulu. "Hey motherfucking scum! You got dog sperm for brains? What you looking at?" Jimmy took a knife out of a sheath he had attached to the inside of his big black leg. "I'm gonna cut me some prime officer heart out, that's what I'm gonna do. And I ain't feeding it to no damn dogs. No siree! I'm gonna eat it all bah mah black self. *Sir*!! I like mah officers warm and raw." Jimmy laughed in Lima Zulu's face and spit on the ground.

Lima Zulu gritted his teeth and backed down but he was like an addict and he'd be back for more. We knew his candy-ass inside and out. Sure enough, about an hour later we heard from him. Lima Zulu was in a chopper and he sent orders down that our team was to zippo (burn) the ville and catch up with the rest of the company in Langvei as best we could. We sat our butts down and waited. We hated doing it. And we hated Lima Zulu. COME ON, MAMA, LET'S ROCK! These were people's homes. This was where children lived. We were sitting there passing a joint the size of Bangkok between us when we heard the crying. Usually crying made your skin crawl. At night the VC would get all messed up in the concertina outside the bunkers and they'd cry until sunrise. Screaming. Until we'd go out there in the morning and shoot them to put them out of their misery. But this was different. This was kiddie crying and it was absolutely the last thing we wanted to hear.

"Shit, Boss," Jimmy said. "Kids is where I draw the fucking line."

"Let's find them, man," I said. And we went looking for

them. It was easier said than done. These were children who had evaded the United States military, the South Vietnamese military, the North Vietnamese military. And it was a wonder that they could cry at all.

"I FOUND THEM!" Titi yelled. "Over here!"

"Damn," Jim said. There were four of them. Three girls and one boy. Jimmy Bo from the Bronx had a place in his big black motherfucker heart for children. And we knew it. He served us notice although the notice was unnecessary. "Any fool messes with these kids will mess with me."

"This is not news," Titi said and he laughed.

"It ain't funny, man!" Jim said. "I'm sick of seeing kids killed. Baby, maybe this is Lima Zulu's crazy war but it's not mine. I ain't killing no damn kids."

The children were huddled in the middle of a hooch that for the most part had been destroyed. The oldest girl looked to be about thirteen maybe fourteen. The others were younger. Much younger. One of the little girls was crying because her leg had shrapnel in it. The leg looked bad and it stank. "Put this one in the jeep," I said to Chris. "We'll take her to surgical in Khe Sanh."

"What about Lima Zulu?" Billy asked.

"Fuck Lima Zulu," I said. "Just fuck him, man. What's he going to do? Send us to Vietnam?" Billy laughed.

One of the little girls walked up to numbah one niggah GI. "Changee money, GI? You want boom boom? I got plenty goodtime. Dirty pictures? You want dinkydao cigarette? I got dinkydao." Maybe she was five-years-old. "GI numbah one." Her eyes were old.

"Come here, precious," Jimmy said. The little girl came to him and he swept her up in his thick arms. She put her arms around his neck and cried softly.

"What are we going to do with the rest of them, Boss?" Billy asked.

"How the fuck should I know!" I was walking around in

my brain for answers. GET OFF, GET OFFA MY BLUE SUEDE SHOES. They were no answers. Titi could speak some Vietnamese. "Titi, tell them we are going to give them some food. And all we can do is check on them later—some other day—to see if they are okay? Maybe." The older girl said something. "Ask her what her name is," I said.

"She says her name is Quong Lee," Titi said. "She says that they were caught in the fighting. The one with the bad leg is her sister. She says her parents are dead."

"Give them your rations," I told the guys. "And put this one in the jeep."

We left the other three in the ville. The ville that we were supposed to have burned to the ground. "Let me stay with them, Boss," Jimmy pleaded.

"No."

"Fuck you, Boss."

"If you stay with them Lima Zulu is going to find out all about it, Jimmy. He may find out all about it, anyway, man. But if we spend the night in Khe Sanh maybe we can bullshit our way out of this and come back in the morning. Okay? Or would you rather have Lima Zulu come around here tomorrow looking for you?"

"Hell sucks, Boss."

"Hell sucks, Jimmy Bo. Hell sucks."

Jimmy and I conviced one of the MASH docs that the kid was worth it. It took the promise of a whole kilo of Thai boom boom dope to do any real talking. Jimmy insisted that the kid be saved. In my dreams I give full bloom to that sleepless night. The doc was a major and he was not a bad guy. Not at all. He was dead tired from operating all day on grunts—the grunts that could make it. Grunts that could not make it were triaged. Most of them were simply left on stretchers to do their dying on. You wanted to be anywhere else. Anywhere, anywhere. Anywhere at all. But not in the fucking Khe Sanh MASH.

You were afraid that somebody might reach out and grab you, look at you, and then die while he held you in some kind of a deathgrip. It hurt too much. And you avoided the MASH unit like it was the plague because it was the plague. In Vietnam wherever you were you walked carefully. You walked carefully in the field because of the mines and the Bouncing Betties. In the hospitals and in the MASH units you walked carefully because a dead man might grab you, clutch at you, scare the living breath out of you. In Khe Sanh you walked carefully because it was Khe Sanh. If death didn't grab your balls despair would.

"I can't save this leg," the major said. She just looked at us with those vastly beautiful sensitive five-year-old baby-almond eyes. Rock-a-bye eyes so soft you wanted to walk into the ocean and leave Vietnam to feed on itself because you couldn't take another minute of the senselessness. "Okay, sweetheart," he said to the girl, "you're going to go to sleep for a little while, now." We named her Tigerlady because she was without a doubt the toughest one-legged female we'd ever met. Tigerlady's bad leg ended up on the floor which was like a pool of thick blood. The blood of soldiers and the blood of Tigerlady. Some of the best people in Vietnam, people who didn't have to be there, really, but they were there because *they* had to be there, were the nurses. Tigerlady got the attention she needed and none of it was regulation.

James LeRoy Washington, black badass motherfucker from the black badass motherfucking Bronx, hardly ever left her side as she fought fate itself to get better. Jim was always at the MASH unit sitting on Tigerlady's bed. Tigerlady wanted very much to live. "Where are you going?" I heard a grunt ask him once.

"Going to visit Tigerlady," he said. He laughed from his bowels that black badass motherfucker laugh. He said it as if she were a whore. Whores were acceptable to visit. "Toughest old woman you'll ever meet," he said to the grunt. "Hey, man, Tigerlady likes candy. You got any candy?"

"Sure, man. Give this to Tigerlady." The grunt threw Jimmy a candy bar.

"Thanks."

"Must be some serious woman," the grunt said.

"Very serious," Jimmy said. "About as serious as your white ass can get."

I watched him go. Titi watched him go. Christopher watched him go. Billy often went with him. In time Tigerlady would become one of the loves of Jim's life. BABY LET ME BE AROUND YOU EVERY NIGHT. I'LL RUN YOUR FINGERS THROUGH MY HAIR AND CUDDLE ME REAL TIGHT. OH, LET ME BE (OH, LET HIM BE) YOUR TEDDY BEAR. I JUST WANNA BE YOUR TEDDY BEAR.

Lima Zulu had a Confederate flag hung over his rack in his bunker. I wasn't surprised to see it. I was, however, surprised to see a Vietnamese woman in his bunker. I had not wanted to go. "Sit down," he said. There was a small table. "Have a drink." I felt out of place. "This here's Jayne Mansfield," he said. And he laughed. "Leastways that's what I call the bitch." Jayne Mansfield smiled. Her front teeth were missing. I nodded at her and sat down. "Maybe we ought to get to know each other a bit better, Boy." Lima Zulu was trying to be friendly. I wasn't interested. I didn't trust him.

"Yes, Sir. Sir."

"Cut the Sir crap." We talked. Or rather Lima Zulu talked. He was already quite drunk—obviously he'd been drunk for a while. He ranted and raved on-and-on about his meaningless life. Not that he thought in any way that it was meaningless. He thought it was nothing less than fantastic. I didn't give a damn about his life, about his wife, about his kids back in the States, about his new brick house, or about how he just wanted to support the President. "Somebody's got to stand up and fight this fucking war, don't they know that back home, Boy? Goddamn demonstrators. I'd line'em all up and shoot every fucking one of them right between the eyes. I'll show them what free speech is all about. We'd fuck'em then we'd shoot the bastards, right, Boy?"

"Yes, Sir."

"I always thought the South got a raw deal in it, anyway. You know, Boy? You wanna be my friend, Soldier? None of you college boys wanna be my friend. Well, fuck you, I say. I say fuck all of you. You ever had a real woman, Boy?" I didn't say anything. Jayne Mansfield just smiled. Lima Zulu stood up, smacked her across the face, and sat down. Jayne Mansfield looked at the ground. He was making me sick. I wanted to pull out my side arm and shoot the fucker right then and there. Just get it over with. But I didn't have the guts to do it. Lima Zulu ranted and raved. He ordered me to fuck his whore. I felt sorry for her. She was as much of a prisoner in that place as I was.

"You're drunk," I said. "You disgust me."

He couldn't believe I was talking to him. He looked around the bunker as if I was talking to somebody else. I had to be talking to someone else. "Are you telling *me* that *I'm* drunk?"

"Go to hell."

"I'm already there, Boy! Don't you know that? You come in here, you drink with me, you tell me that I'm not good e-nough for you, that my whore is too much pussy for you to fuck. You little educated SOB. I ought to . . . " The irony to it, of course, is that Lima Zulu was far more educated than I was. I just looked wet behind the ears. And he hated that. I looked at him right in the eye. Straight into his soul. It was the first time I had ever bothered. And there it was. I saw it clearly the way you can see the calmness of a lake in the morning rain. He wanted me. He didn't want Jayne Mansfield. She was a prop.

Window dressing. I could see it distinctly. Lima Zulu knew exactly what I was looking at. I laughed. I couldn't stop laughing. The son-of-a-bitch wanted me. Me! If we had been somewhere else in another situation he would have still wanted me.

Through his wife, his children, his new brick house, his pain, his whore, and his very own personal war he wanted me. If we had met on the North Pole he would have wanted me. I was unattainable to him here or anywhere. And he knew it. It filled him with suppressed anger and outrage. He wanted me. I finally had something over him. Something hot as ice. He knew that I knew that he wanted me. I could not stop laughing. It was my laughter that threw his flag, his wife, his children, his new brick house, his Jayne Mansfield, and his rage back into his face. How dare I spit on him. It almost left him breathless it enraged him so much to hear me laugh at him. I marveled at this animal. At how much he savored the taste of his own madness. The man fed on his own anger. He wanted me. He tried not to—he hated himself for it—but he wanted me. It made him want to puke but he wanted me. I was merely amused. In that one brief intriguing look into his eyes I saw him wanting me. I know that look, that need, that hunger. I wanted him to fucking starve on it.

Who he really was had become so repressed it'd twisted him. He had reached the point where he could no longer differentiate love from hate, need from rage. He gritted his teeth.

"I'm going to kill you one day, Boy," he said very quietly. I just looked at him. Lima Zulu reached out and grabbed my hand. His grip was iron-like. He smiled and let me look into his eyes again. It was all there. He wasn't trying to hide it this time. I saw his eyes swim with his need for me. He had always wanted me. His voice was low and very serious. "Someday I'm just going to take what I want and then I'm going to kill you. You know that I can do it. And that I will do it. Don't you ever laugh at me again. Not ever. I may be scum to you but I am still a man. You had better take me out, Boy, before I take you first. You're going to have to kill me to stop me and I'm betting you don't have the kind of balls it'd take to take me down." Lima Zulu was the one who was laughing as I left his bunker.

I had to put my hands in my pockets to keep from shaking. Eventually someone offed that SOB. I kept telling myself that he didn't deserve to live. That he was less than human. He had to be . . .

On the psycho-ward of the Bronx VA Hospital the only really safe place to go was the day room, the glitterball. Shuffle shuffle. COME ON, MAMA, LET'S ROCK. It was almost as if some kind of a truce with insanity and rage had been declared in the day room. You could do a lot of things in the day room, talk to your voices, talk to your buddy's voices, but you could not be *Really Crazy* or *Really Enraged* in the day room. If you wanted to be *Really Crazy* or *Really Enraged* you had to go to the art room. WELL, THEY SAID YOU WAS HIGH-CLASS. Or you could flip out in your own room. The hallway was always pretty good. Of course, no one could miss you if you wanted to rock'n roll in front of the nurses' station. Hello, I'm fucked and flying. But being *Really Crazy* or *Really Enraged* in the day room was off limits. Even the hard cores for the most part respected that.

No one knew why.

I was sitting in a psychiatrist's office on the fifth floor—one floor below The Zoo. He was one of those men in one of those positions that you occasionally meet who know exactly what you're talking about. They know who you are and they know who they are. He was one of those all too rare men who know for a fact that they're not God. Men who are willing to meet you one-on-one without any judgments. Men who've been there. And you have to respect them for that. Not because they're officers. Or superiors. Or because they're smarter. Or better. But because they've been there. Inevitably these are the kind of men who will respect you whoever you are.

"Do you mind if I smoke?" I asked.

"Not at all. Would you like a drink? I think I have some Scotch around here somewhere." He rummaged around his cluttered desk.

"Scotch?" I was speechless.

"I'm afraid it's all I drink. Unless you don't like Scotch?"

"Scotch is fine." The doctor poured us both a very warm and very healthy stiff drink.

"Here's to Vietnam," he said. Our glasses touched almost tenderly. "You wanna talk about it?"

"Not really. Were you there?"

"I was in Saigon. They wouldn't let me leave Saigon."

"Lucky you."

"Yeah, I guess maybe I was." There was a long intense silence between us while we evaluated one another. "You saw a lot of it. More than most."

"More than most is right."

"You're not the same person who went over there."

"That's pretty obvious, isn't it? Tell me, does it ever stop hurting?"

"Sometimes," he said. He bummed a cigarette from me. "For some people. They can block it out. And then there are some people who partially block it out. And then there are the ones who will never be able to do that."

"Which one am I?"

"You tell me."

"I'm somewhere in the middle. I killed a man."

"Vietcong?"

I laughed softly. "Shit, man. I killed hundreds of them. No, I killed an American. An officer."

"You're shitting me?"

"Scout's honor."

"You don't have to tell me if you don't want to."

"No, I don't mind talking about it. If it doesn't get to you. I mean, if you wanted to turn me in or anything I'm afraid there's already been an official investigation and all of that. The military did all their paperwork, you know. They assumed it was Vietcong, right, who else. You could have drowned in the bullshit over there."

"Some officers are four star clowns. Assholes . . . "

"He was that."

"Who was he?"

"We called him Lima Zulu. One of the really gung-ho types. He was always telling us to cut off their ears, you know, cut out their hearts. Cut off their balls. Stuff like that. Some of the things I did make me sick."

"It happens."

"Killing Lima Zulu isn't one of those things. Once he asked me into his bunker. I didn't want to go. He wanted to, you know, make friends."

"And did you."

"Not really. He had a few drinks. We sat there for a long time. Just shooting shit. Not really saying anything. I guess I was supposed to be honored that he was trying to be friendly. I wasn't. All this time he had this Vietnamese whore there. She just sat and watched. And smiled. I don't think she understood a word we were saying. It was stupid having a woman there. She was probably VC."

"This guy was your CO?"

"Here's to good old Lima Zulu," I said. The doc poured some more Scotch into our glasses. "May he rot in hell. He wanted me to fuck the whore."

"And did you?"

"No."

"Why not?"

"Would you have?"

"I might have been tempted. If I remember just about everyone was pretty fucking horny."

"For one thing I wasn't about to let this asshole see me in such a vulnerable situation—fucking. And for another thing it made me sick to even think about him watching. And for another thing I like men. I don't have sex with whores or officers. Officers are not men. At least not in my book."

"Oh, really?"

"Oh, really."

"You don't mean sexually."

"Watch my lips sexually."

"Well, you're honest. You've got guts for that," he said.

I shook my head. "If I had any guts I would have been honest about it a long time ago. Maybe I never would have gone to Vietnam. I could have stayed home and . . ." I was looking for a word.

"Just been gay."

"Something like that."

He was quiet for a minute and then he smiled again. "Why is it that I doubt that? Somehow I suspect you would have found your way over there."

"Probably." We drank to honest men. Dead or alive. "It's over," I said.

"It will never be over, will it? Not for you?"

"No," I said. "Not for me. Not ever."

In the middle of horror there are often islands of insane sanity. Like the day room at The Zoo. Like the doc who didn't judge. He just poured some great Scotch. Period. Eventually our team was transferred from Khe Sanh to Landing Zone Sally just outside of Hue which gave us the opportunity to put our little unofficial urchins on a Marine convoy that dropped them off at a place we all called the orphanage. While we were stationed at Landing Zone Sally the only really safe place to go was the orphanage. It was almost as if some kind of truce with insanity had been declared in the orphanage. Although it was not really an orphanage. It was simply an old half-bombed-out house on the old jungle-dirt road which connected Hue to Phong Dien that two French nuns had taken over and it contained God only knows how many children.

No one was counting. No one wanted to know. The United States military particularly did not want to know. The orphanage was one of those mean little contradictions that made the war the fucking bitch that she was. Ironically, there would have been no orphanage if it hadn't been for the military. C-rations until the cows came home. Jeeps and trucks were always pulling up to the orphanage to drop off whatever GIs could get their hands on which was plenty. The obsessed pregnant war machinemonger was a creature of amazing limitless creativity. Her fat bloated belly could cough up anything.

Coute que coute; the French nuns would never turn away a child who came there. For every child who arrived there'd be two who would die. Death was everywhere—it flowed. The Perfume River which ran through Hue was thick with the bodies of the luckless who'd been thrown into the water. The river became a graveyard. It was clogged with the sampans of the barely living and the corpses of the definitely dead. There were far too many other truly important things to do in Hue than bury the dead. Let the dead fend for themselves.

The living needed food. And water. And shelter. And medicine. The streets of Hue seethed with refugees. It was a virtual ocean of wandering homeless tired souls. I feel like I was born a motherless child. The blue the blues. Sing it. It was a glimpse of Saigon yet to come. Huge squealing armies of rats fed off the bodies of the dead in the streets. Hue was a horror that saw literally hundreds of thousands of people die. The US military took away their dead. The North Vietnamese took away their dead. And the dead of Hue were thrown into the river by those unfortunate enough to be left among the living.

If Khe Sanh saw blood running from the green Laotian hills which surrounded us, then Hue with its quiet almost elegant sense of French sophistication saw that same blood flow through its streets and its sewers. It was a tidal wave of blood and no one—no one—was left untouched. Hue is a name that will stay with many GIs until the day their brains cease to function. Even if the rest of the world wants to forget we will never forget. We can't. We wish we could. Many of us have begged God to be allowed to forget. But we cannot forget. The American GI did not always understand what surrounded him in that place. What surrounded him often intimidated who he was. He was an eighteen-year-old boy from Chicago born and bred for killing. Nothing more nothing less. And even that confused and perplexed him. Shake it, baby, shake.

YOU AIN'T NOTHING BUT A HOUND DOG CRYING ALL THE TIME. YOU AIN'T NEVER CAUGHT A RABBIT AND YOU AIN'T NO FRIEND OF MINE. He was an eighteen-year-old boy from Chicago with his hair slicked back who found himself in Hue fighting house-to-house. Urban fighting as opposed to jungle fighting. One was about as honest as the other. He was an eighteen-year-old boy from Chicago with parents who fervently believed that God himself would eventually thank them for what they had done.

And that boy from Chicago will never forget.

In Hue he saw the old ones, ancient timeless Vietnamese, sitting on street curbs, sitting on the banks of the Perfume River, that empty wasted look in their eyes that they all had, smiling vacantly, and most GIs assumed that it was arrogant indifference. GI numbah one was wrong. He was eighteen-years-old. He was Elvis. He was from the south side of Chicago. He was from Nebraska. All he knew about was killing. And that if you took a Ford engine and put it into the body of a Chevy and you took a Chevy engine and put it into the body of a Ford: Both cars would run faster. He did not know why. He could not have been expected to understand or know more than he knew which wasn't much. What looked like arrogant smiling indifference to the average GI was in reality a silent horrible tolerance for what the old ones considered to be the natural inherent misery of life itself. To the old ones life was nothing more than the sick fishbelly promise of eventual death. Please, death. It wasn't the GI they were indifferent to; it was life that they waited out.

And this angered the GI to the core of his childlike American soul.

COME ON, MAMA, LET'S ROCK. After all he was there to save them. Why didn't they appreciate that? And when they didn't—couldn't—appreciate that, often the old ones found death quickly enough. Or it found them. Amazingly, it was the children of Hue who hung onto whatever sweet scraps of sustenance that life offered them. We saw two- and three-year-olds who survived horrors that we knew that we could never in a million years of rock'n roll go through. "Hey, baby," Jimmy Bo would say, "rat bites ain't nothing, man. You ain't *lived* till some rat go gnawing on your meat in your bed. If you got a bed. Hell, I'm fucking home here. These are my people!"

I had to cover for the black dumb big bastard when Lima Zulu came around our bunker because Jimmy was never there. "Yes, Sir! He's helping the doc over at the orphanage." Only there was no doc over there. Just Jimmy. And I was betting that Lima Zulu was too fucking busy to care. "Yes, Sir! We burned that ville to the ground. Nothing left, Sir. Looks like no ville was ever there, Sir. We fucked those zips right in their gook mouths, Sir." As long as I sounded as if I was giving him what he wanted to hear he'd leave it at that. He knew it and I knew it. I hated him. GET OFF. GET OFFA MY BLUE SUEDE SHOES. I often looked for a chance to shoot that motherfucker

in the back if we were out in the field and he knew that as well.
He also knew that I was more than capable. Much more . . .

"You one of them college homo protestors, Boy?" he'd
ask me, scratching at his nuts.

"No, Sir!"

"Well, I hope not, Boy, because if I ever find that you've
been fucking me over ahm gonna stick mah face in your grunt
crotch. I ain't no homosexual. Ah'll just bitecher testes off
an' eat 'em" Lima Zulu always laughed when he said it. But
he meant every word he said.

ONE FOR THE MONEY, TWO FOR THE SHOW . . .

It was dark. Mortars were coming in slow. Maybe one an hour.
Nothing heavy. Most everyone was half-asleep. Kind of awake.
Kind of not awake. "Hey Boss," Jimmy whispered. I pretended
to be asleep. "You ain't sleeping, you lily-white-assed cocksucker. Hey, Boss!"

"What is it?"

"There's a fruit truck coming in tomorrow."

"A fruit what? Oh, man, I don't want to hear this shit." I
put my flack jacket over my head.

"A fruit truck, asshole. Canned fruit, Boss. Somethem
kids ain't had no canned fruit their whole lives."

"Now I know I don't want to hear this shit."

"Hey, Boss. We could get that truck and take it over to
the nuns, you know."

"You really are o-u-t of your mind, man. We're going to
hijack a truck of canned fruit? I'm too old for this war. I don't
want to hear about this."

"You gotta help me, Boss."

"Wrong."

"Somethem kids are starving over there, man. What, you
think I'm some jive turkey? Here, this is serious. You're
gonna help me, Boss."

"Wrong again."

"Kids need fruit. Tigerlady ain't never had no canned fruit. You know, vitamins for the kids, Boss!"

"It's not my problem. My problem, here, is staying alive. Not fucking with no fruit truck, you dipshit. Lima Zulu catches you stealing a truck he'll skin your black hide, nail it onto a tree and let it dry in the sun. Go to sleep, Killer."

"Kids over there are damn hungry. Fuck that sombitch. Someday I'm going to blow that mother to kingdom come."

"He's your commanding officer."

"He's deadmeat you mean if he gets in the way of my fruit truck."

"I'm not hearing any of this. I don't know about any kids. I don't know about any orphanage. I don't know any French nuns, thank God. And I don't know anything about any fucking fruit truck stole by some jerk-off grunt hellbent for trouble. You got that, Jimmy?"

The nuns helped us unload the truck. I'd never seen so much canned fruit in my life. I'm standing there in the middle of the night, hoping that no MPs are on the prowl, thinking that these two scared-looking nuns ought to be very grateful, but no thank you. No one so much as says: Thank you, you stupid grunt, for the stolen canned fruit that you're ignorant enough to bring out here in the middle of the night. In fact, one of the sisters turns to me, with this holy-of-holy look in her eyes and says, "*Qui s'excuse s'accuse.*" He who excuses himself accuses himself. Whatever that meant. Jimmy didn't speak French. They could have put in an order for pâté de foie gras and Jimmy would have merely smiled and gone off to look for another fruit truck. I loved him. But that didn't make it sane.

"*L'homme propose, et Dieu dispose,*" the sister said after we'd unloaded the truck.

"What she call me?" Jim asked.

"She said man proposes, God disposes. Or something."

"Oh, I thought she was calling you a homo, Boss." I

sighed. He was hopeless. Quong Lee was devoted to Jim. She knew that our bringing those children there had saved her life. She wasn't dumb. She turned into the sisters' numbah one right hand helper and the sisters needed all the help that they could get. And then some. Not that any of it was my fucking problem. In no time it seemed as if we were at the orphanage more than we were at LZ Sally where we were supposed to be. The children grew on you. Tigerlady was a champ and she hobbled around on crutches with her stub as best she could. You wanted to put her under your wing but Tigerlady wouldn't have any of it. She was her own person. As was Dragonfly. Being your own person was what got you through the night. And through the battles. And through the amputations. And through just about everything. YOU CAN KNOCK ME DOWN, STEP ON MY FACE, SLANDER MY NAME ALL OVER THE PLACE, BUT, HONEY, LAY OFFA MY BLUE SUEDE SHOES . . .

Dragonfly was the titi one: You need changeee money, GI? You want boom boom? Me got plenty goodtime. Dinkydao cigarette? Dirty picture? Me like soda. Dragonfly behaved as if she were from a Saigon blackmarket cathouse. We figured that somehow the bloat of the war had simply found its insipid way to her ville. Quong Lee explained to the nuns that Dragonfly had survived the wasting of her ville by hiding under the bodies of her family. GIs had shot them and then stabbed the dead bodies but somehow they had managed to miss Dragonfly. It was one of those stories you didn't want to hear. But it was one of those stories the nuns wanted you to hear so you heard.

I tried real hard not to like the two sisters. Real hard. And every time I tried not to like them they reminded me that they were doing twenty times what I was doing for the kids. Twenty times at least. And then some. No one was innocent because no one could afford the luxury. You wanted to turn Dragonfly over your knee because five-year-old girls have no business propositioning American GIs. Dragonfly was a survivor. She loved to ride on GIs' shoulders. All twenty pounds of her. But hold on to your watch. Dragonfly would steal it. You wanted to put her in your pocket, take her home, hold her, kiss her soft brown cheek, tell her everything would be okay, make her eat her oatmeal, and make her behave. Behave, Dragonfly. I tried not to have a favorite. I tried not to like any of them. But if I had been five-years-old I would have married Dragonfly in a minute.

No matter how you much wanted to do something—anything—for them the fact remained that there were thousands of Dragonflies on the streets. Your pockets weren't big enough to hold them all. You didn't have a home you lived in a bunker somewhere that stank. You ate C-rations from a can. And no matter how much you wanted to believe it everything was not going to be okay. You knew it and Dragonfly knew it. Peter Pan was dead. Neverneverland was a graveyard. Elvis was just another junkie. LOVE ME TENDER, LOVE ME SWEET, NEVER LET ME GO.

And then there was the little boy. Maybe he was three. Half-naked most of the time. In the whole time I knew that kid I never heard him once utter a sound. Maybe he was deaf. No one knew. We called him Twirlitoes. He never seemed to go anywhere on his own unless Quong Lee had his hand. Sometimes he'd walk around in circles or twirl. Spin. But that was it. He'd sit down, look at you, and smile. But he never laughed. Even when the universe had gone to the shithouse many of the other children would laugh. They were children. But Twirlitoes was soundless and vacant. Even when he smiled his eyes were vacant. You never really knew what he was smiling at. You didn't want to know. He lived somewhere else. He had one tooth, short hair, and the weeniest little weiner wanger any of us had ever seen.

Billy, of course, used to put Twirlitoes on his lap, gather

the other kids at his feet, and he'd play the guitar for them and sing. Watching Billy play with Twirlitoes was another one of those moments that got imprinted onto me. Titi and Billy would try and get him to laugh. But all he'd do is twirl around. And they'd be the ones who laughed. Somebody had to. TWIRLI TWIRLI TWIRLITOES. OH, TWIRLITOES. OH, TWIRLI-TOES. YOU GOT ME ROCKIN' AND A ROLLING ROCK-IN' AND A REELING, TWIRLITOES, TWIRLITOES, TWIRLITOES. WENT TO A DANCE LOOKING FOR RO-MANCE SAW TWIRLITOES SO I THOUGHT I'D TAKE A CHANCE. OH, TWIRLITOES. OH, TWIRLITOES. YOU GOT ME ROCKIN' AND A ROLLING ROCKIN' AND A REELING, TWIRLITOES. TWIRLITOES, TWIRLITOES. TRIED BETTY SUE, TRIED BETTY LOU, TRIED MARY LOU BUT I KNEW IT WOULDN'T DO. TWIRLITOES. OH, TWIRLITOES. YOU GOT ME ROCKIN' AND ROLLING ROCKIN' AND A REELING, TWIRLITOES. TWIRLI TWIRLI TWIRLITOES . . .

There was a bond between two half-exhausted grunts who were hellbent on somehow saving the world when the reality of it was that they'd be lucky if they could even save their own lives; two grunts and one half-naked baby who had retreated from the world and created his own version of what was real—spinning. Sometimes Billy would twirl with Twirlitoes. He said that it made the world seem like it was going around faster and faster.

If all you did was spin you could convince yourself that you were sitting smack dab in the center of the fucking universe.

They needed powdered milk. So we stole it. They needed more canned fruit. So we hijacked more canned fruit. They needed antibiotics for the kids who might live and morphine for the kids who wouldn't. So we hijacked some very heavy very serious Thai dope. We shot the Saigonese smugglers (who were arvins) and sold the boom boom smoke for antibiotics and morphine to certain docs at the Hue Hospital. The Hue Hospital made the Khe Sanh MASH look like the lobby of the Plaza Hotel. The shots came in syrettes which were collapsible tubes attached to hypodermic needles.

Sister Marie went around with Jim giving the shots. He'd hold the little squirmers and Sister Marie would stab them with a syrette. We called her Sister Willie Peter (Willie Peter was an explosive) behind her back due to her shit-hot French tongue. We heisted some SP packs which were special purposes packages—boxes crammed with an assortment of cigaretts, candy, toilet articles, pens and paper. We figured the kids could eat the candy and sell the ciggies on the black market which they did. I don't know what they did with the pens and the paper. Dear Mom, I'm starving and the nights are cold. They needed blankets so we appropriated blankets from the Seabees who weren't going to miss a few extra blankets. In the summer Hue is hot and miserable. In the winter Hue is cold and miserable.

They needed rice so we promised not to burn a certain hamlet to the ground if the ville leader would give them rice. He went back on his word so we burned that sucker into a black lifeless char. They needed insecticide for the lice. So we ripped it off. Jimmy decided that they needed a rocking chair. He told us about how as a child he'd lived with his grandparents in Huntsville, Alabama. And how his granny had had an old rocking chair out on the porch. WHEN YOU'RE WEARY, FEELING SMALL, WHEN TEARS ARE IN YOUR EYES . . . Jimmy would crawl into his granny's lap. She would rock him and run her old fingers through his hair. It made the bad times go away. So we went to a home that had once belonged to a French rubber planter. It was strictly off limits. But by then our respect for limits had grown somewhat thin. Razor thin. The taut agonized-looking white woman who lived in the wasted mansion let us in passively. She was going to die soon, she knew it, and she didn't care. Take what you want. Everyone else has. So we did. She had a rocking chair. Sister Marie was very impressed.

If they had needed party favors for a birthday bash and a cake with candles we would have found a way to get it. In fact, we arbitrarily declared Tigerlady's birthday and celebrated it. Billy greased his hair back and did his Elvis the pelvis routine. WELL, YOU AIN'T NOTHING BUT A HOUND DOG CRYING ALL THE TIME. YOU AIN'T NOTHING BUT A HOUND DOG ROCKIN' ALL THE TIME. WELL, YOU AIN'T NEVER CAUGHT A RABBIT AND YOU AIN'T NO FRIEND OF MINE. The language of rock'n roll is universal. The kids ate it up. There was candy, canned cakes, and Kool-Aid. There was singing.

I DON'T WANNA BE YOUR TIGER CAUSE TIGERS PLAY TOO ROUGH. I DON'T WANNA BE YOUR LION CAUSE LIONS AIN'T THE KIND YOU LOVE ENOUGH. I JUST WANT TO BE (OH, LET HIM BE) YOUR TEDDY BEAR. Tigerlady sat on Jim Bo's lap and blew out her prayer candles on her canned birthday cake. We were stricken with a case of the subliminal guilts at what we had done, seen, participated in—we knew that we were no better than the people who had put these kids into the orphanage in the first place—combined with a virulent sense of disgust toward the war in general. Here was something we could do. Do! Damn it! Do! And we could *do* it behind Lima Zulu's back which was without a doubt an absolute part of the attraction.

The Hue water supply got real bad. The kids all got diarrhea and dysentery. Half of them died. Most of the time they'd have the good sense to do it quickly. They went fast. They'd just shit, dry up, and die; brown, shriveled, and silent. The Vietnamese are little people. The Vietnamese children seemed microscopic. Jimmy Bo insisted on being the one and only gravedigger. He refused to let any of us help with the graves. "It's something I have to do," he said very quietly. He dug their graves, carried the babies to their holes in the ground, and gently put them in. I couldn't watch him do it. I had a solid year of college. I was his team leader. I was free, white, and (not quite) twenty-one. But let me tell you something: I wasn't jack-shit compared to Jimmy Bo. I was lucky to be able to kiss the ground that numbah one niggah walked on. I loved him.

They needed drinking water and anti-diarrhea pills so we stole cases of beer and Lomotil. The nuns disapproved. Then the nuns got thirsty. The beer got rationed. (Ever see a nun drink a bottle of beer? It's a sight.) The Lomotil didn't help. The bad ones died anyway. Dragonfly got bad fevers. She burned and convulsed in my arms. I cried but Sister Marie told me crying wasn't helping anyone. Not even me.

I was a mess. I really wanted Dragonfly to live. I wanted it beyond reason. I did not believe in God. I swear I didn't. But I prayed to that sick son-of-a-bitch couldn't he once just let one little insignificant dragonfly live? Dragonfly, Twirlitoes, Tigerlady, and Quong Lee made it through the worst of the disease thing which didn't exactly make me believe in any fucking God. For every baby who died another one would show up on the nuns' doorstep. I was the one who had poured beer down Dragonfly's hot little lips. Not fucking God. Disease was the least of it. The fighting in Hue, the taking of the ancient Citadel where an emperor had once ruled this hellhole, had only just begun. We gave the sisters guns to protect the children. It was a war not a mass. They needed. They needed. They needed.

The blues the blues. COME ON, MAMA, LET'S ROCK. Life was charmed. You lived because you had the right charms. You didn't get shot if you walked point because you carried a peanut butter cookie in your pocket that your mother had sent to you last summer. Until the cookie turned to mush. Then you carried it anyway. "Hey man," Billy would say to Jim. "When you're asleep I'm sneaking into your pockets, man, and I'm eating that disgusting cookie." Everyone would laugh. But everyone had their own personal charm. I hated God's guts but I wore a cross around my neck. Just in case. If I heard a mine go off I dove—everyone dove. You landed on the ground. The first thing you felt for was your balls. If they were still there the second thing you felt for was your charm.

Titi's charm was his red bandana. He'd wear it under his helmet. He wore it all the time. Jim had his disgusting cookie. Billy had a picture of Elvis. The old Elvis when Elvis was new and bad and fresh and pouty. The Memphis Elvis not the Las Vegas Elvis. The jailhouse rock Elvis. He had it all folded up—it was about as disgusting as Jim's cookie. None of us had ever heard Elvis sing House of the Rising Sun. Not even once. Billy would argue with us about it for hours endlessly. Yes he had. No he never did. We simply needed something to fight about that had nothing to do with the war. COME ON, MAMA—but Mama was too lost to rock. There is a house in New Orleans they called the house of rock. Billy'd take out the picture, stare at it, and sing like a wolf howling at the moon. Chris had a marble. After Titi was killed Chris threw the marble into the jungle. A man could become extremely morose if anything happened to his charm. And then there was religion. Like incoming it was something that you mainly avoided.

Lima Zulu was religious. He'd line us up before we went out on a search and destroy, put a chaplain in front of us, and the chaplain would lead us all in prayer. "God bless these young men as they go out into the fields of the enemy," the chaplain would say. "Preserve me, oh God, for in thee I take refuge. Thou art my Lord. The beginning and the end. Let me destroy the evildoers I am about to destroy in the name of the father, the son, and the holy ghost."

"I hate seeing ghosts," Jim would say after the chaplain was through. "Every dead zip has a ghost out there walking around in them fucking paddies. Bombs don't bother me, man, but I hate the ghosts."

"He means the holy ghost, asshole," I said to him.

"Ain't no damn holy ghosts where I come from, Boss. Just ghosts." Jim used to wake up in the middle of the night screaming, sweating, stinking with the excess of the dexy smell, seeing ghosts. "Fuck!"

"Hey, babe," Billy would say, "it's only a ghost."

Jim would look at him. "I seen a fucking chink ghost in my dreams, man."

"No, you didn't," Billy would say. "This whole bunker is chock full of gook ghosts, Jimmy. I see one right now." Billy would point into a dark corner, his finger shaking. "Don't let it get me, man! It's coming for me! Auughh!" And then he'd lay down and laugh as if seeing ghosts was the funniest thing in the world.

"It ain't funny, cocksucker. It ain't funny."

Chris would get up. "Will you two let the rest of us get some sleep around here? Screw your ghosts." Everyone would go back to sleep except me because I never slept. And Jimmy Bo because Jimmy Bo was seeing his ghosts. Jimmy Bo once opened fire with his M-16 into a dark corner of the bunker. Any other team would have had him committed to a psychiatric which is where he belonged. Psychiatric was where all of us belonged. But all we did was turn over on our rack and go back to sleep. Fucking ghosts were everywhere. WHEN EVENING FALLS SO HARD I WILL COMFORT YOU. I'LL TAKE YOUR PART. OH, WHEN DARKNESS COMES AND PAIN IS ALL AROUND LIKE A BRIDGE OVER TROUBLED WATER I WILL LAY ME DOWN . . .

The really bad dreams can seem like automatic rapid bursts from an M-60, a lightweight machine gun. The screamers all had machine gun dreams. Bursts of fire. The ratatat ratatat dreams spit at you in your sleep when you were vulnerable, cut you in two, ripped you apart. They'd stop briefly, and then begin again. On the psycho-ward we called them screamers. Most of us had some kind of idea—at least perhaps one deranged abstract fantasy—around what seductive torments plagued the screamers. We knew what they were screaming their guts out about. The Bronx VA Hospital had its share of sleepless solicitude. Nights were the worst. Guys who were afraid of their dreams. You weren't crazy. Really Crazy. And you knew that they were just dreams.

What disgusted you was the relationship of your dreams to the reality of what had been. Oh, they'd tell you, hey, man, they're just dreams. You're just seeing boogies in your sleep. Everyone does. And everyone did. But they were your boogies. And you knew in your bones that they had once been real. It was the fact that your dreams once lived and breathed that tended to make you piss warm urine all over yourself in your pajamas. Even your dreams demeaned who you were.

Talk about losing it.

Our team once had to make an airborne jump from Camp Eagle, south of Phu Bai, to LZ Sally where we were stationed just north of Hue. The last Huey was full of dead. We did n-o-t want to get on that fucking whirlybird. She looked like a flying omen. Not a good sign. Everyone felt for their charms. It was get on or walk. We got on. Nobody had bothered to put the dead into the bags. "Oh, man," Titi said. "I don't want to fucking look at this." We sort of pretended they weren't there. To the gunner and the pilot we weren't any more or any less important than the dead. They'd seen so many dead boys that it didn't mean spit to them. But it meant spit to us. None of my live grunts said much of anything.

You looked at their blue open—dead—eyes. It could have been you. Or anyone you loved. You wondered which was worse; dying or being surrounded, saturated with the death of others. Their boots looked so heavy. Heavier than the rest of them. Their hands looked almost sensitive almost soft. You wanted them to laugh, get up, get up, man, tell me that it's all just another sick joke, but they never did. Every time the chopper banked or took a turn the dead would all roll around onto each other.

They looked like lovers. Touching being so close like that. In life the closeness was only psychic. You only rarely touched each other like that when you were alive. But when you died you were all over the place rolling your lifeless ass over onto the lifeless ass of someone you probably had laughed with, played cards with, smoked reefer with—you sure as shit had died with. We pretended that we weren't fascinated with the cargo. Jimmy Bo started to cry. He didn't say anything to us. We didn't say anything to him. Big dripping tears just started coming out of his puffy basketball brown eyes. He sniffed snot and looked at me.

"Don't look at me, man," I told him. "I had nothing to do with this."

"I'm gonna close their eyes. They're fucking *boys*, Boss."

"It's not my fault," I said. I said it to me as much as I said it to him.

"No, babe," Billy said. "You can't touch them. It's not right."

"Well, they're looking right at me, asshole," Jimmy said. "Somebody got to close their eyes." Jim reached down to them, took in a deep breath, held it, and shut their pretty eyes.

They looked released.

You went through periods where death didn't matter anymore you'd seen so much of it. Hey, it wasn't any more boogey than buying a hamburg back home. With greasy fries. And a Coke. Not a warm Coke. A cold Coke. With ice. Fuck me. I don't care anymore. Grease me. You had to be on the lookout for men who were going through that. They'd go through it, it'd last a couple of weeks, you'd help them pull themselves out of it like it was a quicksand swamp of quickshit not sand, and then it'd be your turn to slide. You'd try not to but down you went. You might even hit bottom without knowing that you had made the trip. It was your buddies who'd be around to help pull you out of the same mental shitsucker. Cocksucker. Pull me. Don't let me slide into it. Here's my fucking hand. Hang on, babe. Hard. Harder. Fucking harder, man! Hey, man, I love you. Love me. Please, love me. Everyone is dying all around me and I'm begging you to pull me o-u-t.

WELL, THEY SAID YOU WAS HIGH-CLASS. AND THAT WAS JUST FINE. WELL, THEY SAID YOU WAS HIGH-CLASS. AND THAT WAS JUST FINE. BUT YOU AIN'T NEVER CAUGHT A RABBIT AND YOU AIN'T NO FRIEND OF MINE. I'd stand up in the middle of incoming and I'd scream at the zips to come and get me. "Come and get me, you zip cocksuckers! I'm over here." And someone would have to sit on me until I wanted to live.

"Asshole's gonna get his head blown off," Chris would say. And he'd pin me down. I'd fight to free myself of him so I could take on all of them, every NVA who ever lived, and Chris would literally sit his grunt butt on my face and hold me so that I could not even move much less take on the whole fucking war. "John Wayne's got it bad this week," he'd say. I'd squirm. Going nowhere. WELL, THEY SAID YOU WAS HIGH-CLASS . . .

One week we made a LURP (Long Range Reconnaissance Patrol) from Khe Sanh to Lao Bao and back again. Lima Zulu had been on my case all week. I no longer cared. About anything. Which amused Lima Zulu to no fucking end. "I think," Chris said, "that we should put a gag in Boss' mouth the next time the Captain wants to talk to him. I mean, really."

I had just told Lima Zulu on the damn radio what he could do with his shit-hot war. Lima Zulu said something about knowing where to find me when he wanted my ass. Someone by the name of General Somethingorother had cut into the exchange. We had both been asked if we were professional soldiers or what? To which Lima Zulu responded affirmatively. And to which I responded in terms of what the General could do with his shit-hot war. The radio went smack-dead.

Sometimes you just said or you just did crazy things. Period. I knew that the General whoever he was would forget it. And I knew that Lima Zulu would forget it. Until he could really get close to my private parts at which time he would probably beat the private shit out of me. Privately. Off the record. The whole damn war was being fought off the private record. Lima Zulu came back on the radio. "Is that cocksucker looking to die?" he asked. I went for the radio but Christopher held onto me. I couldn't move.

"I think so, Sir," Jimmy said on the radio. Lima Zulu sounded as if he were up in a Huey or a Cobra. Again. he said that it gave him a better view of what was going on. Of course it also kept his butt out of the action. Not that he wasn't prepared to do anything and everything he might ask any run-of-the-mill grunt to do. And if you believed that you'd believe that Lima Zulu was Martin Luther King. Or your mama. GET OFF—GET OFFA MY BLUE SUEDE SHOES. The blues the blues. I often wondered if an M-16 could bring down a chopper. "Our team leader seems to be momentarily incapacitated, Sir."

"You are all going to be incapacitated when I'm done with you," Lima Zulu said. I struggled for the radio.

"Yes, Sir!" Jim responded.

"Well, if your team leader *wants* to die let's let him, niggah."

"No, Sir!"

We could hear his chopper pass overhead. "Come on down here!" I screamed. "*Spermbrain*! I wanna kick your ass!" Chris was holding my arms and Billy was holding my feet. I calmed down. It was an illusion. I wanted to kill Lima Zulu. I wanted his flesh. When you get like that your whole body just runs wild with the adrenalin. You don't need the military dexy. You've got your own private sense of madness which is always better than dexy although it doesn't last as long. It's not as tenacious as speed. We ran into a nest of VC. Normally we would have called in air support. A gunship. Why bother. We had me. I ran toward them screaming like an Apache on the warpath. I wanted to kill them. But more than that I wanted them to kill me. I was tired of waiting around for some zip to just do it. Get it over with. Do it.

I fucking dare you.

After I machine-gunned the VC nest I grenaded them. And after I grenaded them I grenaded them again. And then I machine-gunned them. Again. Or whatever there was left of them on the ground. In the trees. Bits and pieces. What was wrong with them why couldn't they kill me. Fucking gooks. Why couldn't they kill someone who wanted to die? I couldn't understand it. So I shot them. And then I shot them again. "Okay, Boss," somebody said. "That's enough." But it wasn't enough. I took my knife out and started stabbing a corpse—the body had its brains half blown out of its head. And I stabbed it in the face. In the brains. In the neck. Over and over again.

Somebody held my arm. Somebody took my knife away. "He's just going to make his dreams worse, you know," somebody said. I thought I saw blood coming out of my eyes. I started screaming. Somebody sat on my chest. They pinned me down. A mortar came in at us. Here they were in the middle of the damn jungle, a crazyman trying to get himself killed, incoming dancing around, and they threw themselves on top of the crazyman because they did not want the crazyman to die.

Even though he wanted to.

It was just the kind of men they were. I didn't want to be put into a body bag alive. I wanted to be put into a body bag dead. Goodbye. Finished. *Bon soir*, Sister Marie. *Autant d'hommes, autant d'avis.* COME ON, MAMA, LET'S ROCK! I had seen boys who were still alive being put into the bags. I didn't want to be one of them. Oh, you knew that eventually, most likely within the hour, if you were one of them you'd die, all right. And soon. But the process frequently got pushed. If they felt you were a candidate they'd put you *alive* into a body bag, zip it up, and that would be the end of it. Hey, Mom, these crazy medics put me in a body bag alive, Mom. Can you believe it? I'm in this thing and it's hot. I can't breath, Mom. Squirm, soldier, squirm. We'd seen them thrashing around in the bags. Trying to get out. Guts all over themselves. The sight would freeze us. YOU AIN'T NOTHING BUT A HOUND DOG. CRYING ALL THE TIME. The blues the blues. Candy, soda, dirty pictures, boom boom dope. Elvis always Elvis. YOU AIN'T NEVER CAUGHT A RABBIT AND YOU AIN'T NO FRIEND OF MINE.

I wanted to die in someone's arms. Not alone. In a plastic bag.

When you're fighting a war you don't get the big picture of it. You don't see that any more than if you were home eating dinner, watching the news, listening to someone in a suit trying to explain it, rationalize it, make it acceptable. Pass the potatoes, please.

When you're fighting a war you see the small things. You see the one sniper who's crawling through the perimeter. You see the female VC on their minibikes who toss grenades into schools. You see mamasans by day who come to collect laundry. They'd return it to you before nightfall—fresh, clean, crisp. And when it got dark the same mamasan who'd washed your shorts would be gunning for your ass. We killed a sniper once who had been able to crawl through the wire, through the mines, past the watch, and she got to within twenty yards of our bunker before she was stopped. She was the same woman who had been doing our laundry all week. And she was coming for us with enough plastic explosives to turn us into memories. You saw laundry women. You didn't see the whole thing.

You could go up in a Huey but even from there you never saw the entirety of it. In fact, it could all look downright peaceful, lush, and green from a Huey. Hey, aren't those tracer bullets coming up after you, streaks through the sky, aren't they pretty to look at? You never saw the big picture. It was the men in Saigon who saw the big picture. WELL, THEY SAID YOU WAS HIGH-CLASS. The men who sat in office buildings. The men who went home at five and stopped off at the Continental Hotel for a drink. Maybe twenty drinks. Now, these were the men who saw the big picture. Office Joes who had an occasional whore now and then. Saigon fuckee fuckee. Men who did as they were told because we all did as we were told. They could see it on the maps they all had in their air-conditioned offices. Men armed with TFES—Territorial Forces Evaluation Systems.

Computerized reports used to evaluate the bigger picture. Room after room of computer print-out sheets. BOQs—officer quarters-types. These were the men who were winning the war. These were the men who day in and day out told the world that victory would only be a matter of time. Just around the corner. And then they needed more time. And more boys. And more napalm. And more boys. And more food for the beast. They could see the big picutre. They had computers. They were winning the war. All they needed was more always more. Just look at the body counts. Every time we lost a thousand men the enemy lost ten thousand. They never understood that the enemy was fully prepared to lose millions. The North Vietnamese were prepared to sacrifice themselves down to the last final living human being that existed. Whatever it took. Charley didn't need a computer to tell him that it was going to take everything.

He just knew.

Our winners were men in offices with technology and rank. When the monsoon came they could buy an umbrella it was that simple. These were the men who fed us, fed the war, and fed the burning heresy that was the black market which was what really kept the whole leaking sampan afloat. While the rest of us watched the sampan sink (with us on it) they were winning the war. The big picture told them that in order for it to mean anything they were also going to have to win the hearts and minds of the Vietnamese.

Never happened. Not even close. That's how wrong we were.

COME ON, MAMA, LET'S ROCK. Hue was itself an omen of what was yet to come. The fact of the matter is that Khe Sanh gave the military a big jolt. None of the TFES computers had indicated that the enemy was going to fight that hard, that viciously, even the Marines had had to dig in. Khe Sanh showed the men with their computers in Saigon that not only was it possible for them to be wrong but that they had been wrong all along. Since day one, mama, the blues the blues. Sing it.

After Khe Sanh you could almost hear the men in Saigon start to sweat. They knew. And we knew. We also knew that they knew. After Khe Sanh they could have thrown their computers, their body counts, their lies, their public relations, and their predictions into the South China Sea. Us grunts never saw the big picture. We were grunts and it wasn't our job to see anything. We saw things like the faces of the fourteen-year-old boys we'd personally decapitated with short bursts of fire. We were short on vision. It was like being blind. We were long on horror.

It all boiled down to a matter of face. We had to cover our balls. The very premise of the war was that sooner or later we'd wear the North Vietnamese down with our technology and our superiority. We'd lose a thousand men overnight taking some hill with a number tagged to it inside a Saigon computer. We'd take it and then we'd be ordered to leave it. The next week we'd take it again. Same hill same number. Different lives. After all, we were right. We had God on our side. You had to actually kill a VC to appreciate the irony of it. You'd kill one, then you'd pull him out of his spider hole, and you'd look at him. You wanted to see what it was you were killing. You wanted to know. You had a right to know. You were armed with seventy pounds of the latest weaponry. And there he was: a sixteen-year-old with one round, one gun, a pair of pajamas, barefoot, and handful of rice in his pocket.

Period.

He changed character in Khe Sanh and Hue. He was no longer a sixteen-year-old. He had Russian tanks. He made the Marines at Langvei, one of the more entrenched and better-equipped base-camps, eat shit and death. The United States Marines retreated. Those of us already in Hue saw the Marines coming down the road. It was a shocker. They looked beaten because they had been beaten. Eighteen-year-old boys with eyes of sixty-year-old men. The bunkers at Langvei were three-feet solid-thick reinforced concrete. They were more solid than the bunkers around Tan Son Nhut. But the Langvei Marines were overrun. Wiped out. The survivors ran for their lives smack dab through the enemy lines.

It was no longer a war against a for the most part unseen sixteen-year-old with one gun and some rice in his pocket. It was now a war of seasoned urban house-to-house experienced horrific killing. Hue looked like Berlin looked like after the

Second World War only Hue had far more refugees. Even when the North Vietnamese had controlled the Citadel, before ARVN Major Trong was able to drive them out at a heretofore unheard of cost, the problem of what to do with the refugees who were pouring into the city from the ravaged countryside was staggering. The NVA took tens of thousands of them back into the jungle, dug holes, and executed all of them. In Vietnam there was one and only one solution to any and all problems.

Death.

It would have been easier if I hadn't had that one year of college. I was a year older than the rest of my grunts. I was the team leader. There were decisions to make. Once after a particularly grueling search and destroy we were set to be picked up by choppers. But the choppers kept getting shot down. Like big ugly black birds. Where there should have been five choppers to pick us up there was one. And that one was a medevac half-full of wounded from another battle from another hill. Stupid son-of-a-bitch should never have put down for us in the first place. My team climbed on. Right behind us were I don't know how many ARVN. God knows they wanted out of there as badly as we did.

"Go, fucker, *go!*" I shouted to the pilot. COME ON, MAMA, LET'S ROCK! He just looked at me as if to say what in hell will I do with these men I'm leaving behind? Of course the only answer was leave them. There were no other options. He hesitated for too long. And the arvins started climbing on board. We were not going to make it out of there with that many men in that chopper. Not no how not no way. We would have been too heavy. I could hear and feel the zip of snipper fire going through the whirlybird. "Shoot them," I said. I said it softly. The noise from the chopper was deafening. You couldn't even hear me say it things were so loud. It was something that had to be said but didn't really have to be said.

I said it. I gave the order. I did not have to scream. Titi emptied his M-60 into the guts of the ARVN. Short bursts of fire. Just like they said in the book. The arvins sort of stopped and looked at him as if to say, hey, it's us. They're doing this to us. And up we went.

The last arvin that I allowed myself to look at was a man I knew. About as well as you could know any of them. He used to carry around pliers in his pockets to yank out the gold or silver he might find in the teeth of the corpses in the hamlets and the villes. I told myself that this was not my country, these weren't my people, and these customs were not mine. That somehow I had to respect them. But I did not respect them. They were not my people but they were people. I'd watch this man open up their mouths and yank the teeth out. Sometimes, inevitably, his victims weren't dead at all. I watched the expression on his face as Titi shot him. It was a mixture of surprise and rage.

Candy, soda, dirty pictures, boom boom dope. Neverneverland. They hung onto the chopper. They clutched at it. Xin Loi. Xin Loi. It was them or us. Half way up the pilot started having the shakes. GET OFFA MY SHOES, MAMA! The stick stuck. He was new. If he hadn't been new he would never have put down for us. He didn't know. Titi told him that if he didn't stop shaking—now—Titi would shoot him as well. We stopped twirling around in the sky like a beer can being shot on a fencepost with a twelve gauge and made it the hell out of there.

I don't know who found me in the latrine. I wanted to die. I did not want to be alive. SAIL ON SILVER BIRD. SAIL ON HIGH. YOUR TIME HAS COME TO SHINE. ALL YOUR DREAMS ALONG THEIR WAY . . . By all rights it should have been enough Thai smack to kill a herd of water buffalo let alone one dumbass grunt. SEE HOW THEY SHINE. My arm ached. I dreamed I was having sex with Elvis. I woke up with my heart pounding like it wanted to jump outta my chest. I was on Chris' rack. Chris was holding my arms down. Jimmy was giving me CPR. Titi and Billy were on either side of me. "Asshole," Jimmy said. "You think we're gonna let some asshole die on us? Who you think gonna be the new team leader, huh? You ever think about that, asshole? Old Lima Zulu'd move himself in here to be the team leader you give that sombitch half a chance. Hey! That's right I'm talking to you. You motherfucker we love your white ass around here. We ain't gonna letcha die on us. So nice and prettyboy, asshole. Hey! I said we need you!" And he slapped me. I just looked at him incredulously. And he slapped me again. And again. My face felt warm.

"Put some more speed into his mouth," Billy said. Jimmy opened my mouth. Chris shoved his grunty fingers down into my throat and they gagged a bunch of dexy into me. I swallowed. Jim poured water down my throat and I swallowed again. I was drenched in sweat.

"Fucking smack doesn't kill him," Jimmy said. "the fucking speed will." I gasped for air. "That's right, motherfucker, breathe! I said *breathe!*" And he hit me again. And then they started walking me around. "You ain't gonna sleep tonight, candyass. Up we go." Jimmy had me on one side. Chris was on the other. I was half-dragged half-walked half-hauled around and around in the bunker. My feet didn't want to move. I wanted them to put me in my rack and let me die. My heart hurt. It wanted to bleed. It wanted to explode. We walked and walked.

"Move them feet, cocksucker. I said move them whiteboy feet. You sombitch ain't dying on me. Hey, man, I need you down that orphanage. Tigerlady needs you. Dragonfly needs you. Twirlitoes needs you, man. Quong Lee needs you. Sister Willie Peter'd skin my black ass if I let you die like this. We're going for a walk, baby. Ain't the sights pretty, prettyboy? I just love fucking Vietnam. I love it. Now, move them whiteboy feet. This here ain't the first time old Jim Bo walked a fucking junkie. Now, let's see them white feet dance. Comeoncandyass. You can do it. I just knows you can do it. Cause I'm gonna make your white ass do it. I said move. We're walking, Boss. Ain't it great to be awake, asshole? And now we're gonna pour some coffee down your lily-white throat till you throw up all over your white self, Boss. Here we go . . ."

We were up most of the night. In the morning my head wanted to pound itself into the earth. We walked out of the bunker—there was a familiar smell in the air. There was a familiar sound in the air. You got to shake rattle and roll. Heavy artillery. We called them big boys. Some of them were aimed at us. Everyone looked south. No one said anything. A huge black raging cloud of smoke was pouring into the atmosphere. The city of Hue was burning. "I got to get to the orphanage," Jimmy said.

"No, man," Chris said. "It'll be impossible."

A mortar came in at us. We could hear the fucker coming and we dove back into the bunker. "Don't let him go," I said. "Nobody can go out in this."

"I got to go."

"He's not to leave this bunker," I told the others. "Jimmy, you won't be much good to them dead."

We sat in the bunker and ate it. The North Vietnamese were determined not to leave Hue. As the old imperial center of power there was much symbolism in that place for them. As far as they were concerned they'd go down to the last man if it meant the total destruction of the city which is what for all intents and purposes happened. From the slit in our bunker we could watch Hue burn. Finally, we got permission to join the rest of our unit on a convoy into Hue. "Permission requested to stop at the orphanage, Sir!" Jimmy asked Lima Zulu.

ONE FOR THE MONEY, TWO FOR THE SHOW. Lima Zulu was in his element. GO-CAT-GO. "There's a war going on, niggah, or didn't you know that? Permission denied. You going into Hue, Boy. You going to really kill you some gooks this time, you hear! Charley really has his act together this time. This ain't no fucking picnic this time, Boy!"

"It'd only take a minute to check on the children, Sir." Jimmy was going to go. One way or the other he was going to make it to the orphanage. Lima Zulu reconsidered.

"Now, I don't suppose that this here is the same place that all these here missing supplies have been going to?" Lima Zulu gritted his teeth. Jimmy Bo said nothing. "And I don't suppose that if I were to stop at this here orphanage I'd find any of the things that've been missing, now, would I, Boy?" All he got was silence. "And I don't suppose that if I were to find any of let's say that missing morphine that I'd bust your negra ass down to southern soup if I did, now, would I, Boy?"

"Permission requested for a jeep, Sir."

"Now, I don't suppose you boys, here, would consider taking my jeep, now, would you. With me in it. I've been waiting for something like this to come along, Mister. Let's go. I wouldn't want to keep a gook lover from his gooks, now, would I?"

Lima Zulu thought he had his sweaty hands around our scrotums. He stopped the jeep. "Where is it, Boy?" Nobody said anything. We were in front of what had been the orphanage. There was nothing left of it except a smoking pile of stone and embers. We had seen it all. Death was not new to any of us. But this left us speechless. Nobody cried. Nobody had the energy to cry. We walked through the ruins in stunned silence kicking through the char. We could hear Lima Zulu back in the jeep laughing. He laughed and he laughed.

Billy looked at me. His eyes were clouded. "They got Twirlitoes, Boss."

"I know. I'm sorry. Let's go."

Jim was just standing there in the middle of the char. He

seemed calm and peaceful. We all went to him. He had been the center of it. You looked at him. But there was no pain. Jim was beyond pain. We stood around him. We all wanted to touch him. He was big and dumb and black and beautiful and none of us could touch him. We were in awe of him. "You all did good here," he said very quietly. Jim looked over at Lima Zulu. "And I'm gonna chew another hole into that white bastard's ass. Let's go." Lima Zulu laughed himself all the way into what was left of the city of Hue.

Whenever I picked Chris up at the Bronx VA Hospital the staff would without fail lecture me on the evils of doing whatever it was we were doing when we went out together. We were treated with a certain amount of justified suspicion. We weren't sure what it was we might be doing wrong. But whatever it was it had to be right. The VA was convinced that it was evil. Two men, one of them in a wheelchair, could not possibly enjoy themselves as much as we enjoyed ourselves unless those men were up to no damn good.

Sometimes all we did was find ourselves a basketball court and shoot baskets. Just shooting baskets. Over and over again. Our wickedness was rather bland. Evil is as evil does. The drop-outs did not object to our presence at the basketball courts near Broadway and 225th in the Bronx near Marble Hill. Somehow we sort of blended in. Sometimes we spent the afternoon at Lincoln Center listening to jazz, just jazz. The blues the blues. We went to outdoor summer concerts as we could afford the price of admission—they were free.

After the concerts we'd sit and eat sandwiches near the Lincoln Center fountain which is where we had some of our better arguments. Chris calls them disagreements. Differences of opinion. I call them arguments because Chris was always wrong. And when Chris is wrong we argue. "Davy Crockett hats were the best," he said.

"No, you're wrong," I said. "They weren't Davy Crockett hats. They were coonskin caps. And Mouseketeer hats were better."

"They had tails and they made you feel like Davy Crockett," he said. "They were useful. What good is a hat that has two big black mouse ears? You can't shoot anything wearing mouse ears."

"Not everybody wanted to shoot everybody else," I told him.

"Maybe in California they didn't. But in Michigan you wore Davy Crockett hats . . ."

"They weren't hats."

" . . . and you shot everything and everyone with cap guns. Even your friends. Particularly your friends. And then they'd shoot you. Grandmothers hated the cap guns which is why we liked them. What good is a gun your grandmother might like? My dad used to take me fishing. Did they have fishing in California?" I handed Chris a sandwich.

"We invented fishing in California."

"He used to wear this hat with flies hooked onto it. Dad went to catch fish. I went to be with my dad. He wasn't a bad dad. He smoked a pipe. When I think of him I remember that cherry tobacco smell. Gloria wanted to play baseball with us boys. Nobody wanted her on their team. God knows I didn't. So she appealed to Dad."

"And?" I asked

"And it was a mistake. Dad made her stay inside while we played ball. Gloria always had to learn the hard way. Dad used to go deer hunting they'd tie the dead deers to the front ends of the cars. I'll bet you can't tell me what Mickey Mantle batted in 1956. I'll bet you don't know."

"He hit fifty-two home runs and batted .353 in 1956, asshole," I said.

"I had a skateboard."

I just looked at him. "My mother gave birth to all of her

children while on a skateboard. You weren't from California."

"I had a skateboard anyway. I was the only kid who had a skateboard. And we had . . ."

"I was the Cheshire cat for Halloween."

"I beg your pardon?"

"I was the Cheshire cat for Halloween."

"What the fuck is the Cheshire cat, pray tell?"

"Didn't you ever read *Alice Through the Looking Glass*?"

"You mean the one with the chick and the rabbit and the queen? *Alice in Wonderland*! Sure, off with her head! I liked the queen. Oh, yeah. The Cheshire cat was the one with the grin. Jesus, they really were weird in California. You were the Cheshire cat? It makes sense. I mean, why not? All the weirdos lived in California. It's where they invented weirdos. The rest of the world is ghosts with sheets over our heads, witches with brooms, but he's the Cheshire cat. I like it. I was Captain Hook. My hook was made out of a coat hanger. I really had a hand. I just held onto the coat hanger, you know, it had a long sleeve. And then I could stab kids with my hook."

"Captain Hook?"

"Yeah, I had a mustache made from my mother's eyebrow pencil. That was a great Halloween. Gloria was Peter Pan but by then she was growing tits so it didn't really work. Gloria could grow tits but I couldn't grow a mustache it pissed me off. She had this thing about how Peter Pan was really a girl, she said. Not a boy. So we used to fight about it. She kept saying that Peter Pan was a girl. So I stabbed her with my hook. And then she wrapped up her tits so they wouldn't show . . ."

"When did you wear your first jockstrap?" It was my turn to laugh. "I really want to know."

"You have a filthy mind, Boss."

"I used to stand in front of the mirror in my room," I said, "with my first jockstrap on, you know, admiring it. I was a man, right. It was my first jockstrap. I locked the door to my room. I pulled down all the shades. And I wore it over my jeans." Chris howled. "Finally I got the courage to take the jeans off. It felt very bizarre wearing that jockstrap."

"I told Gloria they were nose protectors. She believed me. And so then she put my jockstrap on over her face to see if it protected her nose. Boy, was she pissed when she found out they weren't nose protectors. She hit me. I hit her back. And we used to pick apples."

"Apples?"

"Yeah, apples. Before the block got all built up there was an old field where there were some apple trees. Us kids would climb the trees and pick the apples. I remember the smell of fresh apples. Gloria used to eat the green ones because they smelled so good she couldn't wait for them to turn red. The apple orchard is where we played war. We had sticks for swords but whenever we killed Gloria she wouldn't die. She just said that we didn't get her. It was usually a lie. Usually we'd cut her to ribbons and really ran her through, you know, with our swords. But Gloria always refuses to go gently into that good night. Even today . . . "

"You were a violent child, Chris."

"Childhood is a violent period, my friend. Ever look at the cartoons they have nowadays? Body counts all over the place. Any Saturday morning on TV makes Vietnam look like a pleasant afternoon at Lincoln Center. If the younger generation ever fights a war—God help us. It'll be ruthless."

"We had a milkman," I said.

"Everyone had a milkman."

"Not like our milkman."

"Oh, I'm sure that the California milkmen were probably superior. Weirdo milkmen. Probably only dropped off health-milk. They don't have apple orchards in California."

"He had a horse."

"A horse?"

"Yeah, I suppose he could have driven a truck . . . "

"Maybe they hadn't been invented yet," Chris laughed.
"A milkman on a horse? Now I've heard everything."

"Not on a horse. He drove a cart. Or something. The
horse pulled the cart. It had ice in the back. He sold the milk
and he also sold ice. Kids would climb into the back when he
was in someone's house. And they'd steal ice to suck on.
Sometimes the ice was covered with sawdust."

"I can't picture you stealing ice."

"That's because I never did. If the milkman caught you
in the back of his milk cart with the ice he got mad. And then
he'd tell your mom . . . "

"Heaven forbid." Chris laughed again. "You know what
your problem is, Boss?"

"I don't have any problems unless you are considered a
problem."

"Your problem is that you are still afraid of the milkman
and you still lock the door whenever you put your jockstrap on.
Isn't this the fountain Zero Mostel danced in?"

"Zero Mostel?"

"In the movie, *The Producers*? I think it is."

"I'll give you fifty bucks if you dance in this fountain."

"You don't have fifty bucks. You're broke."

"Fifty bucks if you dance in this goddamn fountain. I *dare*
you to do it."

"I don't dance in fountains."

"That's your whole fucking goddamn problem, Boss!
You never danced in a fountain. You never dared being caught
by the milkman. You never showed the other guys how fucking
great you looked in your first jockstrap! It's *important*! If I
could walk I'd throw you in, asshole. You don't dare. You're
so fucking careful. Get in that fountain."

"I don't dance in fountains."

"Fifty bucks."

"Fifty?"

"Fifty."

I was still dripping wet when I returned him to the Bronx VA Hospital. And he was still laughing his head off. The Bronx VA Hospital was not amused. No one there had ever danced in a fountain.

Chris has never paid me the fifty bucks. Even as a kid I never believed in God. Unless God was the milkman. I thought it was a crock. Nor did I believe in spirits, or ghosts, or in Davy Crockett's coonskin cap, or in charms. Certainly, I did not believe in men. If I believed in anything I believed in dreams. Vietnam confirmed this for me. I stuck a lot of garbage into my arms in Vietnam. But it was the dreams that Vietnam stuck into me that turned me as an adult into a believer in the power of dreams. I'm from California I can believe in anything I want to. I was dreaming and I could see them. I could see Tigerlady, Dragonfly, Twirlitoes, and Quong Lee.

It was my old house where I'd grown up. The golden foothills of California. I was an adult and I was playing with them. We were walking through the tall grass that used to grow near the stream that ran past our house. I was the leader. I could smell the cold sweetness of the water. I could feel the grass. The children were behind me. But I was going too fast. I lost them. I didn't mean to. One minute they were there. And the next minute they were gone. Vanished. I was standing there wondering where the children had gone off to when Quong Lee emerged from the grass. She was alive. I didn't know where she was. Or how she had survived. But she was alive.

I woke up. I was in the bunker. We were all bone tired. We ached. We burned with the smell of Hue in our nostrils, in our throats, in our eyes. "Jim, wake up." He didn't move. The man was exhausted. "Jim, wake up. I saw her."

"Shit, man. You dreaming again. I'm tired, Boss."

"I saw Quong Lee."

"Whatchoo mean you saw Quong Lee? Quong Lee's dead, man. She's dead. And that's what you're gonna be if I don't get some sleep."

"I saw her in a dream. She's alive. It's like she was this spirit. I think—I think maybe I know where we might find her." Jimmy just looked at me in the dark.

"Don't play no jive turkey with my head, Boss. You hear?"

"She's alive." We lay there in silence and shared a joint.

"You really think so?"

"I do."

"Where?"

"Tomorrow we'll drive over to the black market. Chinese section. Over by the river."

"Lima Zulu ain't going to let us anywhere near no jeep."

"We'll catch a ride on the convoy."

"And how we getting back?"

"Any way we can, man. You coming or are you going to sit around on your ass while I go!"

"You know the answer to that one, you white motherfucker." And he laughed. He laughed so loud and so hard he woke up the rest of the team. He laughed from his bowels, that loud growl, and he couldn't stop laughing.

"Aww, man," Billy said. "We're trying to sleep. You find that funny? Boss, put this guy into psychiatric. He's wiped, man."

"Quong Lee's alive, Geronimo," Jimmy said.

"Say what?"

"Quong Lee's alive. Boss had a dream. We're going into Hue tomorrow and we'll find her." Jimmy smiled his I don't care if you don't believe it smile. Jim was from the Bronx and he could believe in anything he wanted to.

"Aww man," Billy complained. "Boss sees boogies in his dreams it don't mean they're alive."

"Your mama, it don't," Jimmy said.

"You think so, Boss?" Billy asked. By now everyone was looking at me.

"Go back to sleep, all of you."

"Where is she, Boss?" Titi asked. "Can I come?"

"No."

"You can't stop me, Boss," Titi said.

"I'm coming, too," Chris said.

"Who's going to defend this bunker?" I asked.

"Ghosts," Jimmy said. And he laughed again.

I wasn't the only one who believed in dreams. We found her selling ciggies in the Chinese ghetto. The Black market seethed with action. Candy, soda, dirty pictures, boom boom dope. Neverneverland. She dropped her ciggies and ran to Jim when she saw him. All fifty pounds of her. Another twenty-four hours of no food and Quong Lee would have been history. Jim picked her up and hugged her. His lips covered her with kisses. You never saw a fourteen-year-old eat C-rations with such relish. The six of us sat on the banks of the Perfume River in the middle of Hue in what had once been an imperial park. Bodies and sampans floated by as if nothing about any of it was in the least unusual.

"So now that we've found her what do we do with her?" Titi asked.

"Actually," I explained, "I have been giving some thought to that."

Everyone looked at me as if I was supposed to have all the answers. Again. "I have a friend who's flying a bunch of CAVs back to Saigon in a couple of days. I can get her to Saigon if somebody else can get her to somewhere safe. Maybe one of you might know somebody who'd pick her up. Take care of her for a while. It's the only thing I can think of."

"I know a nurse in Saigon who's just dying to get into my pants," Billy said. We all roared with laughter. Jimmy rolled on the ground. "Well, assholes, it happens to be true. She'll help me. I'll owe her one. But she will help."

We kept laughing. "I can see her now," Jim said. "Probably one of those big ones, the warhorse type. Oh, mama, sit on mah face. Yumyum." We kept laughing.

"Well, then forget it, man," Billy said. "It just so happens this woman would love to sit on my face." We kept laughing. Billy tried not to, he crossed his arms all huffy-like, but Billy laughed with us. His face just cracked up. It felt so hysterical to be able to laugh at all. Whatsoever. We'd jive Billy's butt about it yet we all knew that he'd be a big help. So would his nurse. And, yes, she was a big rockin' mama. She also had a heart about the size of Seattle which is where she was from. With hips to match. For every motherfucking Lima Zulu you met in Vietnam you'd meet someone good. Someone who was there because they knew unconsciously that what it was about was the small picture. If it was about killing and death it was also about survival and life.

Most of these people, many of them were nurses and medics and hospital support staff, were in Vietnam by choice. Because there was nowhere else, really, for these kind of people to be. They had to be in the middle of it. The big picture sucked but there was nothing on God's earth that any of us, whether we were the good guys or whether we were the bad guys, could do about any of it. It wasn't a question of good guys or bad guys. It was a question of making it from one day into the next. We smuggled Quong Lee into Saigon and Billy's warhorse nurse picked her up and adopted her until the end of the war.

Sister Willie Peter, Tigerlady, Dragonfly, and Twirlitoes, all died. They were bombed, shot, burned, raped, greased, offed, zapped. Whatever. We would never really know. Quong Lee survived. She doesn't remember how she survived. It comes to her in flashes, bits, pieces, small pictures in her mind, mostly at night when she's asleep. Vulnerable. In her dreams. The blues the blues. In her dreams she runs. She says that she can feel the wind on her face as she runs. She can hear them telling her to run, Quong Lee, run. And she ran. She ran until she dropped. Until she could run no further. Until she dropped onto the ground like any other corpse. Sister Willie Peter, Tigerlady, Dragonfly, and Twirlitoes all exist—alive—in our dreams. In our dreams there is no place left to run.

Two weeks after we'd received word that Quong Lee had arrived safely at Tan Son Nhut, old Lima Zulu bit the big one. He walked into a latrine and the latrine blew to shit and pieces. Lima Zulu done gone to hell. YOU AIN'T NOTHING BUT A HOUND DOG ROCKIN' ALL THE TIME. Someone had jury-rigged his latrine so that when the devil opened the door a grenade went off. Bang, you're dead. That's all she wrote. We were all sure that he died grinding his teeth the way he always grinded his teeth. There was justice somewhere in the fact that that SOB died in a toilet. I liked it. Top brass made a report. Top brass said that it had to be a VC infiltrator. But our unit knew better. We knew. We knew. ROCKIN' ALL THE TIME. No VC was going to risk infiltrating past mine fields, past watch, past razor wire, past hell itself for the sublime opportunity to hook a grenade onto a latrine. Our team never really discussed it. We knew. We knew. Some things are just too close to home. Top brass said it had to be VC.

And I'm your mama.

YOU AIN'T NEVER CAUGHT A RABBIT YOU AIN'T NO FRIEND OF MINE! The blues the blues.

Part Five

DANCING AT THE WALL

—the chemical musicians
sing prince songs
as we dance at the glitterball
shuffle shuffle
marching wherever we are told
to march
bare and pure fragrant and nude
our heads were full of thorazine
and daddy ran his fingers through
your gentle boy brains
bleeding shuffle shuffle
anywhere and fire raced through our eyes
even our eyes were a part of the indigo hoax
singing daddy's song because we
were unconditional and could not see our vision
was as bare and as cold as our naked
prince soldiers tin and dancing
anywhere where big brother's hobby-horse
rocked babes to sleep in their
daddy's arms so soft so
sweet with fever at
the glitterball
where boys are babes and babes
dance reuseable till dawn
where quiet daddy ran his prophetic fingers
through
our tender intoxicated
eyes of love—

BABY LET ME BE AROUND YOU EVERY NIGHT. I'LL RUN YOUR FINGERS THROUGH MY HAIR AND CUDDLE ME REAL TIGHT. OH, LET ME BE (OH LET HIM BE) YOUR TEDDY BEAR...Our Greenwich Village apartment living room could be a very busy place. It did double duty. Sometimes it did triple duty. Chris used to say that it did so many duties it was downright howdy duty. I had no fucking idea what he was talking about. The living room served as Michael's bedroom and it was the headquarters of the Forging Faggots. Until the Forging Faggots became the Wheelchair Wahoos. Until the Wheelchair Wahoos (thankfully the name was short-lived) became the Wrathful Wrecks. The Wrathful Wrecks finally became the Fighting Furies. It was somewhat difficult for them to decide who they were. They were six gay men in wheelchairs. And they kept changing the name of their group. Whoever they were in any given week was usually contingent upon whatever controversy they had decided, usually somewhat abruptly, to confront.

Gay rights, of course, was a given. But then so was a confrontation they had with Ma Bell about putting pay phones lower where they could be reached by people in wheelchairs. They petitioned the City of New York for the construction of a workout obstacle course in a park that would have been designed for people in wheelchairs but the City of New York thought they were mad and simply ignored them. They looked great wheeling themselves down the middle of Fifth Avenue in the Gay Pride Parade. But they wanted to do more than that. Gay pride parades were cute but they weren't enough. They wanted a challenge. Challenge boiled in their blood.

I swear all of them had burrs up their butts. It was, of course, Christopher who paved the way—they became a basketball team. It was inevitable. I suggested to Chris that they instead become arctic explorers. They could be the first wheelchair convention to the North Pole. I was told that the North Pole would not be challenge enough, thank you, but no thank you. They met weekly in Michael's bedroom which was my living room which was their meeting headquarters and occasional bar facility. Whatever it was it was crowded.

Christopher was their leader, chief organizer, chief bartender, and chief basketball coach. Michael and I were named honorary cheerleaders although we would have been too embarrassed to actually do any real cheerleader cheers during any of their games. We usually sat in the bleachers and cheered from the sidelines. Silently. Oh, sometimes we'd stand up and yell. Usually something brilliant like: Go, Chris, Go. Chris called us Mickey Mouse Dick-and-Jane cheerleaders. This was something of a slur. He said that we were a sorry sight as cheerleaders go and this I admit was somewhat true. Go, Chris, go was about as enthused as we could get unless we got riled or mad.

If we were angry we'd stand up and call whatever team they were playing a bunch of pansyass motherfuckers. But only if we were irritated. Usually we only got mad when someone from another team got rough. Wheelchair basketball makes professional basketball look like champagne cocktails with Jayne Mansfield in her tub. With bubble-bath. Wheelchair basketball is serious where professional basketball is occasionally amusing. Someone from the Fighting Furies was always having his wheelchair flipped. Dumped out and ran over. Men in wheelchairs can be downright merciless when it comes to other men in other wheelchairs.

It was a wonder that the Fighting Furies didn't have wheelchair burn marks branded down their backsides they were run over so many times. Wheelchair teams can play dirty if it comes to that. Most of the time it did. So Michael and I would call the other team obscenities. Whoever said that the screaming of obscene nasties at the top of your lungs during times of stress and passion never makes a situation any better was quite simply wrong.

Michael and I would stand up in the bleachers and call the opponents of the Fighting Furies dipshits and spermbrains. We didn't have any pompoms. We would have looked silly with pompoms. It wasn't quite like being a cheerleader and doing cheerful cheers but it was the best we could muster.

It made us feel good.

We would encourage our team to dump their opponents o-u-t of the enemy's wheelchairs on the theory that what's good for the goose ought to be good for the gander. This usually happened when the Forging Faggots or the Wrathful Wrecks or whoever they were that week were getting creamed which was, sadly, most of the time. Their original stated intention said something very lofty about playing wheelchair basketball to simply play the game. Physical fitness and all of that. It was a barefaced lie. The fact of the matter is that they played wheel-chair basketball because they had a lust for blood. They liked winning.

They were men.

There was a lot of discussion about the team name. As the Forging Faggots they got a lot of attention which they had a tendency to bask in until the attention started making everyone who knew them think of them as gay men in wheelchairs. Ironi-cally, the Forging Faggots didn't see themselves like that at all. As individuals they tended to see themselves as *men* in wheelchairs. Who were gay. The *men* part came first. And then somewhere in there there was the wheelchair part. And then there was the gay thing. As the Forging Faggots the name was inevitable doomed. No one really liked the name. They just liked the response that the name evoked in people. In the beginning for a long time they didn't even have a name. They were informal.

But none of the other wheelchair teams would play them. You had to have a name. After they became the Forging Faggots and got one rather notorious newspaper article written about them all of the wheelchair teams in town lined up to whip their asses. More teams wanted to play them than they had the time or energy to commit to the cause. It was, however, now a cause of honor and honor is always the final cause.

Always.

Most issues in life boil down to a matter of balls. Who has balls. Who has the biggest balls. They weren't half bad basketball players. Sometimes they won. Sometimes they didn't. The name changed when the word faggot no longer amused them. As the Wrathful Wrecks they got real serious about winning and staying in shape. They were challenged to a game by the Nam Gnomes; a wheelchair team that creamed them with no small amount of rubbing their gay noses in the sublime smell of obliterated defeat. Again and again. Try as they might they could not beat the Nam Gnomes.

The Nam Gnomes eventually changed their own name (it was contagious) to the Nam Knights which made matters worse. The Nam Knights really creamed them. Again and again. In fact, the Nam Knights would wipe them off the floor of the court. The Nam Knights were the top wheelchair basketball team in the country. They were the LA Lakers of the wheelchair division. Finally, Chris' team changed its name to the Fighting Furies and their purpose in life was to somewhere, somehow, someday beat the bejesus out of the Nam Knights. I DON'T WANNA BE YOUR TIGER CAUSE TIGERS PLAY TOO ROUGH.

And I'm your mama.

During meetings my poor apartment was so crowded that nobody could turn his wheelchair around unless everyone else turned their wheelchairs in unison. Out of the six members of the Fighting Furies, two, Chris and Tony, were Vietnam vets. Chris was a bum and Tony was a counselor at the VA. Thom was oriental and owned the Golden Buddha Restaurant on Spring Street. Thom had a standing offer. If they won Thom paid for the beer. The Golden Buddha was a lot better meeting place than our apartment. I accused them of using the apartment because they all thought that Michael was cute and they liked looking at his underwear which he usually left around on the floor. I was told that I was wrong. I was told that the reason they used the apartment was because I made the best sandwiches in Greenwich Village which was true. They were spoiled rotten.

Edward was a stockbroker. Rick was a black ex-drag queen who now worked in marketing at Macy's. And George was another bum who had inherited a fortune somewhere and was living (quite well) on it. Chris had put an advertisement on the bulletin board at the Gay Community Center and slowly but surely the Fighting Furies evolved into the group of frustrated philosophically liberal basketball fanatics that they all were. WELL, THEY SAID YOU WAS HIGH-CLASS . . .

Michael and I were sitting in the bleachers of the Upper West Side YMCA watching the Nam Knights pound the shit out of the Fighting Furies. Their best player, Rick, the ex-drag queen brother, was their best player. But try as he might he couldn't carry the whole thing himself. Chris was very good. His best asset was the fact that he was very built which meant that he could go very fast in his chair. But you could tell that the other guys dreaded letting him have the ball because Chris could never make a basket. He missed constantly. Oh, he'd be down there before anyone else, he'd aim, and he'd miss. After years of making baskets from a standing position, relearning how to do it from the confines of a moving chair was a slightly more difficult proposition than it looked. Michael and I would glance at each other as if to say: Oh, no, here we go again. Sometimes the score would be as bad as 27 to 110. Go, Chris, go.

Really humiliating.

Sometimes we pretended that we just happened to be total strangers who were passing by. By mistake. That we really didn't know any of the losers. And when we cheered we did it softly. Under our breath. Of course the other men, the Nam Knights, had by this time seen us so many times that neither Michael or I could fool them. When the Fighting Furies lost the Nam Knights would point at Michael and myself in the stands, laugh, and give us the finger. Pointing at the Fighting Furies, laughing, and giving them the finger had lost its bite. It was redundant. It grew boring. So they switched to humiliating the cheering section. Eventually the cheering section got blamed for the accumulated failures of the Fighting Furies. I pointed out one evening in the Golden Buddha that this was somewhat unfair. I was informed that in love and war everything is fair. Shake rattle and roll.

"Why do we keep coming to these games?" Michael asked while we watched Chris miss a basket.

"Well, personally I like chests," I said. "If you like hunky chests you get to see some really serious chests at wheelchair games."

"I hadn't noticed."

"That's because you're cursed with being straight which is why you never pick up your underwear. They lust after your underwear, you know."

"They do not."

"Trust me."

"Do you lust after my underwear?"

"I lust after your 4.0 GPA. I am beyond underwear."

Chris had the ball again. We stood up. "Go, Chris, go!" we whispered. Actually, we just thought it. Chris got to the end of the court, threw the ball, missed. We sat down.

"I got a phone call from Gloria, this afternoon," Michael said.

"Oh, really. How's the reefer queen doing?"

"She wants to know if she can pay us a visit. I think Gloria's left Chuck, you know, her husband."

"Don't tell me," I said, "and she wants to move in with us. I just love women's liberation as long as I don't have to pay for it. I wonder if she picks up her underwear."

"I'm not sure. Well, maybe she might move in for a while. Of course I told her I'd have to bring it up with you and Chris."

"What about her kids?"

"I think my mom has them."

"How lucky for her."

"She'll be here tonight."

I looked at Michael. "Tonight?"

"That's what she said. She said that if we couldn't put her up she could sleep in the street."

"Where are we going to put her? In the tub?"

"She said it'd just be for a while."

"I love big families," I lied.

"Liar."

George had the ball. He could pass it to Chris or he could pass it to Rick. Chris was closer to the basket. The look on George's face was one of sheer agony and the Nam Knights were closing in on him fast. "Over here!" Chris yelled. George threw the ball to Rick. Rick made the basket which brought the score to 36 to 112. We stood up and smiled. We should have cheered but 36 is a long way from 112.

That night I met Gloria at the Port Authority bus terminal. "Welcome to New York, Luv. Did you bring money?"

"I'm leaving my husband, my life is a crisis, the world is going to the dogs, I'm going to have to find some kind of a job. And he wants to know if I brought money? No, actually I thought I'd live off you guys for awhile. I brought marijuana."

"I no longer smoke marijuana. I'm trying to set an example for Michael. He's now a college student at City College, you know."

"That's what I hear. Do you think if he becomes a lawyer he'll handle my divorce? I mean for free. I'm family."

"I think he has a way to go before he becomes a lawyer. Right now he buses tables at the Golden Buddha. Maybe they need someone to wash dishes?"

"Oh, great. I leave my job as the happy homemaker. Everything's a crisis. My kids hate me. I come to New York. He wants me to wash dishes."

"Life is shit and then you die."

"You're telling me? Honey, I'll wash dishes. I'll answer phones. I'll do anything. It doesn't matter. I can be a cashier. Anything. I'm really quite good at rolling joints. You know, where I come from women aren't really trained at too many things. Where I come from life isn't shit and then you die. Life is let's have a bunch of babies and then you die. You know, I was a cheerleader. Maybe someone needs an old cheerleader down on her luck? Kind of frayed at the edges. But really quite good with the cheers. You wanna see me do one? My pompoms are in here somewhere."

That night I was in bed with Chris. I had my head on his big lunk chest. I was trying to decide whether to go to sleep or nibble on his nubs. It was dark. Gloria and Michael were smoking joints in the living room. I was mostly talked out. "I really do like your sister," I said.

"Oh, you'll like my mom, too," Chris said. "She wants to know if she can move in next week."

"We can put your mom in the laundry hamper. I think she'd fit."

"Gloria will get her act together."

"Do you think so?"

"She's a survivor."

"She did some cheers."

"Some what?"

"We were in the Port Authority and Gloria showed me her Eastern High School basketball cheers circa 1965. Give me an E. Give me an A . . ."

"Seriously?"

"Seriously. She's afraid she doesn't have any skills. She says homemaker sounds about as good as cheerleader on a job application."

"She can roll joints."

"I noticed."

"We're a family of bums, I guess. 'Bums,' my dad used to say. 'I raised a family of bums.' Maybe he did. Look at me. I collect SSI and VA benefits. I play basketball and do Elvis imitations."

"Well, you kind of play basketball. You kind of do Elvis. Kind of. Maybe if you practiced more throwing the ball into the . . ."

"Not funny. You could try being a little more supportive."

"Maybe Gloria could teach me some cheers."

"Do you think Billy's Elvis was better than mine?"

"Billy's Elvis always sounded like he was from San Diego. Your Elvis sounds like it's from Michigan not Memphis. I call it a draw. Either way imitating Elvis is definitely a skill."

Chris was showing me some of his other skills when we heard them put some Elvis on in the livingroom. BURN MY HOUSE, STEAL MY CAR, DRINK MY LIQUOR FROM AN OLD FRUIT JAR. BUT HONEY, GETCHER FEET OFFA MY BLUE SUEDE SHOES! "She can't be hopeless if she's still playing Elvis."

I kissed him. "Nothing is hopeless," I observed, "as long as there's a little Elvis in the world."

The Golden Buddha Restaurant on Spring Street in Manhattan is not a gay restaurant. It's only kind of a gay restaurant. It's not chic enough to be a gay restaurant. The rice is kind of lumpy. The decor is 1959 Hong Kong hotel red. The best drinks are the Pink Squirrels. Most of the Golden Buddha's customers are either down and out punk poets, gay men too cheap or too poor to eat in Greenwich Village, or men in wheelchairs with bar tabs the size of Queens. Thommy's fortune cookies all have the same fortune: *A Tall, Handsome Stranger Will Come Into Your Life.* And I'm Jayne Mansfield. You could open sixty thousand of Thom's fortune cookies and all you'll ever get is his enigmatic, tall, handsome stranger whom you will supposedly meet some romantic night at the Golden Buddha over a scrumptious meal of mugu-something. Post abstract mugu-something. Thommy's steamed chicken tastes suspiciously like warmed over wet rubber dipped in soy sauce.

"Thom," I said. "All the cookies say the same thing. Where's my tall, handsome stranger? Every time I come in here I look for him. But I never see him."

"I'm right here, baby, let me in your life. But first let me in your pants." Thom laughed.

"You're it?"

"I'm it." Thommy Chan is about five three. He can't weigh more than 120 pounds. He caught a bad case of polio when as a child he lived in Taipei and since then he's spent most of his life in a wheelchair. He's very bright. Very cute. And he has a mouth that can only in the best of times be described as charitable. Thommy is one of the good guys. He's an incorrigible flirt and a wicked basketball player. He can make his wheelchair travel at the speed of sound. I swear I've heard him pass the sound barrier as his chair flashes across the basketball court. I'd marry him but I just wasn't cut out to work as one of his waiters for the rest of my life.

"Oh, wonderful!" Gloria said. She was reading her fortune. "I'm going to meet a tall, handsome stranger. Just what I need. I hope he's had a vasectomy."

"I thought your tubes were tied," I said.

"Well, supposedly they are. But my doctor was a man."

"So?"

"Never trust a man over the age of four."

"I thought that you loved men," Chris noted.

"Oh, I do. I just don't trust them."

"How good are you at making drinks?" Thommy asked. "I need a bartender."

"Gloria was born to be a bartender," Chris observed. Gloria just looked at Thommy and kind of batted her unemployed false eyelashes somewhat obnoxiously.

"How do you make a peach blow fizz," Thom asked Gloria. It was something of a test.

"Well," she said, "First you take the juice from half a lemon. Add egg white, two teaspoons of grenadine, a half-teaspoon of powdered sugar, one ounce of sweet cream, and then two ounces of dry gin. Shake with ice, strain into a highball glass over ice cubes. Cubes not shaved ice. Fill all of this with carbonated water, get on your knees, blow yourself, and stir. I can make them in my sleep. Where I come from women do many many things. Making peach blow fizzes is one of those things."

"Three hundred a week plus tips you've got the job," Thommy said.

"Four hundred a week plus tips plus health insurance and I'll blow the best peach fizzes in Manhattan," she said. Thommy kind of turned pale, he sort of gasped, but Gloria got the job. It was more than Thommy wanted to pay. But he needed someone who knew how to not only tend bar but how to shoot the shit with his customers.

"You got any more family that needs work," Thommy asked Chris.

"My mother wants to come to New York, burn her bra in front of Gloria Steinam's office, and then have an affair with Germain Greer. She'll need work but she's not cheap."

"Germain Greer is straight," I noted.

"That never bothered Mom," Chris said.

"Can she wash dishes?" Thommy asked.

"Honey," Gloria said, "all women can wash dishes. It's what we're all told from the beginning that we were *born* to do. The women where I come from were washing dishes before they were out of diapers. Someday we're all going to wise up, you know, the women of the world are going to unite and refuse to wash another fucking dish. Poor Mother. Every time I look at her I feel guilty because she thinks she likes what she does. It just happens to be all she knows h-o-w to do. Well, fuck all of that. I'm over it. Now, if we'd been the ones who'd been sent to Vietnam instead of you men, here, we would have put an early end to that nonsense."

"How's that," I asked.

"Well, as I see it the problem in Vietnam was not communism. It was lack of day care."

"Lack of day care?" I said.

"Lack of day care. Most problems in the world can be traced back to lack of day care. Ask any mother. We women would have turned South Vietnam into a giant day care center. This would have solved everything. You see, if the Vietnamese women had had day care then they would have had time to take over the government and run things the way things ought to be run. But, oh, no. There's never enough day care. This keeps your average woman at home in the suburbs or in her hooch. Suburbs, hooches, they're all the same. Barefoot so to speak. And pregnant. Unable to take over governments. And other such things. You see, if the women of the world ever get tired of the bullshit you men make us go through we'll show you how things *ought* to be run. But first we have to run our own lives for awhile to get some practice if you know what I mean. Then look out." No one knew what she meant. Gloria promised that she would show us what she meant. Personally.

But first she had to whip the Fighting Furies into fighting shape. "If there's anything I can't stand to see it's a bunch of gay wimp underdogs getting creamed. It's unAmerican. Are you all really gay?" she asked. Gloria knew that gay existed but not in such concentration.

"They're all gay," I said. "Except for the cheering section. We're straight."

"And I'm Connie Chung," Thommy said. "All the good-looking men in New York are gay, Gloria."

"Such a waste," Gloria said. "But you know. About right now I need a straight man in my life like I need a hysterectomy. Who needs straight men, anyway?" Gloria sighed. "What we need to do is whip this gay team into gay shape! I'll tell you a secret. Nothing gives old Gloria, here, more of a thrill than seeing some straight men whipped at something. Anything. It's a very bad case of repressed revenge. It's not exactly a sexuality. But it's close. I've had lots of practice at getting basketball teams into shape. I know just how to work a basketball team o-u-t, honey. I'll have you guys winning games in no time. It's all a question of physical fitness and the cheers."

"The cheers?" I asked.

"The cheers make you or break you. If you don't have decent cheers you can't win anything. It's why we lost the Vietnam war."

"Oh, really," I said.

"Yes, there was the lack of day care and then the cheering section quit when they saw that the game sucked a big one. Any cheerleader could have told you why we were losing the

Vietnam war. Us cheerleaders could see it coming." According-
ing to Gloria most challenges in life involved two things: the
cheers and the availability of decent day care. She had Christopher up and out of bed by eight in the morning every morning
which was something of a record. She'd wheel him down to
Washington Square where there were baskets. Chris practiced
and practiced.

Gloria practiced her cheers. "What this team needs," she
said, "is a little morale booster. Give me an F . . .!"

"F," I said. Softly. I didn't want anyone to know I was
with them.

"Give me an I . . !"

"I."

"Give me a Gee . . .!"

"I'm afraid I don't always understand Gloria," I said to
Michael.

"That's okay," Michael said. "Gloria doesn't always understand Gloria. Sometimes she sounds like Bella Abzug.
Other times she sounds like Judith Krantz. Gloria is one of
those mysteries of life. Just when you think she makes sense
you realize that she is totally gaga. They kicked her off the
cheerleading team in high school, you know."

"No, I didn't know that."

"She mooned everyone at homecoming."

"Everyone?"

"Everyone. She made cheerleading history. And then she
moved to California and lived with the weirdos at the New
Buffalo Commune. If you can imagine."

"Is this another one of her runaway periods?"

"I don't think so. This time I think she's gone for good.
This time I don't think they will let her back. Ever. If you
think gays scare your average Lansingite you ought to see what
a semi-liberated woman does to them. If Gloria ever went back

they'd all run for their lives."

The term "magnetic" is an intricate somewhat scientific complexity that defines itself not all that far linguistically from the concept "magic." There are, perhaps, twenty words in the English language that position themselves between "magician" and "magnate," which, according to Webster, equates as a very important or influential person in any field of activity. Magnate being related to the Greek word "magus" which literally translates back into the word magician. Which brings us, again, linguistically at least to magnetic—a concept that ranges from that which is a magnetic force to that which is magnificent—beautiful, exalted, rich in splendor. All of these concepts are related. One could not theoretically exist without the others. Certainly Christopher was very much a "magnetic force."

God knows he was attractive. If the unkind naked truth were known I would have to (not proudly) admit to the fact that there is at least a small part of me which secretly likes the reality that, yes, Chris depends on me. I wanted him to depend on me. There are simply times when I have to be there. Sometimes Chris can't make it from his chair to the bed because he hurts and his body won't do what he wants it to do. Chris is very strong-willed. But he has limitations and they're real. Somehow not being there for Chris has become like not being there for myself. Just being there is often half the battle. If I wasn't there for him, to haul him out of his chair when he just can't make it into the bed, then Chris would have to virtually sleep where he sits—immobilized. And I refuse to allow him to be more of a prisoner than he has to be. Suffering isn't necessary.

Life is too fucking short.

Sometimes I wondered what it'd be like if he just left me. If we broke up whatever it is we eventually became. Together. And I realize that Chris would hardly leave me—lightly. I am, indeed, an important part of his support system. But the bottom line between us occasionally slaps me rudely in the face with the knowledge that Chris is with me because he wants to be with me. It's true. I do a lot for Chris. Not because I feel sorry for him but because I want to. Nevertheless, I know that Chris knows where the door is. And if he had to use it because he had to use it, for whatever reason, he sure as hell knows how. Which isn't to say that if he ever leaves me I won't drag him back, tie his chair to a tree with a rope, strip him, and fuck him until he sees the light.

He needs me. And I need him. We have reached a stand-off.

When he sleeps I find that I can almost fit into his warm naked form something like a fetal glove which is a long way from that first terrified night we slept together in Hong Kong at the Hong Kong Hilton—it seems like yesterday. Me in my underwear with a boner. And Chris with his arms around me. I didn't sleep at all that night. But now I would find it difficult to sleep without the son-of-a-bitch beside me. I would give anything if Chris could walk. And reality dictates that I have to see the beauty in who he is and what he is. I no longer see who he was. I simply see him the way he is. I like him naked, my arms around my babe, because there is a very real part of me that protects him. Chris has difficulty dealing with it but the fact remains that he is vulnerable.

No matter what he says.

There is a very specific and powerful beauty in the way in which Chris is, yes, vulnerable. His spirit and his tenacity are alive, well, and living in every breath he takes. They don't make'em any tougher than Christopher. He broke the mold when it came to masculinity. Yet when he's naked, in our bed, childlike, and he can't move, and he's with me, you had better believe he's mine. I DON'T WANNA BE YOUR TIGER CAUSE TIGERS PLAY TOO ROUGH. I DON'T WANNA BE YOUR LION CAUSE LIONS AIN'T THE KIND YOU LOVE ENOUGH. I JUST WANT TO BE YOUR (OH LET HIM BE YOUR) LITTLE OLD TEDDY BEAR.

If Chris was a magnetic force, the Flying Furies were a magnetic storm: a worldwide disturbance caused by gay sunspot activity. They attracted attention. They attracted people who, normally, were quite content to remain on the sidelines, yet these same people found themselves joining—spontaneously—into their games. Just shooting baskets. Men who were stockbrokers and just walking through Washington Square would stop, throw a few baskets, and more than a couple found themselves, minus jackets and ties, involved in full-fledged games. To hell with Wall Street for awhile. The Fighting Furies attracted energy. And it was not at all unusual to find them playing with various assorted drug dealers or students or cops or with shirtless foolish young hunks who did not seem cognizant of the fact that the Fighting Furies lusted after their shirtless foolish delicious young bodies.

Just shooting baskets.

"Never could shoot a basketball worth shit," he said. It was a voice we were not expecting. Although neither Chris nor I could say that we were in the least surprised to hear from Jimmy Bo. "Ranger," Jim said, "you ain't exactly the Harlem Globetrotters on wheels, man. Hell, my bookie wouldn't take odds on you. And my bookie will bet on anything. Well, almost anything." It was a sight to see a white man in a wheelchair planting wet crazy kisses on a big black motherfucker. Even for Washington Square. Jimmy simply joined into the game like everyone else who simply joined into the game.

Jimmy got the ball. "Okay," he said, panting, sweat dripping down his face. "You look at the basket, Chris. Then you close your eyes. You see the hoop in your head. You become one with it. You shoot." Jim threw the ball toward the basket.

There was a grace to it. A union. The ball went up, hit the hoop
rim, swirled around twice, and dropped. They played basketball until sunset. The rest of the Fighting Furies left for a few
beers at the Golden Buddha. Chris and Jim stayed in the park
until dark. Shooting baskets. Shooting baskets. They were, of
course, doing more than just shooting baskets. Chris was like
the North Pole and Jim was like the South Pole and the unseen
magic in between them simply . . . pulled.

It was late. Jim, Chris, and I were sitting at our small kitchen
table which was covered with Michael's textbooks, Gloria's
ashtrays of marijuana seeds, a few dirty dishes I had decided to
ignore, and a set of photographs. The photographs were of
oriental children. I could not look at the photographs. I just
couldn't.

"Well, you could at least look at them, Boss," Jim said.

"I can't."

"You mean you won't."

"All right then I won't. How's that . . . ?" I started to
pick up the dishes from the table and put them into the sink.

"Man," Jim said to Chris, "what are you doing with your
goddamn life?"

"Hey, man," I interrupted. "Who the fuck are you to
come in here and ask us what we are doing with our fucking
lives? Maybe it's none of your damn business anyway. You
ever think of that? Who the fuck do you think you are?"

"I'm Jim, Boss," he said very very softly. "Remember
me?" Then he practically yelled at me. "And if anybody got the
right to confront cher lousy white ass, motherfucker, it is me!
You got it? You hear me?!"

I sat down and looked at the pictures. "They're from
Pnom-Penh," Jim said. Calmly. "The refugee agency I'm
dealing with estimates that in the next six months there'll be
over a million refugee children who'll cross over into

Thailand. Probably most will die. It's the same war, Boss. The one we left. Same people. Same issues. Same killing. Just next door. It never changes, you know. Come on, Boss. Take in a deep breath." Jim took in a deep breath with his big chest. I could hardly breathe at all just looking at the faces of those kids. "Breathe in, Boss. You can smell it. War and blood. Remember napalm? Nothing like it. You smell it? Motherfucker, you can't help but smell it. It's in your goddamn dreams."

I could smell it. I was there. I put the pictures back on the table. "Right now," Jim said, "they're in a refugee camp just across the border into Thailand. Soon they'll be in Bangkok. And then they'll be here. Quong Lee and I have put everything we have into this." Jim thumbed through the pictures. "The camps are full to bursting. You remember how that was. Remember how they all left Hue and went to Da Nang? Remember Da Nang, Boss? Remember how a hundred thousand people ran out on the Da Nang airport runway? And remember how people trampled over one another to get onboard the one and only seven-forty-seven that landed to get people the hell out? And remember how people latched onto the wings, hell, they were in the fucking jet's wheel-wells. They didn't even dare raise up the wheels on the plane because there were people in there. Some of them fucking froze to death on the way to Saigon. And some of them lost their grip. Remember any of that, Boss?"

"I try not to. Do you mind. I really try not to."

"And what the fuck are you doing with your life, Boss? Cleaning some high school bathroom toilets? Big fucking deal, man. The two of you ain't doing shit and you know it. I'm talking kids here."

"In case you haven't noticed, Jim," Chris said. "I live in a wheelchair. You're talking about us coming to New Mexico to help you out with this thing. Jimmy, look at me. How're your arms feeling after shooting all those baskets from my wheelchair today?"

"They hurt."

"Yeah? Well, mine always hurt."

"Shit!" Jim said. "The self-pity is so thick in here you can taste it. Hey assholes, we need you. Quong Lee and I can't handle these kids by ourselves. Not ten of them we can't."

"Jesus Christ," I said. "You idiot. Ten?"

"Ten. Count'em. We got the place. We got the money. You know, everyone who came back from Nam didn't become a goddamn *bum*."

"Now you sound like my father," Chris said. He had a big smile on his face.

"Ten is just the beginning, assholes. I'm dealing with the Red Cross, the State Department, more agencies you can count."

"The beginning of what?" I asked.

"The beginning of what we started in Hue but couldn't finish. Well, I'm going to finish it. We owe them kids something. You wanna know what I see in my dreams, Boss? I don't see Titi. I don't see Billy. Leastways not dead I don't. I see them alive. And I see Sister Willie Peter. Alive. I see her all the time. I don't see Dragonfly. I don't see Tigerlady. Hey, man, remember old Tigerlady hobbling around on that leg? Kid had more guts than the two of you will ever have. I don't see Twirlitoes. And you know what?"

"What?" I asked.

"I wish I could. Sometimes I really want to see them in my head. I get out the pictures but it doesn't mean anything. The pictures don't do it for me. I wish I had dreams with the kids in it. The way they were. But I don't see it. I see the villes. I see old Lima Zulu, that sick SOB. I see the damn whores. And I wish I could see the kids. I did one good thing over there. One insignificant meaningless good thing helping them kids. And I can't even see it in my dreams. I wish I could. I've tried real hard. So I just got to do this. I need you. Quong Lee needs you.

We can't do it alone. The kids they need you. Look at them pictures. These kids are beautiful, man."

"Need us for what, Jimmy?" Chris asked. "We can't help you, man. How could we be of any help to you? I don't understand."

"Ten kids ain't no damn picnic," Jim said. "And these will be kids who are going to need a lot. An awful lot. Look, right now it's just the beginning. Look at these pictures. Now, isn't this beautiful?" Quong Lee was standing in front of a large adobe house in what was obviously the mountains of New Mexico. "I built the place myself. Contracting pays good money. I need help. I need two men who can help me with my new kids and my house and my business. And I know the two men I want. Hell, I could go out there and hire me two men in two minutes. But I want you. I need you. I ain't going to let you say no and you know it. So what's all this shit about? Come outside. I have something I want to show you."

"Show us what," I asked.

"You'll see." We went downstairs and out onto the street. Jimmy walked up to a brand-spanking-new Chevy van. He opened the side door of the van and a hydraulic wheelchair lift buzzed itself down. "Get in, motherfuckers, you're going for a ride in your new mama." Jimmy laughed that deep laugh he has which is more of a growl than it is a laugh. I hesitated. "Look at it like this," he said to me with his big black arm around my shoulders, "it's like shooting baskets, Boss. You've been trying real hard. But you've been missing the basket. You tell yourself that, well, that's okay. It's okay to miss the baskets because what's important isn't making points or baskets. What's important you think inside your mind is that you're just playing the game. But in your guts you know it's a big lie. You know in your soul that you want to do some winning. You want to make some points. You *want* the ball to go into the basket. And none of that other bullshit about just playing the game is gonna change that. You are playing to win. So now what you gotta do is close your eyes. Look at the basket in you head. Become one with it. Throw the ball. No, no, don't open your eyes, Boss. You got to throw the ball with your eyes closed. You got to become the ball and become the basket. And that's when you start winning the game. You're just breathing, Boss. You got to start winning, man. Nam is over. It's time."

That night we got into the new van and drove all over New York. It had everything because Jimmy wanted it to have everything. He didn't settle for less than what he wanted. It had stereo, a little bar, a table, a fridge, and it drove like a dream. It was three o' clock in the morning and we were driving through Washington Heights on Broadway when we went by a deserted concrete playground. Jimmy stopped the van. We got out and shot baskets until the sun rose. Shooting baskets. Just shooting baskets. We were like three crazy kids. I felt exhilarated. Alive for the first time in a long time. If I closed my eyes I made points.

They were my points and I was winning.

Jim was driving us home. "I want to do this," Chris said.

"Do what?" I said. "You don't know what you're getting into."

"I want to get out of this chair."

"Yeah, and I'd like to sprout wings and fly."

"I mean it. When I'm playing basketball sometimes I don't think. I'm in the chair, Boss. And whenever there's a little kid on my lap, you know, it's like I'm a human being. I'm not a crippled human being. I'm just a human being. Boss . . .?"

"What?"

"Little kids don't even see the goddamn chair. All they see is me."

"You don't know anything about little kids. Except for the fact that you are one." I sighed. "I suppose that when you were a kid you would have climbed into the back of the milk-man's cart for the ice."

"I would have been sucking ice till you could have skated on my lips. You know what your problem is, Boss?"

I rolled my eyes. "Okay. Okay. But when the milkman tells on us—that we're frauds, baby—well, don't ever say that I never warned you. We'll do it. When it doesn't work I won't say I told you so."

"Yes, you will."

"You're right. I will. I'll say I told you so. But I'll tell you right now, Chris. There's no coming back. If we go we go to stay."

"I gotta get out of this chair. Kids don't even see it, man."

"I wonder if they even play basketball in New Mexico?"

It was time to win a few.

Three days later Chris and I found ourselves dressed in suits at Kennedy International. The suits were for the officials and there were a lot of them. Jim was so nervous his hands shook. The plane from Bangkok was late. Eventually it landed. It was crammed with over four hundred refuge children. They were shy, afraid, quiet, a few cried. Rock-a-bye eyes so many rock-a-bye eyes. The agency officials on the plane had every-thing organized into groups. Nevertheless there was a sub-liminal chaos. All of the prospective adoptee parents were there although Quong Lee was in New Mexico getting their place ready. Jim and his ten children would be flying to New Mexico that afternoon with his Red Cross contact. It was going to be a long haul for the kids but Jim felt that the sooner they were all "home" the sooner they could start to adjust.

The woman from the International Red Cross who was with Jim's group introduced her small entourage to Jimmy Bo. Black motherfucker from the Bronx. Hi, daddy, who the hell are you? I didn't catch all their names. They were so fragile it was almost overwhelming. One little girl was named Mai. She

caught my immediate attention. Jim picked her up and sat her
on Chris' lap. She was carrying a doll that someone had obviously just recently given her. The doll was new. Most dolls that
little girls really cherish do not look new. Eventually they
looked dragged around and worn. The doll looked new. Mai
was about five-years-old. Jimmy picked her up in his bear-like
arms. "Come here, precious," he said. All I could see was
Tigerlady. Dragonfly. Twirlitoes. These were different children. Yet they were just as homeless, just as terrified, just as
lost.

Hell still sucked.

We put Jimmy and his new family on a domestic flight to
New Mexico. I told myself that I wasn't going to have any
favorites. But when I gave Mai a kiss I knew that it was another
one of those lies we like to tell ourselves. She managed a small
smile. It was her rock-a-bye dark almond eyes which embraced me. Jim had his hands full and then some. "Maybe
they'll sleep till we get there," he said. All Chris and I could
do was laugh. "Hey, man, it ain't funny."

"No," Chris said. "It's hilarious, man, hilarious."

"Don't take forever, now, getting there," Jim said. "I
need your goddamn help. I told you this ain't no jive turkey,
assholes. Quong Lee says I can't swear in front of the kids.
Now, that will be a change."

"We'll be there in a week," Chris said. And he handed
Jimmy his goody bag. The one with the comic books and the
Pampers.

"You don't really think I'll need these do you?" Jim
asked. He was referring to the Pampers.

"One never knows," I said. "I'm looking at what appears
to be a two-year-old right now who's got this big wet spot all
over his legs."

"Oh, no, man!"

"Instant fatherhood," Chris said. "Daddy, you better
tend to your son." The last we saw of Jimmy he was walking

onto a jet with a two-year-old under his arm like the kid was a football. "See you in a week, man," Chris said. "You black motherfucker I love you."

"I'll miss you," Gloria said. "But can I have your apartment? Somebody has to look after Michael, here. The kid needs day care." We gave Michael and Gloria the apartment. Gloria went up on the roof and rearranged Chris' flowers. She potted some marijuana seeds and declared that if it was the last thing she did she'd learn to become a farmer. "I will grow the best marijuana in New York City. People far and wide will once again call me the reefer queen. I have a reputation to uphold."

Michael helped us pack the van. He was very silent. "Hey," Chris said. "You'll come visit us, okay? It's not like I'm going to Vietnam."

"Better not," Michael said. "Or I'll be the one who kicks ass. Yours." We were on the street. Chris pulled his brother into his lap and gave him a sloppy disgusting wet kiss. It was Greenwich Village. No one gave a damn. That night we drove up to the Upper West Side YMCA where the Fighting Furies had their final battle with the Nam Knights. Gloria was dressed to the teeth for the occasion in full cheerleader drag with pompoms and ponytail. She looked like a flashback to the sixties. COME ON, MAMA, LET'S ROCK! I noticed that Gloria had tears dripping down her face.

"What's wrong, Gloria?" I asked.

"I told myself I wasn't going to cry. But I just realized something. I'm dressed in this outfit, you know, for the first time in a long time. And it made me realize something. I've been a fucking cheerleader all my life. I've always been cheering someone else on. Go, team go. Good old Gloria the keeper of the team spirit. And you know what?"

"You do look kind of silly."

"I don't care. Now I realize after all these years, after cheering other people on all my life, I realize that I want to cheer me on. *Me!* Tonight good old Gloria cheers her last cheer for some other team. I have to start being my own team. I *want* to be the one who gets cheered on. Even if I have to do it myself. I want to play in the game. I'm just as good as anyone else and I know for a fact that jockstraps aren't nose protectors." We all laughed. "I guess tonight will kind of be symbolic or something. Tonight old Gloria hangs up her pompoms forever. Tonight I graduate from cheerleading."

"How does it feel?" I asked.

She smiled through her tears. "What, to grow up? It scares the hell out of me. Tonight I'm going to cheer my guts out and quit. Good old Gloria wants to be more than a cheerleader. Can you believe it? I can't."

The Nam Knights had grown somewhat accustomed to winning which is when you stop winning. The Nam Knights didn't have Gloria. The Nam Knights didn't have a cheering section like the Fighting Furies. Now, we were a cheering section.

"Give me an F . . .!"

"F!" Michael and I screamed.

"Give me an I . . .!"

"I! You motherfuckers we're gonna whop your butts tonight!" The cheering section was in full enthusiastic attendance. Go, Chris, go. Christopher never missed a shot. The Nam Knights never knew what hit them. Basket after basket.

"Give me an F!"

"F!"

"What's it stand for," Gloria yelled.

"Fuck them! Fuck them! Fuck them!" We won.

It was about fucking time.

The staff at the Bronx VA Hospital used to take us temporary crazies up to the roof where we had hot dog barbecues. You ate hot dogs and chips in your pajamas and your robe. You had to keep putting your dick back into your PJ pants if it popped out of the hole in your PJs—you never got used to it. You had to have slippers or they wouldn't let you go up on the roof. You could stand next to the tall wire fence that surrounded the roof and stare out at the Bronx. Many of the buildings that can be seen from there are shells—they look bombed out. It looked like Cholon after Tet. I was back. I had to grab ahold of the fence. I was back. I kept expecting to see the dark bug-like images of choppers coming to get us, insects hovering on the horizon, coming to take us to the ships.

In the distance was La Guardia. It could have been Ton Son Nhut. Jets taking off. There was a satanic-like noise to Ton Son Nhut. It screamed with tinbeast technology. All of the technology was useless. It didn't mean anything. Watching jets come and go was like shooting baskets. Just shooting baskets. Flying east out over open water. No one ever jumped from the roof of the Bronx VA Hospital. The fence was too tall to climb. And jumping from the roof was against the rules.

As the war dragged on during those last few remaining months of voracious carnivorous lunacy, the surge of wandering refugees turned into a grim tidal wave. A tidal wave that traveled south always south. South toward Saigon. We saw them in Khe Sanh. We saw their ranks swell in Hue. From Hue they went to Da Nang. By the time they got to Da Nang there were hundreds of thousands of them. Now, many of them included renegade ARVN units that had seen what was coming. It was a nightmare of panic. The air filled with the smell of panic like an overabundance of half-dead flowers. In Da Nang a World Airways jet did, indeed, land at the Da Nang airport to pick up 200 refugees and fly them out. Over a hundred thousand people really did overrun the Da Nang runway in the mad scramble to get aboard the aircraft. A unit of South Vietnamese marines, the top unit in their military known as the

black panthers, pushed, shoved, and shot their way through
the crowd. The evacuation plane that was orginally intended
for civilians was taken over by the Hac Bao. There wasn't a
single civilian aboard.

As the jet took off hordes of people hung onto whatever
they could grasp. Some managed to squeeze into the wheel
wells where a few actually survived the ride. Others hung onto
the wings and they did not survive. As the war slowly burned
its way south the US military, those men in Saigon offices with
all of their accumulated and collective rank, decided that
perhaps more complex technology could save the day. The day
was long past saving. It was the dead of night and in the distance an orange fire raged.

We had all heard of cluster bombs although none of us
had ever seen one. Officially they were known as CBU55s.
When we finally saw what one could do it left—even
us—speechless. A CBU55 is a highly complex type of bomb
that contains specially constructed gas canisters filled with a
secret mix of gases and propane. When the thing explodes it
releases a fire cloud that can be seen fifty miles away. You'd
swear the thing was nuclear but it isn't. Nevertheless a CBU55
has much the same effect.

We exploded a CBU55 north of Saigon. The astonishing
thing about the weapon is that it didn't burn everything and
everyone up instantly. Most of the people in the destructive
zone of the bomb weren't even burned at all. They just lay
there on the ground, dead, with stunned expressions on their
faces. The CBU55 burns so rapidly and with such intensity it
uses up all the available oxygen around it for miles. It creates a
ferocious whirlwind inhuman vacuum of air. The vacuum
literally sucks your lungs out of your body. You can't breathe.
You choke to death on yourself.

The men in Saigon dropped one CBU55 smack dab near
the end of the war. It was not Hiroshima. Not even close

although the CBU55 that was dropped had just as much potential. It was becoming apparent even to them that this was not a war they were going to win. YOU CAN KNOCK ME DOWN, STEP ON MY FACE, SLANDER MY NAME ALL OVER THE PLACE. DO ANYTHING YOU WANT TO DO. BUT, BABY, PLEASE PLEASE PLEASE, BABY, GETCHER ASS OFFA MY BLUE SUEDE SHOES!

What was left of the South Vietnamese military now surrounded Saigon. They were there to defend what was left to defend and to keep as best as they could the mass of refugees o-u-t of the city. The city itself was quiet and tense. I helped load a C5A transport plane with four hundred children from various hastily organized orphanages who were bound for the States. There are four levels to a C5A and it took several hours to load the giant plane. The three bottom levels do not have seats and the children had to be strapped down to the floor. A C5A is at least as big as a football field. When it flies it looks as if it lumbers through the air—slowly.

I stood there with about a hundred other grunts and watched the huge plane take off. You could still see it when it was out over the water. A rear door blew open. It rained babies. They were sucked out. The pilot should have won the Congressional Medal of Honor. He was about four miles up going for eight miles which was cruising altitude. When a door on a plane as large as a C5A blows it can send structural shivers throughout the entire aircraft. The pilot banked and made a crash landing in a rice paddy. He was two miles from where I was standing in the middle of Ton Son Nhut. The survivors were simply put on another plane and flown the hell out of Vietnam. Out of Vietnam. Everyone wanted out of Vietnam. They were leaving on anything that could fly. Anything that could float. Anything and everything. They were flying to Hong Kong, Hawaii, Japan, Australia. O-u-t. Just o-u-t. Anywhere.

Anywhere.

Saigon is a city that has a deep historical ingrained genetical respect for and understanding of one basic thing. And that thing is money. French. Vietnamese. American. It doesn't matter. Money is money. People with money could easily buy their way out. Bribes flowed through the streets of Saigon where blood had flown through the streets of Hue. You wanted out. You had to pay your way.

American GIs made sweeps through the whorehouses. A whore could afford to pay. Some merchant seamen got married three or four times a week. Long lines formed at every agency that had a stamp. American civilians, contractors, drug dealers, the unofficial support system of the war; this scum would have to pay through the nose. It was the final slap in the face. These were the people who had done everything they could do to keep the war machine alive and ticking. And now they were going to have to pay and pay—and pay—to simply get out.

Alive and ticking.

Chris and I were part of the team that was putting whatever and whoever onto the choppers. We were supposed to be checking passes and stamps. And I'm your mama. You wanna ride with numbah one GI? Getcher ass onboard. We stuffed those choppers with anything that could walk or get to our roof. One at a time. Sometimes ten at a time. Saigon was real nervous. Anxiety had a bad smell to it. We got Quong Lee and Jim out without a hitch. It was night and we'd be spending that night just like we had spent so many other nights. Crouched down with our guns in our laps. Smoking joints. Our backs up against some wall. The choppers couldn't land at night. They would continue with the evacuation in the morning. We watched fires north of the city glow as if they were laughing sunsets.

"How long do you think it'll take them," Chris asked, "to take Saigon?"

I half-laughed. "Not long."

"I never understood any of it."

"No one did."

"What if we don't make it? What if this is the last of it? Damn! And what if at the last minute we don't make it, Boss?"

"Then we'll just kiss our asses goodbye. Just like anyone else."

"But what if . . . ?"

"Stop it, Chris."

"But what if this is the last time we'll ever talk to another human being?"

I laughed at him. Not angrily. Not bitterly. But because I loved him. "Well, if you feel that this might be the last time you ever talk to someone what is it you want to say?"

"I don't know."

"Neither do I."

"I want to tell you that I've—I've really enjoyed living. I liked my life. I liked fishing with my father. I liked Taylor. I liked knowing him. I loved him, Boss."

"I know."

"No, I mean I really loved him."

"I know."

"I liked making popcorn with my sister, you know. I liked John Wayne movies. I liked playing doctor with the other boys. We were always playing doctor. I don't think one of us ever really ever became one. I liked Christmas. I liked scaring other kids at Halloween. I liked basketball. Did you ever play basketball with the guys, Boss?"

"Not really."

"Oh, Jesus, playing basketball with the guys was the best. Someone's going to shoot me. I just know it." Chris was

looking up at the black sky. You could see the stars better from
the roof.

"No one's going to shoot you."

"I can feel it. Did you ever feel anything that was going to
happen? And then it happened?"

"No," I lied.

"I wonder if it hurts right away?"

"I don't think so," I said. "It takes a couple of minutes.
And then the hurt starts."

"I liked horses. I always wanted one. But I never had one.
I always wanted to live somewhere where I could have a horse.
I'd name him something original like Trigger." Chris laughed.
"I always wanted a horse."

"I love you." I couldn't believe I said it. I was embarrassed to say it.

"I know," he said. His eyes never left the sky. "But you
don't know how."

"It's hard. I wish it wasn't so hard."

"If this was the absolute last time we were ever going to be
together, Boss, what would you want to say to me. Or do?"

I took my hand, reached out, and touched his lips.
"Don't talk like this."

"Someone's going to shoot me. I can feel it."

"If this were the absolute last time I'd ever be able to tell
you something I'd want to tell you that I think you're full of
shit." We both laughed.

The sun was just beginning to show her nasty self in the
indigo east when we heard the choppers coming. Chris stood
up to look. I never heard the shot. I saw it hit him. But I didn't
realize right away that that's what was happening. It kind of
pushed him forward. I couldn't even figure out where the hell
it had come from. Or what was going on. Or why. He just fell.
Limp. Oh, God. Oh, God. I threw my gun down, ran to him,
pulled him to the chopper. I practically threw him in. GO!
FUCKER GO! JUST GO. GET THE FUCK OUT OF HERE!

JUST GO. GO NOW! DAMN YOU, GO! They looked at me as if I were slightly mad. And then they realized I'd thrown a bleeding man into their chopper. GO! DAMN YOU!

Just go.

Michael and Gloria followed us outside to where the van was parked in the loading zone. "Someday you'll get your kids. And you'll all live happily ever after," I said to Gloria.

"Do you really think so?" She was dubious. So was I. It was one of those mornings where even the air in New York seemed fresh and almost cold. The van was packed with our junk. We couldn't believe we had so much junk. Stuff we did not want to part with. Like Billy's guitar. At the last minute I gave the guitar to Michael.

"But I don't know how to play the guitar," he said.

I pushed his hair back with my hand, stepped back, and looked at him. "A little grease you'll look just like him."

"Who, Elvis?" he asked.

"No. Your brother about ten years ago." I got into the van. Gloria kissed me.

"Take care of my lunk brother, okay?"

"Somebody has to," I said. We waved goodbye. We weren't sure what we were going to find in New Mexico. I had to stop being afraid of the milkman and do something with my life. Somebody (ten somebodies) needed us. The challenge of it was scary. We didn't know what the fuck we were getting into. Or what would happen. But we were on our way. There was a wall between us and New Mexico. Between us and Jim. Between us and the children. A black wall of death. They call it the Vietnam Memorial and it sits on a grassy knoll in Washington DC like a long dark wounded gash on the face of the love me tender earth. In order to get to New Mexico, in order to really get to wherever it was that we were going, we were going to have to negotiate that wall. Climb over it.

Make some kind of horrible peace with it.

The thing about the wall is that it's so fucking silent. Yet it says so much. Names. Just names. We sat there in the van for the longest time looking over at what was the wall. We didn't get out of the van. WHEN TEARS ARE IN YOUR EYES I'LL DRIVE THEM ALL—OUT. I'M ON YOUR SIDE. OH, WHEN TIMES GET ROUGH AND FRIENDS JUST CAN'T BE FOUND LIKE A BRIDGE OVER TROUBLED WATER I WILL LAY ME DOWN. LIKE A BRIDGE OVER TROUBLED WATER I WILL LAY ME DOWN . . .

"I'm not going to cry," Chris said. "Boss, please don't let me cry. I'm here *because* I don't want to cry anymore. I'm too dry to cry, Boss."

"Nobody's too dry to cry." So we cried. We sat there like stupid idiot babies and we cried. We didn't want anyone to see us like that. So we stayed in the van until we couldn't cry anymore. Chris got into his chair and the hydraulic lift buzzed him down to the ground. We started looking. The black marble is smooth and unforgiving. It does not embrace you. It reflects who you are. We searched for a long time. We were not alone. Small groups of people here and there were looking for names of boys they knew. Touching. And when they found the name of whoever it was they were looking for they cried. Oh, they told themselves, no, I can't cry anymore. I'm cried out. And then you found his name. He was just a boy. Someone you loved only you never really told him how much you loved him. He'd be back. And everything would be the same again only everything could never be the same again and nobody could ever be the same again. It was impossible. OH, WHEN DARKNESS COMES AND PAIN IS ALL AROUND LIKE A BRIDGE OVER TROUBLED WATER I WILL LAY ME DOWN . . . You touched the name with your fingers. This—this stone was all that was left of him. And then you cried again.

The Vietnam Memorial is not awesome as memorials go.

It is beyond awesome. It grabs you and it won't let go. Ever. It hurts and yet it nurtures. It refuses to allow anyone who sees it or better yet touches it to forget. We touched Taylor's name. We cried. We wondered if it had been about anything. And we climbed over the wall—we left it. Emotionally. In our guts. It was time. We will always hurt with it. Those wounds will never totally heal. Yet seeing the wall, touching Taylor's name in stone, helped us to stop bleeding with it all over ourselves. Candy, soda, dirty pictures, boom boom dope. Tigerlady, Dragonfly, Twirlitoes, Titi, Billy, And Kai . . .

Goodbye. We loved you.

The van drove smooth, cool, like a dry martini at five o'clock. We were somewhere in the midwest. Driving west toward whatever. I kept hearing Jimmy in my head telling me that he needed us. Us! Us cripples. Somebody needed us and we needed to be needed. Oh, how we needed that. "Jim says that they're making these new chairs," Christopher said, "that have batteries and motors, now, you know, that you don't have to push yourself. They just go where you want them to go."

I looked over at him and smiled. I loved him with all of my heart. "What, you think you could get used to being motorized?" There was a long silence.

"No," he said. "Not really. I fully intend to run."

The sun set in front of us with the same kind of brilliant, glorious orange that she used to show us at sunset in Vietnam. Uncompromising and intransigent. Bloodred and indigo. Candy, soda, dirty pictures, boom boom dope. Elvis in my head. YOU AIN'T NOTHING BUT A HOUND DOG ROCKIN' ALL THE TIME. YOU AIN'T NOTHING BUT A HOUND DOG ROCKIN' ALL THE TIME. AND THEY SAID YOU WAS HIGH-CLASS, WELL, BABE, THAT WAS JUST FINE. YES, THEY SAID YOU WAS HIGH-CLASS AND THAT WAS JUST FINE. BUT, OH, MAMA, YOU NEVER CAUGHT A RABBIT AND YOU AIN'T NO FRIEND OF MINE . . .